The Shadow Was Gone.

Allanni changed her mind fast enough. It was her own special peripheral vision that saved her, when movement caught her eye—movement in a doorway ten meters away. She had turned halfway around when she knew what she was seeing: a man leveling a weapon.

Reflexes took over. Without finishing the turn, she threw her go-bag. And an eye-searing light flooded the corridor as a plasmer beam reduced the flying satchel to rapidly-diffusing molecules and a few charred bits large enough to fall.

Lord of Light—he's using a pulsar beamer!

Already she was snatching up and throwing her boots. She drove herself after them while they were still in the air. One boot smacked heel-first into Shadow's forehead. His next shot, incredibly, was a stopper beam, aimed for Alanni's head . . .

SPACEWAYS

SPACEWAYS

#1 OF ALIEN BONDAGE
#2 CORUNDUM'S WOMAN
#3 ESCAPE FROM MACHO
#4 SATANA ENSLAVED
#5 MASTER OF MISFIT
#6 PURRFECT PLUNDER
#7 THE MANHUNTRESS
#8 UNDER TWIN SUNS
#9 IN QUEST OF QALARA
#10 THE YOKE OF SHEN
#11 THE ICEWORLD CONNECTION
#12 STAR SLAVER
#13 JONUTA RISING!
#14 ASSIGNMENT: HELLHOLE

SPACEWAYS #14

ASSIGNMENT: HELLHOLE

JOHN CLEVE

BERKLEY BOOKS, NEW YORK

SPACEWAYS #14: ASSIGNMENT: HELLHOLE

A Berkley Book / published by arrangement with
the author

PRINTING HISTORY
Berkley edition / November 1983

ISBN: 0-425-06407-7

for the Atlanta Connection,
Jeff & Kathy

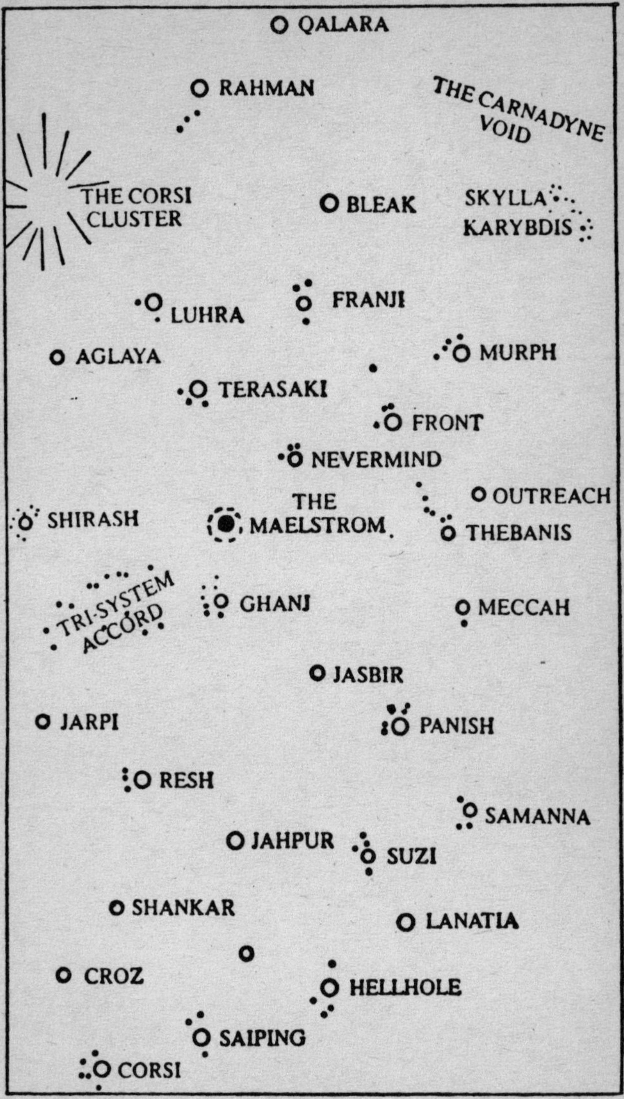

A: All planets are not shown.
B: Map is not to scale, because of
the vast distances between stars.

SCARLET HILLS

Alas, fair ones, my time has come.
I must depart your lovely home—
Seek the bounds of this galaxy
To find what lies beyond.

(chorus)
Scarlet hills and amber skies,
Gentlebeings with loving eyes;
All these I leave to search for a dream
That will cure the wand'rer in me.

You say it must be glamorous
For those who travel out through space.
You know not the dark, endless night
Nor the solitude we face.

(reprise chorus)

I know not of my journey's end
Nor the time nor toll it will have me spend.
But I must see what I've never seen
And know what I've never known.

Scarlet hills and amber skies,
Gentlebeings with loving eyes;
All these I leave to search for a dream
That will cure the wand'rer in me.

—Ann Morris

Cults come and go. They've been coming and going for too many thousands of years. They're better when they are going, and humanity is a lot better off then, too.

—*Carnadyne of Iceworld*

TGO or not TGO, that is the answer.

—*Trafalgar Cuw*

1

Alanni Keor drove the tractor onto the dike at the south end of the greaseroot paddy. She kept going until the seeder fell into place at the end of its hitch behind the tractor. By the time she could stop the rig with everything on solid ground, she was nearly out of dike.

The day was warm, though not quite hot. The work certainly wasn't as bad as it would be when the greaseroot started sprouting—adding stink to heat. Damp, Alanni slid down off the tractor's seat, pulled off her broad-brimmed skulkerhide hat, and fanned herself with it. Then she ran a finger down the front of her shirt, opening it halfway to the waist.

That action revealed nothing much that hadn't showed before. The shirt was cut low to begin with and Alanni was so constructed that she couldn't hide her contours in less than fur or a spacesuit—and not always in those.

There came no sudden sag, either. Alanni didn't, except in gravity much heavier than this; Eagle's .96-standard. Anyone who tried picking her up quickly understood why. He'd be lifting a compact package wrapped neatly in cinnamon-colored skin and weighing a surprising sixty-five kilos.* Her shoulders were wide and her ribcage deep for her 170 sems, and everything else was in proportion.

And in fighting shape, too. Alanni weighed maybe five kilos more now than she had as a TSA policer, and she liked herself this way. (A little extra jiggle had its points—two in

*65 kilograms; about 143 *pounds,* Old Style.

front, notably—as well as its curves.) Beneath was muscle, as a few people had discovered when they tried to pick her up with unfriendly intent. It was a discovery that those who survived didn't need to make twice.

Now she pulled the chillpack from under the tractor seat and unhooked the transmitter for the farm's remotes from the control panel. The transmitter went on her belt while she popped the seal on the pak.

She nearly choked on the first swig, but giggled on the second. Dear ingenious Bouncy! He'd filled the pak with ice-cold Starflare beer imported from Thebanis, then sealed it so tightly that the brew hadn't been able to go flat. Starflare outpointed water about six to one any time! Even more, out in the field.

Alanni didn't hang up the pak until it was empty.

Wiping her mouth with the back of one hand, she pressed a button on the transmitter with the other. The antenna shot out half a meter. Quick touches of four buttons set the frequency. Another touch—at *Transmit* this time—and the receiver on the automatic sluicegates at the north end of the paddy would "hear" her signal. The gates would open and water from the irrigation canal would commence flooding the paddy, submerging the newly planted greaseroot seeds and triggering the enzymes that made them fertile.

The delicate operation divided the good greaseroot farmers from the bad. Also, usually, those who made a living from those who wound up selling out and moving to Starlight—the planetary capital—or Braca's Landing. Let the paddy dry out too soon, and the seeds would turn to stone-hard little husks. Taint the water with some chemical that wasn't supposed to be there, and the roots would produce low-grade or contaminated oil. Farming had grown a lot more technological, but little easier over the centuries.

Greaseroot oil was about the best vegetable lubricant around. Otherwise the Eaglers would probably have left the plant as what it was when the first expedition hit the planet—a weed that choked swamps and crowded out food crops. They hadn't. They had made it pay. Now greaseroot farmers gave Eagle half its offplanet trade income. (They also saved it the need of any sort of petrochemical industry; low-grade greaseroot oil proved readily usable in making plastic.)

Now greaseroot farmers were the aristocrats of the countryside of planet Eagle of the Tri-System Accord, and no one seriously argued that it should be any other way.

Right now Alanni Keor didn't feel like an aristocrat.

She felt hot and still thirsty, not to mention unsure as to how long to leave the sluicegates open. The weather people reading the satellites said the *gahmsin* wind was ten days away. Alanni was a greaseroot farmer's daughter who had no link to weathersats but who read the sky and the feel of the breeze on her skin. They told her the *gahmsin* was overdue, and a couple of sems too little water might bake the paddy dry.

She looked up at the bronze-tinted blue sky, shading her eyes against Posidonios's glare.

That's when the tractor radio said *wheee-eep!*

The signal sounded so much like Bouncy's vocal call that Alanni half expected to see it rising out of the ground or floating down from the sky. The Jarp had been a domestic servant when it was a slave, and learned to move so silently that its mistress usually forgot it was there.

(That was how Bouncy had gained its freedom, too. Bouncy heard something to connect its lady-mistress with bribes to greaseroot inspectors. That something got to Lieutenant Alanni Keor, Tri-System Police. She agreed to leave the lady's name out of the indictment—in return for her freeing Bouncy.)

(Alanni didn't like slavery or slavers very much.)

The sound was only the radio this time. Her other junior partner was calling.

(Jaykennador Eks of Outreach was a retired computer-software thief. Captain Alanni Keor, T-SP, had left his name out of another indictment. Her thinking was that with one more chance he might get up the courage to go straight. So far she'd been proven right.)

" 'Lanni. Jay here. Tilno just called. Says he has a message for you."

"Message? Who from?"

"He didn't say."

"Tell him to get on the tractor's frequency. It's–"

"I already did. He says the message is confidential."

"Sweet of him. Did he say anything useful, Jay?"

"Pos. He's on his way over here."

"*Is* he! Well, give him a parking space and a drink, and tell him he's going to have to wait. If he takes that Hummingbird onto the dikes again, I swear I'll run the tractor over it!"

Jaykennador laughed. He must remember as well as Alanni the damage Tilno's elegant little car had done to the dike's top the last time he'd wanted to see her. "Pos, 'Lanni. Anything else?"

"Sit on any more calls," she said sourly. "I don't care if it's a proposition from the First Councillor of the TSA. I'm not home and you don't know when I will be."

"Will do. End transmission."

"Uh." Alanni flexed tight shoulder muscles. If Tilno had something so confidential he wouldn't transmit it, it was either another proposal of marriage or something she didn't want to try imagining right now. Not with a greaseroot paddy holding a third of the year's income in need of water.

She looked at the sky again. Squinting, she made out a peach-colored haze on the southern horizon. Too light for what her father's generation called the *Gahmsin*'s Scouts, but still . . .

Thirty sems of water should do it, she decided. A person could sometimes add more if she had to. With too much, the greaseroot was done and so was she.

She sighted on the marker pole, made a couple of gestures of aversion (which was as close to praying as she came), and punched the *Transmit* key.

Twenty minutes later Alanni's father would have been proud of her. She was even pretty proud of herself. She was just backing the seeder into the garage when Jay stuck his head out the window of the farm office.

"*Gahmsin*'s on the way. They just broadcast the word. Sounded a little ashamed of themselves, too."

"Kali take me if they shouldn't!" Alanni turned off the tractor's engine. "Tilno in sight yet?"

"Neg."

"Good. I'm going to shower and change. If he comes before I'm through, plant him by the pool."

"Will do."

Alanni headed for the house.

Originally the place was a rich merchant's country retreat. It possessed a few features one hardly expected on a working farm—the pool, for instance. Also a master suite with opaquable windoors opening onto a balcony, and a spiral staircase from the balcony down to the pool. Balcony, staircase, and the suite's paneling were all exotic woods from at least a dozen different planets. Alanni discovered a new one about once a month.

Most of the other luxuries were the kind that showed money rather than good taste. All had come with the house—once the merchant went bankrupt and had to sell out—and most of them left immediately. Alanni cleared half a year's income on the sale, although she'd been tempted to use some of the intriguingly distasteful furniture and rugs for landfill. She still couldn't forget the bow-curved divan, with what must have been intended as erotic carvings all over it. She and Tilno had tried to soar on it only once. He'd got the droops and hadn't recovered until they had pulled the cushions off onto the floor and tried again.

Thinking of Tilno brought back the question of why he was coming over. She scanned it from several angles while she climbed the stairs and from several more as she broke clothing melds, dumped the sweaty clothes and climbed into the shower.

She really hoped he wasn't coming to propose again. That would make five times. She wanted to think better of Tilno than she could of a man who couldn't take five no's as an answer. Or maybe he thought he could change her mind if he kept nibbling away at her like a root-grubber? That would be even worse.

And there's another question too, O woman of pride.

What is it, O ill-natured not-still-enough inner voice of so-called wisdom?

Why won't *you marry him?*

Because he's grateful to me, damn it.

Oh? What's wrong with that? When you broke up the Gryphon's House gang, you let his son go. The boy was just along for the fun, you thought—and it seems you were right. The man should *be grateful!*

He is.

He's also interesting to look at, intelligent, witty, charming, rich, no more than half again your age, and incredibly sexy. Good at it, too.

The showering Alanni rolled her eyes and this time answered that mental "voice" aloud: "Don't remind me about that!"

Her plea was much too late. The water trickling down her belly and between her thighs suddenly took on the feel of Tilno's mouth. Those lips had often followed the same path. She growled low and far back in her throat, knowing that her nipples were hardening, and swore at her inner voice.

He's all of those things, true, but he's not in love with me. At least not enough really to want me around all the time, day and night.

That's important?

Yes, you idiot! Lord of Light, I asked for a conscience and what did you send me? No, don't answer that! If I don't know by now I never will.

And you might not want him around all day and night either?

Suddenly her Voice was saying something useful. Alanni realized she really didn't like the idea of the way she used most of her time depending on another person. Tilno wouldn't be whimsical or cruel or selfish, but he would have his own notions on the subject. Alanni wasn't sure she could live with anyone's notions, now.

Of course with the T-SP she had hardly been sole ruler of her time. Far from it. She had also been doing fascinating work, though, that gave her a sense of purpose.

She wasn't ruler of her own time on the farm, either. Still, weather and grubs and jammed sluicegates (not often, since Jay was a first-class maintenance tech) weren't the same as another person. She hadn't realized until now just how great the difference would be.

Maybe the not-so-still small voice had a point. She should have realized it. Why hadn't she?

Because Tilno is a change, and you're getting bored with retirement to the farm.

Bored?

Bored—and don't play daughter of the soil with me, little falcon!

By degrees the voice in her mind took on a personality; until it was the voice of Prefect Kilwar, dismissing her from T-SP for practicing her own notions of justice too often.

"You gave us a third of your life, 'Lanni, and you gave yourself a fine name. You might have ended up in my chair. I'd have been glad to let you sit down in it, too. That's not the way it's going to be, though. You said you are actually going to take your pension and bonus and buy a farm?"

"Pos."

"Well, if you can regrow your old roots in Eagle's soil, that might be the best thing for you and for us. The Lord of Light knows none of us wishes you harm. Yet if you've been away from the farm too long, and find you can't go home agaih . . ." The prefect seemed to lose either the thread of his words or the nerve to finish them.

"Pos. If I find that I can't go home again–?"

"The moment you know that, 'Lanni, get moving. Don't stay married to the land until they plow you under it."

He'd bent across the desk then, and for the first time kissed her with more than professional respect.

Now it was three years-Eagle later and the moment was here. She wasn't just bored. She felt stale, except when she and Tilno trysted, sliced, soared. That would be an even worse reason for marrying him than any of his reasons for wanting to marry her.

The Voice was silent now, and Alanni was grateful. It had brought her this far, then left her to make her own way. She would have to, although she'd be cursed if she knew where it would end!

Meanwhile there's a crop to raise and a farm to run and Tilno to entertain and generally no excuse for sittin' and feelin' sorry for myself. She overrode the shower's program and turned it to full COLD. That should get her mind off memories of soaring with Tilno!

2

Myths about cold showers die hard. So does a good case of garden variety lust. By the time Alanni stepped out of the shower, she wasn't sure whether her nipples were hard with the cold or firm from thinking about Tilno. That was all the progress she'd made, aside from the gooseflesh.

The vibroset on the bed gave her an all-over massage and rubbed oil into her skin at the same time. When it shut off, she sprayed the soles of her feet deep violet, then lay back on the bed and waved her legs in the air to dry the coloring. It occurred to her and she grinned: this pose and action would be incredibly obscene from the right angle.

A few twinges in her thighs made her swear for the fiftieth time to go back to her combat exercises. Farmwork kept the muscles in fair shape, but she liked the way she had felt in the T-SP. She'd been able to take on some of the combat instructors and roll them up in their own mats.

Back then, she reflected, and made a face.

She rose to dress. A reelsilk wraparound from waist to ankles, green with a decor of golden chinthes. Nothing under the wraparound and nothing above it except a pair of wildman blooms—one on each breast just above the nipple. The long trailing crimson petals pretended just enough modesty to make a man wish for less of it. Her midnight hair went up on top of her head to be held in place by a silver comb set with freshwater pearls from planet Hellhole. It wasn't her best comb or her best decoration, but it was the first gift Tilno had given her.

Just because I'm not going to marry the man doesn't mean I have to pretend I don't like him at all!

She glanced over at the mirror she had decided to keep along with a few other of the house's original furnishings. Round, it was set in the center of a Mandelbrot-Meiku mandala; fractal art in six colors and eleven hues. It always looked just on the point of starting to spin.

Alanni added the final touch to her own decoration: bracelets of raw filigreed copper on both wrists. They came from the top drawer of her jewelry box.

(The contents of its lower drawer were rather less ornamental. One bracelet there could hide a short knife, another *shurikens*—the throwing stars almost deified on Terasaki. A twist of the weighted blue stone on the third and it sprouted a length of monofilament wire, with the stone as weight. Alanni could wrap it around someone's neck with a practiced whip of her arm and wrist—and had. The delicate-looking silver slave-style bracelet stiffened her wrist should she use old-fashioned chemical-explosive weaponry with their heavy recoil.)

(Sometimes she wondered why she kept her combat jewelry. It seemed incredible that she would ever want or need to use it again as other than decoration. Magic, maybe—so long as she kept it, somehow the good hard policer she had been wouldn't disappear completely into the rich soil of the farm.)

By the time Alanni got down to the pool, Tilno had not only arrived, he looked as if he'd grown roots in the inflatable lounger. His boots and high-collared tunic were off and his shirt was open halfway down his chest. One long-fingered hand curled around a half-empty drinking plass of frosty blue. Now it bore real frost, too.

Only two things about Tilno weren't long and thin, and only one showed when he was more or less fully dressed—the beard. He finger-combed a few drops of juice out of that thick dark nest on his chin, set the plass down, and thrust himself leggily to his feet to kiss Alanni. Then he stepped back and held her admiringly at arm's length.

"What's this? Queen of the Lost Colony?"

Alanni wrinkled her nose. "Tigere Sanyana I'm not."

"Thank the Light! I don't care how much gene-juggling

they do on those holomeller stashes. There's got to be a line drawn somewhere as to just how much chest a woman can flaunt and still stand up! You're on the right side of the line."

A finger gently ran up each proof of that fact to her bare shoulders. Alanni waited for the fingers to glide back down again and continue their travels. Most of the time Tilno was as sensitive to pheromones as a human could be. She *had* to be registering on him, she thought.

Instead he squeezed her shoulders and dropped his hands. He picked up the pitcher and poured her glass full. "Sit down, 'Lanni. We have problems."

"What do you mean, *we?" If that's his idea of an opening to a proposal–*

"I'm in it because I volunteered to play messenger. We."

"I won't know whether that's a problem until I've heard the message." She took a massive swig from her plass, knowing without caring that she looked as if she was bracing herself for bad news.

"Have you ever heard of the Invisible Wisdom, 'Lanni?"

Although that wasn't the question she had expected, it was one she could answer. "Uh. An archeological find from the Empire period, isn't it. A crystalline cube about thirty sems on a side and weighing–oh, fourteen kilos. Completely invisible except under certain lighting conditions. They mounted it in a prass frame with a handle so it wouldn't get lost easily. Definitely non-Galactic in origin. One theory is that it's a giant memory chip from a long-lost race's super computer, so they didn't try anything destructive on it. For about the past century it's been treated more or less as an expensive curiosity. The last I heard, it was on Ghanj."

"You're up to date, 'Lanni, except for the last. Now it's out on Hellhole, in the Master House of the Brotherhood of Servants of Tarf al-Barahut."

"The cult?" she asked, prodding a hazy memory.

"Firm. They think the Invisible Wisdom holds a message that will prove they know the One True Way."

"Very good. As long as the Brotherhood stays on Hellhole and I stay on Eagle, I don't care what they have or don't have."

"There you're out of luck," Tilno said, and she watched

him sigh. "Someone on Eagle wants the Invisible Wisdom for his art collection. Someone who can make the TSA cooperate. Someone who can make both the Tri-System planets and T-SP finger *you* for the job, 'Lanni . . . the job of going out to Hellhole and bringing the Invisible Wisdom back here to Eagle."

Alanni managed not to say "Oh shit" and this time she had enough pride not to gulp her drink. She took a small sip and found that her throat was closing against any more. She wasn't sure what her stomach would do, either.

She set the drink down with a clonk of the colored plass. "Fourth Councillor Nortay."

Tilno's eyebrows tipped up at an angle until they formed a shallow V. She knew what that meant: *You're right but I can't admit it.*

"So. I guess I'm not all that surprised, but why me? Why not one of the professional criminals the Council certainly has a line on, or an offplanet pirate-for-hire? Sounds like just the right kind of job for Shieda, for instance."

The V grew deeper, which meant something really bad coming. "Alanni," he said formally, "because Nortay doesn't have any kind of hold on any of them, including fat Shieda, the way he has on you."

Alanni couldn't have lived with a long silence, and so pushed the words any which way. "If I don't go it's my pension and bonus, maybe everything in my account . . ." She hushed herself, knowing she could stand silence better than seeming hysterical.

Tilno was nodding. "You'd be stripped bare, including the farm. They might not stop there, either."

Prosecution for her "abuse of discretion" back when she was a T-SP officer? No doubt, but–

"They wouldn't need to go further," she said, terribly quietly.

If she lost the farm, what would happen to Jay and Bouncy? Bouncy was free, but Bouncy was also a Jarp. Jarps weren't all that popular—except as slaves—because their sexuality and *differentness* made too many people feel uncomfortable. Jarps with no money had been known to be found guilty of something or other that carried a sentence of slavery. Some had had to sell themselves, to avoid starving.

Jaykennador of course was human. He was also an ex-criminal. That could be as big a weak spot as being a Jarp, if one had a powerful enemy. *If I told Councillor Nortay to go bugger himself, Jay would have just that: a mighty powerful enemy.* Jaykennador Eks of Outreach hadn't been away from the dubious pleasures of the criminal's life quite long enough for Alanni's peace of mind. He just might decide that being straight wasn't worth the trouble, with adversity piled on.

Alanni sighed. She had taken on obligations she could not walk away from. Now she'd just have to go where those obligations forced her, and right now that looked remarkably like the planet named Hellhole—for good reason. She also remembered another reason why Nortay might have picked her, apart from her skill and her vulnerability to his squeezing.

One of her early successes was in a computer-fraud case she had built against Councillor Nortay's biggest business rival. It was never proven that Nortay had anything to do with it . . . and it was never really disproved, either. Nortay had a reputation for staying angry a long time and turning minor grievances into running feuds. Did he consider that he was at feud with her?—consider her dangerous to him? The concept made a certain sort of sense, or might to him. In that case, did it make sense to leave Jay and Bouncy?

They might be damned if I do . . . and damned if I don't!

Tilno flipped five, making her realize she'd muttered the last few thoughts more or less aloud. He said, "If I had the answer to that, I'd tell you. I can say that I brought the message because somebody—whose name you'd recognize—asked me to bring it. He said you might say things somebody else could/would testify to in court. *I'd* hold my tongue, even if you didn't."

"Hmm!" That sounded a lot like Prefect Kilwar. *If he's taking an interest in this and if he's at all on my side, Bouncy and Jay might be safe as long as I went to Hellhole. Certainly will be, if Tilno keeps watch too.*

She stood, no longer at all aware of her more than fetching appearance.

"I smell all sorts of vermin in this one, Tilno. Big ones.

Firm, then: I want five thousand birds in my credaccount tomorrow, and the scrute on the Brotherhood by the end of the week. I want hard copy, not computer transfer. I get that and I'll assume it isn't just a set-up, firm? I'll go to Hellhole, and Blackarse Nortay can have either my blood or the Invisible Wisdom. D'you happen to know which he'd rather think about when he's jerking off?''

She yanked the comb with its Hellhole pearls out of her hair so fiercely that strands went with it. The pain only fed her anger. She hurled the comb at the statue in the middle of the pool, wishing the comb was a *shuriken* and the statue Councillor Nortay. Dislodged pearls plop-plop-plopped into the green water like a handful of gravel.

Tilno came up behind her and slid an arm around her waist. The distracted Alanni went on full automatic and slammed both elbows back into his ribs. Tilno sat down on empty air, and went right on back into the pool with a mighty splash.

Alanni stared down. The ripples cleared to show Tilno floating just below the surface. He seemed oddly motionless and suddenly she was more scared than she'd been angry. She must have insulted him by ruining his gift, and now *what if I've really hurt him–!*

Tilno jackknifed and shot upward. Both long legs shot out of the water and clamped around Alanni's left calf. With a scream of mingled surprise and relief, she followed him into the pool.

She didn't stay long. Normally he couldn't lift her, but with the water making her buoyant he hoisted her up onto the rim of the pool. By that time she was wearing only the bracelets and the flower on her left breast, although her straggling hair now covered her as well as the flowers had done. Tilno industriously burrowed his face between her thighs. They opened. So did Tilno's mouth. His tongue slipped forth and darted into the bottom of her invitingly-placed cleft. Neither flower nor hair covered her there!

His lips and tongue worked their way up to the top, then down one side and up the other and then back to the middle. By then she sprawled with her back arched and only her head and buttocks touching the patio. One hand clutched his hair while the other stuffed a handful of her own hair into her mouth to keep the screams inside. Light, but he knew how to get to her!

She had just finished, dizzily, when he settled down to work—which didn't take long.

When he too had soared, she shuddered and heaved herself right off the patio, to flow down over his head and torso. Her breasts weren't quite large enough to reach his ears on either side, but they made a nice comfortable cap he showed no signs of wanting to take off.

At last he got his mouth out of her stash enough to mutter, "Up on the lounger, woman. If you're going into training, we'd better say goodbye now."

"Mmmmm . . ."

"Up, I said!"

"Urmmmphhh!"

The conversation failed to reach a higher level and soon they were both completely bare, Tilno in the inflatable lounger with Alanni on his lap. He raised his knees so that she slid neatly down into place. Grinning, he began rocking gently back and forth while she nibbled at his neck and locked her legs tightly behind his back.

"Uh–uh," she said, which was about the best he could do, as well.

Inflatables have their uses, she mused. *We could never get in all these extra movements on something rigid!*

On the other hand, rigidity has its advantages and uses, too . . .

Rigidity was now the most distinctive quality of the second part of Tilno that wasn't thin. That part burrowed comfortably up inside her while they rocked back and forth. Very comfortably, and getting more so by the second. And not just for her.

"Woman, this is–going to–kill–me!"

"So–o d–d–die ha–happeee! Turn–uh!–about is f–f–fairrr . . ."

"Gggrrhhh," he commented, and that bit of intelligence gave way to a slurping as he got his lips down to her warheads.

She moaned, locking her hands as well as her feet behind him, and pulled her un-petite self more tightly against him.

He heaved, partly to increase the contact and partly to keep from suffocating between her fleshy breasts.

"Eeee-yrrrphh!" she declaimed, as his movements became completely yet agreeably unendurable. "Uh-uh-uh–"

"Arrr!" was all he could get out, on the same occasion.

"Psssssshhhhh!"

The final comment emanated from the lounger, as a seam burst–on the side toward the pool. That which inflates, deflates, and the air rushed out. In seconds the lounger tilted and its two entwined occupants went with it. They were too limp and their minds too much elsewhere to stop what they were doing before they rolled into the pool.

Jaykennador Eks came up to the window behind Bouncy just as the happily coupling couple below ended in the pool with a great splash. He waited beside the Jarp until Alanni and Tilno surfaced, trying to splutter and laugh at the same time. Then he touched the window's opaguing button and glared at his companion.

"I didn't mean to be spying on them," Bouncy said apologetically. "But if they don't seem to care whether anyone sees or not . . ."

Jay sighed. Having some idea of the news Tilno had brought and what came next, he was quite sure that 'Lanni and Tilno hadn't cared. That, however, was not the point at issue. The point at issue was Bouncy's. It was clearly visible, since the Jarp had taken off its shorts and now just as clearly risen. No doubt Bouncy would like for Jay to give it an occasion to have risen to.

Tanned Outreacher gave orange Jarp a look. "So now you're horny?"

"Uh–"

Jay sighed again. Jarps were odd in more ways than that shockingly orange skin and luridly red hair crowning sentimentally sweet faces and mouths unable to pronounce any language save their own. They were hermaphroditic, each with male and female organs and the ability to beget and bear—more Jarps, not Galactics or humans.

The natives of Jarpi were also the most sexually active race known.

Jay supposed that made sense, really. With twice the sex organs, a Jarp had four times the opportunities. (Was that mathematically sound?) So—maybe four times human horniness made some sense. Jarps did not, however, stop there. In fact they damned near didn't stop at all, which was why their sunny, pretty world wasn't on the list of those Protected from interference—and more importantly, from slavers. With no idea of wrongdoing, they had hospitably "raped" the crew of the first ship to land on their planet, which was definitely getting off on the wrong foot as to Jarp-Galactic relations.

Jarps had been screwed ever since, one way or another.

(There were exceptions to Jarp horniness, or so it was said. There was the Jarp known as the Frozen One, who was said to have had not a single sexual thought for an entire day-Jarpi. Opinion varied as to whether that strange individual was sick, mentally disturbed, or purely legendary.)

Jay sat down on the windowsill and kicked off his sandals. "We're not saying goodbye, you know. We're staying right here."

With its scarlet halter in one hand, Bouncy was executing the little jiggling step that had given it its nickname. Like most Jarps, its breasts were too taut and hardly large enough to jiggle along with the rest of it. That didn't stop them from feeling mighty good under a man's hands, and Jaykennador Eks well knew it.

Bouncy stopped jiggling at Jay's words and the little mouth pursed into the Jarp equivalent of a frown. "We aren't saying goodbye *now*. But if Alanni goes and doesn't come back . . ."

"I really sort of wish you hadn't brought that up," Jay said.

Bouncy gazed at its Outie friend, brows up above positively huge and absolutely round eyes. "Would it have been less a possibility if I hadn't mentioned it?"

Jay sighed. "Neg." He stood and opened the frontmeld of the shorts that were his only garment. Bouncy made a happy noise that its translator didn't turn into words, and ran one six-fingered hand up the man's muscular arm.

This could be the beginning of the end for us. I'll miss the Bouncer if it is.

Jaykennador Eks would probably have punched anyone

who called him a "Sunflower," the usual epithet for a Galactic who treated Jarps as people. He might well have killed anyone of any species who or which tried to rape Bouncy. The Jarp had done its share to make 'Lanni's farm the first real home Jay could remember. He'd flashed with a lot of women who hadn't done that that much, and most of them weren't as sexually good as Bouncy, either.

"Think we ought to consider popping down and joining them?" Bouncy asked quietly, pinching its own nipple.

"Neg," Jay said. "And here, let me do that."

3

The second-class passenger lounge of Hellhole's orbital depot Skyraft definitely was. Chipped, hard mud-brown chairs, flatscreen view of the planet below, and what were called "refreshments." Alanni sipped a vile substitute for coffee, smelled an even viler substitute for tea in time not to order any, and sampled (once, briefly) fossilized life forms masquerading as biscuits.

Had the fossilized life forms been edible when they were alive, before their remains spent a million years turning to stone in Hellhole's tidal mudflats?

Her fellow passengers waiting for the shuttle to Bassar offered even fewer prospects of ecstatic pleasure or intellectual stimulation. People who came to Hellhole without having their passage paid for them fell into overlapping categories of the desperate, the adventurous, and the certifiably masochistic.

Alanni could have come more comfortably—the tachyon ship *Darda's Gift* had cabins for twelve as well as a dormitory for fifty. Anyone on the passenger list in one of those cabins would have been conspicuous enough to require more explanation than Alanni's cover story could provide. A second-class passenger dressed like a worker down enough on her luck to try Hellhole would be just another part of the scenery, no more conspicuous than another fixture on one of Skyraft's patched plasteel walls.

(The other safe option for Alanni would have been a comfortable cabin on a cheap ship, without tachyon drive. That wasn't open to anyone in a hurry, which she was. The man she would call Councillor Nortay until she knew otherwise not only wanted the Invisible Wisdom, he wanted it *fast*. That meant either hitting the Tachyon Trail or rearranging the Galaxy to reduce significantly the distance between Eagle and Hellhole. The first course was definitely the more practical.)

With nothing better to occupy her attention, Alanni began noticing that the man sitting next to her hadn't bathed for a good while too long. Since the lounge was less than half full, she changed seats.

The new one gave her a better view of the screen. It was also in the front row. She put her bag out in front of her, propped her feet in their well-scarred equhyde boots up on the bag, leaned back as far as the seat would let her, and contemplated the screen.

It showed nothing but a stagnant pool of clouds the color of well-used dishwater, with a few umber blotches that might have been high mountains. Alanni understood that the clouds looked better from beneath, once one got used to them. That happened fairly quickly or one was in trouble, since the cloud-cover was solid eight days out of ten.

Alanni opened the sadly mistitled WELCOME TO HELLHOLE pamphlet and unfolded the four-color map in the middle. She'd not only seen but memorized under hypnosis far better maps. This one at least showed the gross outline of land and sea.

Hellhole was larger than Eagle but had only .91-Standard gravity—few heavy metals, obviously. It followed as regular an orbit as any planet could in a triple-star system—two live yellow stars, Menzel A and B, plus the dead star Tarf al-Barahut. Between them, the two live suns gave Hellhole a permanent steam bath for a climate. Al-Barahut provided no head but it had enough mass to scramble Hellhole's tides and crust at regular intervals, as it waltzed around with its two live companions.

(One could call the arrangement a threeway, Alanni supposed, except that would imply that Menzel A and B were necrophiliacs.) Most of Hellhole was tepid ocean, swarming with life forms she wouldn't care to meet in a dark alley, and still less in their native waters. It had two continents, Treasure Trove and Fog Coast. Alanni's business lay in Bassar, capital of the Fog Coast, which was why she waited in the lounge.

Bassar provided one shuttle a day, instead of the four to each of the three cities on Treasure Trove—Golden (the planetary capital), Shaitansford, and Sodium Peak.

Treasure Trove produced gold, aluminum, chemicals, and assorted exotic plantation crops. It accommodated four Hellers out of five, not to mention the planetary government—if one wanted to rape both language and logic by referring to it as a "government." A contact was waiting for Alanni in Shaitansford, with everything she'd need to get offplanet after she had the Invisible Wisdom *and* showed it to him.

(Nortay was apparently determined to win the maximum return from a minimum amount of speculative investment. No doubt he'd become rich that way and saw no reason to change his methods.)

The Fog Coast exported pearls, coral (raw and worked), rare woods, and marine creatures to eat, admire, wear, or sleep with (depending on tastes). These exports supported three of the corporations whose obscenely-interwoven Boards of Directors made up the "government." They didn't support nearly as well the men and women who always shortened and often lost their lives on land and sea to find or catch them.

Bassar "governed" these people, entertained them (for a price), bought their catch, repaired their gear, burned them if their bodies were recovered, and sometimes sheltered them in sickness and old age. It also sheltered the people who'd broken hearts, fortunes, or health trying to settle inland beyond the Coast Range.

The land there would make the fortune of anyone with the courage to tame it—or so the government said.

That enthusiasm didn't extend to providing a few other things needed besides courage: medical care, transportation for cash crops, and essential prefab buildings. The land itself might grow hair on a stopper, but if it didn't grow any of these minor necessities, what the Shaitan's good was it? Or so people said, when they staggered back through the passes and down into the cheap lodging houses or charity hospitals of Bassar.

Hellhole has an arsehole, and I'm about to climb up it.

Prefect Kilwar didn't disagree when Alanni said that. He

continued to reserve comment when Alanni wondered aloud whether there were any worse inhabited planets, other than Bleak.

Grumping aside, she knew there were. If Nortay had sent her to one of them, she'd have considered selling up the farm and giving Bouncy and Jay their shares so all three of them could run.

She would have considered that, then picked up the same bag now sitting under her boots, packed it with the same gear, and taken the same train to the nearest spaceport.

The bag had a false bottom and hidden side pockets. In the bottom and the pockets was a basic outfit of gear for high-powered burglary, all of it non-metallic and when folded up not even looking particularly suspicious. (Except to an extraordinarily well-trained and alert policer—or burglar.)

An open patch in the clouds on the screen showed a huge mountain peak, with a diamond choker of snow around its summit and steam trailing from a fissure farther down one flank. As the mountain vanished under new clouds, Alanni noticed that the smelly man who'd been sitting beside her old seat was no longer where he'd been.

Moving her head as little as possible, she scanned the lounge. One of her natural assets was exceptional peripheral vision. At angles where most people could see only a blur, Alanni Keor could recognize faces. At angles where most people could see hardly anything at all, she could detect man-sized objects and sometimes the beginning of attacks.

It didn't take her long to find the man. He was sitting alone in the middle of a half-row of six seats. Apparently her nose wasn't the only sensitive one!

The man was also sitting where, without moving his head enough to be noticed, he could watch Alanni and both doors to the lounge.

Now just what legitimate reason could he have for doing that?

He could be looking for a quick slice.

Maybe, but from a cake dressed the way I am?

Alanni looked down at herself, to be absolutely sure her clothes hadn't done anything to spoil her cover story. Exsecurity guard and spacefarer for a one-ship line, on leave when the one ship went Forty Percent City to evade pirates, after that out of a job. Paid her fare here to Hellhole out of what the insurance left for paying off the few surviving employees, with not much left over for fancy clothes.

She looked as raddled and travel-weary as ever. Of course someone who smelled the way he did might have so much trouble finding women that he was desperate, but–

No buts. Start looking for an illegitimate reason.

He's watching out for Nortay's investment.

Your two hostages back on Eagle do a better job of that. Also cheaper. Try again.

The competition. If there is any.

Why shouldn't there be, for the Invisible Wisdom?

No reason at all, but let's be sure.

The silent dialogue faded away. Alanni's training took over. Picking up her bag, she walked to the women's room—and stopped just inside the door. She couldn't pick out details of the man even with her peripheral vision, but she'd memorized his location. She'd see when he left–

There he goes, moving toward one of the exits. Gone to find help?

He sat down in the last seat of the back row. Now he could see both doors and almost every seat in the lounge. He might not be able to follow her quickly if she left, but he could see when she did, and if he did have help he could call–

No way to find that out but the hard one. Or at least no way that wouldn't leave her either without the scrute she needed or with at least one live enemy on the loose close to her back.

Alanni looked at the clock over the screen. Two hours before the shuttle to Bassar would even be boarding. *Plenty of time to be placidated—even Poofed.*

She spent a convincing amount of time in the women's room, then strode briskly out the door toward the exit at the far end of the lounge. She covered floor fast, trying to look as if she wanted to walk kinks out of her legs.

Her destination was vague. Some place where she could ask her shadow a few pointed questions. (She was carrying the points hidden in her boots.) Odds were good on finding it, if Shadow would just cooperate by following her.

Skyraft had been built on the cheap over Hellhole's centuries of settlement. It consisted of a few special-purpose modules, more worn-out spaceships, and lots of old cargo pods, all connected by a tangle of shafts and tubes. A king-sized version of a child's first toy-construction. Unless Alanni's Shadow had made a full hypnoscan of a recent plan of Skyraft, she'd have the edge in knowledge of the territory.

And if he made a scan too, that's more evidence useful to have.

(Fine, as long as you live to use it.)

A shadow of a Shadow detached itself from the lighted rectangle of the lounge door.

Here he comes!

Alanni shifted her bag to her right hand, to seem even less alert. If the Shadow really had something nasty in mind, he would learn soon enough that in combat Alanni Keor was close to ambidextrous.

She also felt the old familiar acceleration of pulse and breathing. All her senses felt enhanced, as if she was soaring with Tilno or somebody else as good. She'd narrowed down the whole universe to herself and the Shadow, but she sensed every part of that miniverse acutely.

I've come home.

This is home?

It was for ten years.

The corridor ahead divided three ways. Alanni took the leftward branch, past a blue-lit door marked GARBAGE DISPOSAL. Ten meters farther on, she knew the Shadow was following.

Alanni made it easy for her shadow to trail her. As useful as it would be to learn if he knew Skyraft, it was more important not to lose him. Besides, he'd be off his guard if he thought she was too naive or stupid to notice that she was being followed.

Ten minutes after they left the lounge, she was moving even more slowly. She wasn't quite sure where she was.

Hypnoscans were good, not perfect. The corridors in Skyraft were so complex that she wondered whether they might make an interdimensional singularity. She might accidentally find herself keeping company with the spacers that went Forty Percent City, and their crews.

At least she and her shadow were going to be settling matters privately. The compartments on either side of the corridor didn't look as if they'd been used or even cleaned since before Alanni left the TSP.

This could go on until after the shuttle leaves for Bassar, dammit.

Or until he herds you into the hands of friends up ahead?

Thanks for the reminder.

Alanni dodged left into one of the empty compartments, making just enough noise to be sure she was heard. She knelt and pulled off her boots faster than she had thought possible. And she waited long enough to give Myrzha* Shadow time to move into position outside . . .

When she stepped back into the corridor, she thought she'd misjudged her timing. The shadow was gone.

She changed her mind fast enough. It was her own special peripheral vision that saved her, when movement caught her eye—movement in a doorway ten meters away. She had turned halfway around when she knew what she was seeing. A man, leveling a weapon.

Reflexes took over. Without finishing the turn, she threw her go-bag. And an eye-searing light flooded the corridor as a plasmer beam reduced the flying satchel to rapidly-diffusing molecules and a few charred bits large enough to fall.

Lord of Light—he's using a pulsar beamer!

Already she was snatching up and throwing her boots. She drove herself after them while they were still in the air. One boot smacked heel-first into Shadow's forehead. His next shot, incredibly, was a stopper beam. Its incredibility didn't matter, since it hummed over the racing Alanni's head.

Then the shadow's intended prey hit him with both feet and all her weight moving at full speed, airborne to back up those

**myrzha:* the simplest translation from Erts is the ancient "mister."

driving feet. Shadow was slammed through the doorway behind him.

Alanni landed rolling and bounced up onto hands and knees. She had clamped a hand onto the weapon before she noticed that the man had not gone down all the way. He was half-sitting, his head at an implausible angle and his eyes blank.

She rose to her feet to look sourly at the sharp, metal-shod edge of the dusty shipping crate. It had sunk three sems into the back of the man's head. There wasn't much blood, and there wasn't any pulse at all when she fingered his wrist.

Only perfectionists asked to be sure where people were going to land before they started knocking them about. Alanni had been trained by combat instructors who were perfectionists, and she had argued the point with them more than a few times. Lord of Light, when an assailant had a plasma pistol, one needed to *hurry*. A corpse could not answer questions beginning with Why and Who, or course—but a cloud of molecules couldn't *ask* questions.

That knowledge did not stop Alanni from wanting to kick the corpse—hard. Then kick herself, harder.

She knelt by the dead shadow and started searching him.

He had Poofed her bag, which she admitted was considerably preferable to his Poofing her. The problem was that most of what she would need for any sort of quick snatching of the Invisible Wisdom had been in that bag. Most of it wasn't going to be replaceable in Bassar, even if she found the right people. Maybe the agent in Shaitansford would help her—if he could. Maybe he wouldn't. And maybe he couldn't even if he wanted to.

She certainly was not going to be able to gamble her farm and Bouncy's and Jay's futures on the agent, her contact here.

So. I'm on my own.

Yes, and with less equipment than she had expected. Not to mention one more opponent—and now one fewer—than she might have expected! If she could just learn something about the almost-competent flainer . . .

The dead man had been dull enough to swallow her minor

trick, and Poof a harmless object. Unfortunately he hadn't been so just-plain-stupid as to carry ID on this sort of job. He looked as if he might be from Resh, but so did a few hundred million other Galactics.

She did satisfy herself that the late and unlamented shadow wasn't on his own. His weapon was something she'd never seen before and had heard of only as a theoretical possibility. Two barrels stacked vertically, mini-plasmer on the bottom and a stopper on top, all arranged for one-handed use, and the power-cord running up his arm inside his sleeve to a chest-and-shoulder power-pak. Somebody with this piece could do an equally thorough job on either human opponents or real estate, so long as the charge lasted.

That wouldn't be long, with a piece this size and the little power-pak. On the other hand it was easily concealable and could go where a standard plasmer would almost certainly be detected and so prove not usable at all. *A* weapon was always better than *no* weapon, when the browser bull charged.

This semi-competent bug had used an ideal piece for illegal or covert work—and a well-made weapon, too. Whoever had designed and built it hadn't been content with just building something new, exotic. He had wanted good engineering, too. That meant expense. Alanni was looking narrow-eyed at a costly weapon. Something an ordinary hired placidator wouldn't have been carrying without backing.

Pos, but would someone expensively back such a bug as our late friend here with something as expensive as this nasty little piece?

Maybe the boss didn't know all its troops that well.

Maybe. That presupposes a big organization, though.

Firm. It does, doesn't it?

There was one time-dishonored response to that. It was *gulp*.

Alanni's pulse and breathing accelerated again less pleasantly than before. This time fear was lurking darkly within her, like it or not. She squatted beside the corpse of a man *sent* to kill her, and stared at piled crates that told her nothing. No matter; she wasn't seeing them.

Logic said she faced well-financed, possibly well-crewed

opposition who knew she was here and why. They were capable of a mistake; a first-class job had been entrusted to a second-class enforcer. She had left the first move to him, which had run up the odds of her having to kill him. Then she'd let him destroy her equipment by throwing the bag instead of a boot. Even if she hadn't killed him, she'd have been unable to question him thoroughly.

So we were both second-class.

The excitement of being "back home again" had hidden from her how badly her old edge was dulled. So far she hadn't done as well as Captain Alanni Keor would have expected from anyone more than a raw recruit, let alone her exalted self! Oh, she was still fast and tough. Exercises could do that. She could also remember telling recruits that being fast and tough was only part of the job of a professional!

I really wish I hadn't just proven that so unLighted thoroughly!

There was no going back now. Futhermore she had to calm herself before she went forward. If she tried facing really first-class opposition with second-class control, she might as well step out the nearest airlock right now.

With a sigh she rose and started dragging the body to where it couldn't be seen from the corridor. The really nasty part was forcing his head off the puncturing crate-edge. . . . Out of sight of any passerby, she sat down and took the Lotus position, facing away from the corpse. The familiar tension on muscles and an equally familiar pattern of deep breathing worked. Ten minutes, and she was ready to dispose of the body.

She considered that. Since she couldn't carry a ninety-kilo (very) dead weight very far, she moved thirty-kilo crates instead. A dozen or so would make a convincing pile so snug there'd be no sign of the body inside—until it ripened, at any rate. Just to confuse matters further with all the dust about, she would wear the dead man's boots while she was playing stevedore!

She sat down, got them on, stood, moved a crate. On the second, she had help. Bent over with both hands on the big case, she looked its length at the man, who was bent over with both hands on the case. He smiled.

" 'Lo. Need some help?"

"I don't believe this!"

He shrugged and showed her a boyishly ingenuous smile. One hand rose from the crate to make an elaborate gesture that rippled his shirt's full yellow sleeve through the air.

"Happens all the time. 'scalled coincidence. When it's fiction, some people scoff. When it's real life, they say 'I don't believe this.' Captain Alanni Keor, isn't it?"

He straightened, a good-looking devil whose boots matched his shirt and whose very snug, six-way stretch pants were not just blue but *royal* blue; whose sash was red and whose eleven-gallon hat was white.

"Traf! Trafalgar Cuw!"

First he put a finger to his lips and said "Sh!", then he made her a sweeping bow that would have filled D'Artagnan with envy.

"It isn't 'Captain' any more, Traf. I'm retired."

He raised his brows as exaggeratedly as he bowed and gestured. "Oh? Well, you know, when I see a person cleverly wearing a still-warm corpse's own boots to leave *his* tracks in the dust while she makes a nice little house of crates for his body, I just don't think of her as *retired.* As I was saying—want some help, Alanni?"

"I really don't believe this."

"Again or still? We already did that. Here, let's get at it. Lord, lord, you never know who else might come bonkin' along to check a storage room. Whew—looks like permanent storage from all this dust, doesn't it?"

"Uh."

She said nothing else until they had blocked off her late assailant. Her flamboyant assistant took the boots, went up and over their wall of crates, and came back smiling.

"Remind me not to get a job dressin' corpses," he said. "Hard work."

"Trafalgar," she said conversationally, picking up the plasmer/stopper combination weapon, "what *are* you doing in a storage room?"

He pointed to one of the big packing cases. "My employer," he smiled easily. "TMSMCo—mining. Remember? Tell you what—I am *not* going to ask you that question. Old enemy who tried to get you for an old grudge?''

Alanni had remembered about everything, and no longer had visions of Prefect Kilowar stripping her captain's insignia off her shoulders and sending her back to academy. When the body was found, quite a bit of time was going to be spent on how the man had concealed his own body. Taking a look at such trickery from the policer's viewpoint, she knew how such confusion could make big trouble for investigation and pursuit. As to explanations to Trafalgar Cuw of Outreach—certainly she owed him none. Besides, he'd just provided a perfectly logical one.

She nodded. ''Exactly. I'm here for another reason altogether—and I really am out of T-SP.'' She smiled. ''I haven't gone the other way, either.''

He shrugged. ''I seem to've indulged in an illegal act or two, in my time. Chances are you can't help me, then, but I'll ask anyhow. Some friends and I are sort of scouring the spaceways for a woman. An Aglayan—you know, pale pale skin, pale pale hair, eyes the color of a pigeon's breast. Her name's Janja—come to think, some rascal provided her with Outie papers and she's Janjaglaya Wye, now.''

She stared at him, one eyebrow up. ''Some rascally Outie. A woman off a Protected planet. A slave?''

''No, she sort of freed herself, just under a year ago. Owns a spaceship now, ain't that something?''

''And this sore thumb has disappeared and you are . . . *scouring the spaceways for one person?* How many thousands of you?''

''Just her ship's worth. Hey—I helped. And my lips are sealed. You seen her? Heard of her, Alanni?''

She shook her head with solemnity, meeting his gaze directly so he wouldn't question her, until he waved a hand and heaved a sigh.

''All right. No one has, but we're crazy enough to be determined. We are, uh, rich, you see, and really don't have a hell whole of a lot else to do.''

Alanni rolled her eyes. ''That's disgusting, Traf Cuw! So you're looking for this—whoever you said. No, I've been out of T-SP for quite a while, and the name you said is totally unfamiliar. Anyhow—you're looking on *Hellhole?*''

''Theba's dangles, No! Just on Skyraft—I hope. She disappeared on Terasaki. We've already checked a few other places.''

''She's dead, Trafalgar. Or a slave again. Give it up. Why not come down onplanet and have dinner?'' Suddenly she heard herself sounding cold, and added, ''Traf? You—can you be in love with her?''

''Alanni! Please do not talk dirty in my presence! No. Look, she and I and a few others have been through several hells together. We, ah—we love each other, I guess. Something like that. You know, Alanni. We give damns. You're going to pitch that interesting weapon, aren't you?''

She hefted Shadow's weapon. ''I have to go down onto Hellhole. I sure won't try to carry this thing through Customs!''

''So—we waste that lovely—not to mention obviously expensive—monstrosity on the nearest Poofing chamber.'' He held out a hand. ''Please? Once it's inside my shirt, I'll head straight back to my ship and stash it. Excuse me. *Secrete* it. Lord, I'll even swear to give it to you the next time I see you!''

Alanni had to laugh. One could go a long way without meeting another Trafalgar Cuw! He went a step or three past ''unique.''

Just handing him the over-and-under handgun went against the grain. On the other hand—why not? She had been about to chuck it into a disposall, just as he'd said. She handed it over and watched it vanish into the blousy shirt above the tight pants.

He glanced around. ''Well, that's did. Nice job, too. Either your late would-be executioner came in on a ship about the time you did—surely too much coincidence, hmm?—or he picked this thing up here on Skyraft, or the fix is in with the inspector, right?''

''Seems so. I came in on public transportation, don't have a fix in with anybody, and had better go catch a shuttle for planetside. You just go back to your ship and slice—'scuse me, *secrete* that gun.''

The Outie laughed aloud at her twisting his joke back on

him. Then he threw wide both full-sleeved arms. "Give us a hug, Alanni. Mind the bulge in my shirt, now!"

They exchanged a hug, and Alanni enjoyed it. "Spacer *Sunmother,* in case you miss your shuttle," he called. "We have a source of alcohol you'll never believe!"

Probably not, she thought, and watched him stride off, a little wistfully. She did not breathe easily until she was on the Bassar shuttle and it plunged into the omnipresent clouds of planet Hellhole.

4

The screen showing the shuttle's passengers the approaching planet died with a hiss just after the shuttle hit atmosphere. Alanni imagined a thin whine from outside . . . and didn't have to imagine shudders and jolts passing through the thin padding of the seats to her spine. She tightened her seat belt.

At least she wasn't missing scenery. Hellhole's cloudscape would never have inspired Tilno to one of his pastoral poems. It didn't inspire her with anything except a passion to do her job and never see the planet again.

Still, if a screen died suddenly, what did that say about the maintenance of the rest of the shuttle? Not to mention Alanni Keor's chances of ending as part of a smoking crater in the side of a Hellhole mountain?

At least that would save Jay and Bouncy. Councillor Nortay couldn't honestly claim that the shuttle's crash was my trying to betray him.

(Or could he?)

It would, Alanni decided, be much better for everyone (starting with her) if the shuttle didn't crash.

It didn't. An hour after leaving Skyraft, Alanni stepped from the passenger ladder on to the cracked and stained plascrete of Bassar's spaceport. She was the last person out. The other twenty passengers were already scurrying off toward the terminal. Alanni followed, hoping to beat the stain of blackness in the clouds overhead, spreading toward the field from the west.

From safely inside the terminal door she looked back to see a rust-streaked yellow tractor hook on to the shuttle and begin hauling it toward the freight terminal. Then the rain washed out her view of anything more than ten meters away. A gust of wind blew rain rudely into her face. Yells and curses erupted behind her. She heaved the door shut and sat down in a corner seat, uneasily aware that she had much less idea than usual of what to do next.

At least the Customs inspection was behind her, and thank the Light for this small favor, since she clearly wasn't going to receive any big ones on this planet! Like more civilized worlds, Hellhole put its Customs people up on the orbital depot, where one post could sort out everyone landing on the planet—or at least all those who landed legally.

The inspectors hadn't done their work very well. Their missing the false bottom and hidden pockets in Alanni's bag didn't count. Her assassin-Poofed equipment was supposed to be proof against any search up through T-SP standards. One could be a long way short of those without being a sleepwalking incompetent.

But their letting her onto the shuttle without a second look or a single word, when she appeared *without* the bag and hadn't checked it either—that was sloppy and unprofessional, by people who were paid to do better.

Ten per cent of her mind raged at that. Ninety per cent gave heartfelt thanks. Being stopped on Skyraft would have been awkward, even without the additional presence of her little shadow. On a planet there was always somewhere to run if one was fast and smart and only a little bit lucky. On an orbital depot there was no room to do anything except fight or take the first ship out, even if that meant being ship's hust all the way to Bleak or some azaafrunn farm on Nevermind.

So she was free to go wherever she wanted, in what she wore (green tunic, black trousers, dark blue boots) with what her clothes concealed. That wasn't despicable. On Hellhole, gold was about halfway between credaccounts and barter in respectability. Alanni had enough gold in her boot-heels for three Heller days of high living—or ten days of eating light and sleeping cheap.

She also had three different concealed weapons, all supposed to be proof against anything short of a complete demolition of her clothes by people who knew what they were looking for. (Not to mention invisible skills that would make her dangerous as long as she had one arm and one leg working—and even after that, it wouldn't be smart to get within reach of her teeth.)

She wouldn't really have been badly-equipped at all, for a smaller job than this one. If she'd been supposed to go down into Bassar and get a job as hostess in a drug-drop bar, for example . . .

However, the job wasn't going to shrink by her wishing it would do so. The Invisible Wisdom had to be made visible to Councillor Nortay with what she had. This was the last moment she was going to waste wishing for what she would still have but for the stupidity of her own kneejerk act.

So why not go down into Bassar and take a job with the Brotherhood of Servants of Tarf al-Barahut?

A straight inside job?

Why not? Of course, your briefing didn't say much about their security–

Oh, marvelous. I never would have realized that if you hadn't reminded me. I'm eternally grateful.

Alanni pulled the plug on the internal dialogue before it became completely ridiculous. Still, the idea of simply presenting herself at the Temple of the Brotherhood as someone wishing to join them wasn't completely fobby.

Ideally it was always better to study a target from the outside before trying a penetration, open or covert. Realistically, Alanni couldn't spend too much time studying *anything*. She'd either starve or have to find work that might take more time than she could hope to spare, just to stay alive.

At least she'd spend one day in Bassar just studying the city before she even asked the way to the Temple. Briefings were no substitute for personal "eyes-on" work.

Alanni walked over to the insect-specked mirror in the corner of the terminal lounge and adjusted her headband. That was all the vanitizing she could do now, and the familiar hand movements left her mind free . . . to work on a list of what to look for in Bassar.

Outside the terminal, the rain thundered against plascrete and light-metal sheeting.

Right: Hellhole!

• • •

An hour after the shuttle's landing the rain slacked off. Another half hour, and Alanni saw a watery yellow glow in gray clouds overhead. Hints of a second glow tantalized above the hills east of the field. Menzel A was approaching the zenith, with Menzel B dogging its tracks.

If the two suns hadn't been separated by such a generous interval on their daily rounds, Hellhole might not have been inhabitable for Galactic races outside of domed cities. As it was, the heat built steadily. The rain hadn't done a thing to cool—and precious little to dry—the air. The only clothing in which Alanni would have felt comfortable was none at all. The terminal's cooling systemry fought a valiant but foredoomed rearguard action against the heat.

Alanni wiped the sweat off her forehead when it threatened to trickle into her eyes. Otherwise she tried to ignore the heat. She told herself that she'd faced as bad in high summer on Eagle. (Maybe if she told herself this often enough she'd believe it.)

It didn't take her long to wear out "What to do my first day in Bassar" as mental exercise. She started listening to the other passengers. The Hellers at least were talking more freely now that they were onplanet. Two men and a woman in red coveralls were arguing with a second woman in a purple third-cousin-twice-removed to a kaftan. The subject was the best way to travel north from Bassar along the coast to Pearl Haven.

"–breaks up six kloms out in the forest, what comes out of the trees is just as bad as anything you'll find in the ocean," one of the men said.

"He's right," the first woman said. "And it *will* break down, the Dark Brother swallow me if it won't!"

"A boat can sink too," the second woman muttered dubiously.

"It can, but the new ones won't," the second man said. "There's lots of those. Wait a day or two, look around, and you'll have a good choice. Or try your luck with us. We know Aykar of the *Lotus*. She's new."

"Even a new boat can meet a storm or hit a reef," the

second woman just had to say. She seemed determined to go down fighting, like the cooling systemry.

"Aykar knows the coast like he knows his wife's stash," the second man said. "As for storms, I'd rather meet one at sea than crossing one of the coast bridges. It's a turtle-eating long way down from one of them!"

Alanni's briefing mentioned reliable hoverbus transportation up a so-called coastal highway as far as Trail's End, three towns north of Pearl Haven. It began to sound as if the briefing was out of date, since three native Hellers preferred going by sea. Pearl Haven was on the open coast, exposed to the full force of the monthly storms. The road journey must have turned into a real downer.

The idea of a big round hole in her data didn't make Alanni terribly happy. People could fall into that kind of hole and disappear as if they'd fallen into the Maelstrom. The only consolation was that if the boatyards were doing a brisk business she might look one up for a job. All she knew about boats was that they had a bow and stern and were supposed to float. She was handy with enough different tools to make the right sort of impression on anybody who needed anything built.

She was considering asking the travelers whether they knew any boatbuilders in need of workers when the terminal superintendent ambled through the door.

"Brothers and sisters, the bus for Bassar is here."

A look at the timetable (stained yellow-brown and peeling at one corner) stuck up beside the door told Alanni the bus was three-quarters of an hour late. She joined the trickle of passengers toward the door.

The blue-and-white hoverbus crawled toward the terminal, lurching, swaying, and weaving from side to side. Either the lateral controls were gone or the driver didn't know how to use them.

Light, grant that the weather stays good and the road to Bassar is wide and level!

Alanni knew too much about hoverbus crashes. She'd picked bodies out of two, besides taking down survivors' accounts and breaking the bad news to bereaved relatives.

The passengers arranged themselves on the benches along

either side of the main compartment. As they did, a red light glowed from the terminal tower.

Two bare-chested human handlers and a creaking robot platform slid the passengers' baggage into the rear of the compartment and slammed the door. As they stepped clear, the red light turned green. Alanni heard the familiar rumble of a shuttle building up thrust for takeoff.

Stark fear and more than a little self-pity clawed at her throat and kicked her in the stomach until she was afraid she would choke or vomit or both. She fought a mad urge to plunge out of the bus and dash across the field to the shuttle, screaming and pleading to be taken on board and lifted out of here to somewhere else, no matter where!

Then the shuttle reached full thrust and the induction catapult fired. The fat silver arrowhead raced down the rising plasteel track into the sky above the far end of the field. Its drive flared an eye-searing blue for a moment before the clouds swallowed it.

Now there was no way off Hellhole, even in fantasy.

Alanni bowed her head and wound her fingers into her hair until she felt strands pulling loose. The pain restored some of her sanity. She could put herself in the path of being squashed by Councillor Nortay and company; she couldn't do it to Jay and Bouncy.

The holomellers are full of worm droppings, she thought. *Being a hero doesn't give you more choices. It gives you fewer—at least if you take the job seriously enough to do all the work as well as have all the fun.*

When the hoverbus started its engines, Alanni felt as helpless as Akima Mars chained in the hold halfway through "From Resh With Love," not to mention rather less likely to be rescued anything like soon enough.

5

The hoverbus ride into Bassar did nothing to make Alanni feel less helpless. It wasn't quite as bad as she'd expected, which was the most she could say for it. The road into the city lay along the right-of-way of what she remembered as an aborted railroad. Its builders had dreamed of linking the whole Fog Coast; the poor dolts ran out of money before they even finished the section from Bassar to the spaceport.

The builders had left the ground fairly level, and now the road carried enough traffic so that the undergrowth was mostly chopped back. The bus had to stop for the driver to pull branches and leaves out of the intakes only twice. Alanni helped and the driver was sober enough not only to notice, but thank her.

Maybe a job in the hoverbus garage . . .?

Piles of weed-grown plasteel beams and plascrete slabs left over from the railroad kept the trip from being too carefree. The driver seemed to want to steer over or even through the piles rather than around them. He always swerved in time, and usually gave Alanni incipient heart failure before he did. Some of the other passengers also turned a fascinating variety of colors. One woman fainted. The people arguing about the best way to Pearl Haven must have taken this trip before; they went right on arguing.

(Alanni was too busy clutching the back of the bench until her knuckles turned pale to listen. She never did learn how the argument ended.)

The last part of the trip was all downhill, with no obstacles jumping out in front of the bus at the last moment. Alanni forced herself to relax her grip and look around while the bus whined the last few kloms down into Bassar.

The hillsides were studded with what must once have been luxurious homes. Alanni didn't think kindly of building hillside homes in a seismic area. In seismic areas on Eagle, nobody built except on flat land a good way from any hillside that might fall on them. At least most of the homes looked abandoned or shelters only for squatters and vagrants.

Down out of the hills they came, the causeway carrying the road into Bassar from the west. Beyond the city, a rocky peninsula thrust up its shoulders to stretch bluely over a hundred kloms to the north. On the map it looked something like a bent arm ending in a clenched fist, with Bassar perched precariously on the bicep. So much for shoulders and maps.

The causeway carried the road only a couple of meters above the sluggish brown-green water of the tidal flats. The same water, Alanni knew, filled the canals that carried most of Bassar's traffic. Most of the city lay no more than seven meters above high tide and some of it a good deal lower. Half the Bassarites found their feet and sometimes their knees getting wet at least once a year. They stayed even that dry thanks only to a few dikes, judiciously placed to fill in the gaps in the Ahriman Reef just offshore. Those dikes were the best-built structures on the whole Fog Coast and they'd survived major earthquakes before. Still, worse ones were possible, and if one of them cracked the dikes during a storm . . .

Having a lot of boats in and around Bassar made sense. One fine day the whole city might have to sink or swim.

The Bassar City terminal served coastal shipping and canal boats on one side, busses and the few taxis on the other side. Between them lay a huge empty space that must originally have been intended for the railroad. It was large enough for all the students at the T-SP academy to drill there—not just the present pruned-back enrollment either, but all the students of Alanni's own academy days, when the TSA took its policers a little more seriously.

Along the walls nestled a dozen or so booths, roughly built for the most part of timber and salvaged plas or metal sheeting. They poured out clouds of steam and the smells of beer and hot spiced food—which reminded Alanni that she hadn't eaten a real meal since she had left *Darda's Gift* at Skyraft. Her stomach let out a positively feral growl. After counting the coins she'd slipped into her belt pouch from her boot caches, she hurried toward the booths. She wanted something in her stomach to quiet those growls before she set out to learn her way around Bassar.

The smallest of the booths was also the most elegant. The metal sheeting was painted with crude but colorful floral patterns in ruby and amethyst and garish emerald. The wood was not only new but smoothed and varnished to a sheen that showed several layers of grease and grit. Alanni picked that booth simply because she liked the owner's pride of workmanship.

First time I've seen it on this planet, too.

Everyone on Hellhole or even on the Fog Coast couldn't be completely indifferent to whether things worked properly or not. Bassar would be rubble and its people dead of disease or starvation, otherwise. Nevertheless, Alanni had the feeling that the number of people here who gave a Bleaker stell for doing anything right was pretty close to the absolute minumum for keeping things from falling completely apart.

If the Brotherhood could do something about that problem–

You want a cult to do useful work? What next, wanting rootworms to sing?

This isn't getting us lunch, smartass.

I was just about to say the same thing.

Alanni's stomach growled again and she took her place in the short line to the booth.

The plates and mugs were plass. Alanni remembered another policer's joke about such a booth. "Ought to be closed down by the Health Authority or forced to use some other kind of plate. Now, you can't tell where the plates stop and the food begins."

The beer was a long way from Starflare. It tasted a lot more of the original grain. It was still potent. Even better, it was *cold*. Alanni swigged down two mugs before she started on the food. That way she never knew whether it was the beer or the cooking that made the rest of the lunch taste so good.

The fish was fried a crisp golden-brown in some sort of nut

oil, not even vaguely rancid. The bread needed more than its legal share of chewing, but went down smoothly after that. Something called ''hornfruit'' left glue-sticky yellow juice all over her chin and tunic but tasted so good she didn't care.

Solid food left Alanni's stomach purring instead of growling and blew the fumes of the beer out of her brain. She counted her ready money and decided to find someplace cheaper for her next meal. Also some privacy for pulling more coins out of her boot-cache; if there weren't at least half a dozen light-fingered types within shouting distance, she was Setsuyo Puma.

Alanni was looking for the door to the street when a shout from behind slapped her ears.

''Hayaaa! You jumped the line!''

''I did not!''

''You did!''

''He did not!'' Alanni turned, recognizing the voice of the owner of the stand where she'd eaten.

''You let him jump because he's a Brother-lover like you and I'm not!'' the first speaker shouted.

The jacko was small and roughly dressed in a dirty green coverall, but looked tough and certainly had a 250-sem temper in a 165-sem body.

''You love no one, Shirpon, not even yourself,'' the accused man said. ''Nor do I blame you for the last. Who could love—arccchhhh!''

Shirpon had punched him in the stomach.

''Peace, there,'' the stand's owner shouted. ''All of you! Or the policers–!''

The warning came too late on both counts. ''Brother-lovers'' and whatever the opposite of that was were busily grappling and throwing punches. The four policers from the bus side of the terminal were on their way over. Two more nippers were hurrying in from the river side.

Alanni noted with a professional eye that all six needed to trim their waists and clean their uniforms. (Even when clean, those tan suits must have resembled mud. Dirty, they resembled something equally sticky and far more unpleasant to fall into.)

Only one policer had a stopper, but all six had clubs and

cans of what looked like Soothe. Two had locally-produced chemical-explosive handweapons and were waving them around in a way that gave Alanni the acute desire to be behind something solid enough to stop their slugs.

The policers' tactics impressed Alanni even less than their weaponry. They piled into the crowd catch-as-catch-can, hopelessly vulnerable to flank or rear attacks aimed at their weapons if anybody had been thinking of launching one.

Fortunately for the nippers, both factions of the crowd seemed to have reached a consensus in favor of the fastest possible departure from the scene. From being well outside the riot, Alanni was all too swiftly propelled right into the path of the fugitives.

She had time to see several people pushed against the polished stand, hear wood crack, and see the stand go over. While the fugitives blocked her view, someone under the wreckage screamed horribly. Here came a swirly clot of fugitives stampeding past, with one of the policers herding them along. The bastard was taking wild swings at their buttocks with his stick as he ran.

A harder look showed her that the policer was in fact aiming his stick very carefully at the place where it would inflict the least injury. Looking brutal, he was really chasing people to safety, without putting them in danger of worse than a bruised rump.

As he passed, Alanni saw one of his comrades flailing with his club at the tangle of bodies around the stand. Someone else screamed—high-pitched and desperate. A third someone tried to jump to safety over the wreckage of the stand. It was Shirpon, the small man who'd started the riot.

He traveled just far enough to be a nicely-silhouetted target against the pale gray of the terminal wall, with no one behind or on either side of him to confuse even the most inept marksman. One of the pistol-toting policers saw him. His shot smashed at Alanni's ears. Shirpon's head was suddenly red jam from nose to lower jaw.

The impact hurled him off the stand and and against the wall. He slid down into a half-sitting half-lying slump, leaving a glistening crimson trail on the wall.

Alanni swallowed and remembered a computer-precise lecturer at the academy discussing explosive-propellant weapons:

"They are manifestly less efficient than stoppers. However, their noise, flash, usefulness as clubs, and gross physical effects on human anatomy give them certain psychological advantages. It is *not* a mark of a professional law-enforcement person to depend on these advantages—at least not in T-SP."

By the time the voice faded out, Alanni had taken three firm steps toward the not-so-professional law-enforcers.

She had only the vaguest notion of what she was going to do once she reached them, other than that they would probably not like it.

She had an extremely precise notion that she was going to throw up if she didn't do *something*.

She was halfway into the fourth step when the voice returned, not at all computerlike and behind her left ear, stead of inside her skull.

"Don't. If you do and Sergeant Zayain has his way, you won't live to stand trial. You won't want to, either."

A hand like a waldo claw clamped down on her shoulders

Alanni's wits were just far enough ahead of her reflexes to make her turn partway around before going into action. She saw that the hand was attached to the left arm of the policer who'd been driving the fugitives without trying to hurt them.

She had time to see that he was only a few sems taller than she and not unpleasantly round-faced. Then he swung his club at her head. Now her wits were on top of the situation and she took her cue. She screamed and fell, rolling away from the man and clasping one cheek as if he'd actually hit her. The club came down again, hard enough to frag her skull if it landed. She rolled again.

She rolled a third time when he launched a kick. A boot aimed halfway between crotch and warheads rode up and over one rounded hip. Jarring, but harmless. Alanni curled into a fetal ball and lay there, whimpering and gasping convincingly.

Down on the gritty plascrete floor with gravel gouging her cheek, she had time for a thought:

He trusted me a long way, hoping I'd see his act and play along with it. If I hadn't been playing, I could have him down and be taking him with me right now, Sergeant Zayain or not!

She lay curled up until she heard the sound of booted feet receding, then fading out entirely. She stayed down until the silence seemed to have lasted forever . . . and a little longer. When she heard groans and scrabbling fingers, she sat up.

Except for Shirpon's indisputable corpse and two conditionally living people, she was alone in the terminal. One of the living people was kneeling beside the other, making a rough physical examination with one hand. His other arm dangled uselessly.

Alanni stood. She realized that someone else had to be around. Neither the patient nor the doctor was groaning. A little more concentration, and she knew the groans were coming from under the wreckage of the stand.

She was dismantling the pile of lumber and sheeting before it occurred to her that she was now hopelessly "involved." Giving unauthorized help to riot victims was almost as bad as rioting oneself, on a good many planets. Was Hellhole one of them? Alanni couldn't remember. She hauled away on the planks even more desperately, as if the answer might be found under–

"Oh, Lord of Light!"

The groans were from the stand's owner. He'd fallen against the fish-fryer when the stand went over. Hot oil had splashed all down one side of his face and neck onto his chest. Blackened hair, an eyelid fortunately closed over what must lie behind it, shriveled lips drawn back from decayed teeth–

Suddenly Alanni's lunch said emphatically that it wanted *Out*. She scrambled clear of the stand, leaned against the wall, and was desperately sick until her stomach was empty and even a while longer. While her guts slowly unknotted themselves, she became aware of someone wiping her face with a cold cloth.

"Have you any hurt?" a voice said, from her right.

Alanni turned, nearly toppled over, and leaned back against the wall until the three revolving terminals turned back into one. Stationary, too.

"I don't think—so," she said cautiously.

Still more cautiously, she flexed arms, legs, and neck. *Nothing more than bruises and aches tomorrow,* she decided. *Nothing at all, compared to that poor bastard* with . . .

She closed her eyes and felt her stomach twist again. When it stopped she shook her head.

"Then—in the name of the Brotherhood of All, can you help me with the brother and sister who lie here in need of healing?"

The speaker was darker than the usual Heller, a good ten sems shorter than Alanni, and hairless as the Invisible Wisdom itself. He wore sandals and a knee-length saffron robe, with a much-darned blue sash holding up a small black equhyde pouch. The skin around his eyes was subcutaned crimson, so that he seemed to be wearing a mask.

"Are you of the Brotherhood of Servants of Tarf al-Barahut?"

The man gave what Alanni knew was one of the ritual answers:

"Whose quest for the Way is without ceasing."

This saves a whole big fat bunch of time in finding the Brotherhood! "Right now, let's go on a quest for a way to help these poor bugs. Where's the nearest hospital?"

"The First Temple of the Brotherhood is close and its Healers are true-sworn."

"Are they any *good?*"

The Brother took a deep breath. "They are no worse than any Healers who will treat these people elsewhere. Perhaps better. Certainly better than leaving them lie here until the lawless givers of the law think of them, which they may not do at all."

Alanni felt like hugging the man—and remembered his injured arm just in time. Anybody who shared her opinion of those disgrace-to-the-name-of-policers had to be more on her side than not.

More practically–

"What's wrong with her?" She pointed at the woman the Brother had been examining.

"Her knee appears injured."

When Alanni used one of the stand's knives to cut open the woman's chartreuse pants, the knee looked worse than injured. It looked a fragged, bloody mess. Boot or club? No way of knowing, but one thing certain: it was either a major regen job or amputation for the victim. Hellhole being what it was,

Alanni suspected it would be the second. Either way, this poor bug needed first aid about half an hour ago! The burned man needed it even worse—Alanni knew of no way to amputate an injured head.

Alanni used strips of the woman's pants to immobilize her knee as much as possible. Fortunately the "patient" stayed unconscious through the work. Alanni hoped that didn't mean a head injury.

The terminal was still empty; no one had returned either to help or interfere. That was a bad sign as far as Alanni was concerned. If people were so afraid of the policers that they'd abandon the injured rather than risk coming back and getting into trouble . . .

It looked rather as if she and the Brother were on their own.

She collected enough rags from other stands to make a rough sling for his broken arm. By the time she'd finished that, the stand's burned owner had also fainted. She showed the Brother how to put him out again if he started to reawaken.

"Boil cloths at one of the stands, soak them in cold water, put them on his burns, and keep soaking them. Can you do that with one hand?"

"I can do no less than my brother asks of me."

Alanni hoped this meant "Firm," but she wasn't about to wait for a translation. Sooner or later *someone* was going to screw up its courage to return to the terminal, then call more of the alleged policers if they weren't already on the way. Alanni felt an overwhelmingly strong preference for being elsewhere before that happened. She turned a hopeful look at the Brother with his crimson "mask" of subcutaneous dye.

"Can we reach the First Temple by water?"

"We can reach a place where the Brothers keep watch for those needing aid."

"Then I'll go call us a boat."

"The boatmen have not the spirit of Brotherhood, but the spirit of Gold."

"I can appeal to that spirit," she told him. "Don't worry. Now go and start working on our burned friend!"

"Your spirit is true, though your tongue shapes unholy words."

"Uh." Alanni practically ran across the terminal, to get out of range of any further moralizing. Were all the Brothers going to be like this one? If so, it seemed unlikely that they would really do much practical good, Healers or not. Certainly nothing to justify her getting involved with them in the hope of making things better on Hellhole.

You're not here to make things better on Hellhole, you vacuum-brain! You're here to make them worse by one Invisible Wisdom—if the thing was an asset here in the first place. Then we redshift this . . . Hellhole so fast you'll be home on Eagle before they know you've left Hellhole! Helping riot victims may let you feel good again after Skyraft, but it's not a bit of use for the real job!

Oh? Then why am I doing it?

Silence, which lasted all the way to the canalside door of the terminal.

6

Alanni couldn't expect that the boatmen at the dock hadn't heard the riot in the terminal. Nobody within three hundred meters who wasn't dead or deaf could have avoided that. She only hoped they hadn't all fled like the stand owners. No way in the Galaxy she and a temporarily one-armed Brother were going to haul two badly-hurt and helpless riot victims all the way to the First Temple.

When she stepped out onto the dock the sky was turning black again, as if Hellhole had no suns at all, rather than two. A rising damp breeze warned of more rain. Most of the boatmen were preparing their craft to ride out the storm or were already huddled in the sterns, swathed in rain gear. Alanni was able to find a two-person boat without giving everyone dockside a good look at her.

While the sky turned steadily blacker, she and the boatmen bargained over the price of the trip itself, of having the folding shelter erected amidships, and of helping her carry her helpless charges from the terminal to the boat. By the time the bargaining was done, one of her boot-caches was empty and the other halfway so.

She told herself it was money spent in a good cause, even if it meant less survival time in Bassar without a job. (Although if in Bassar riots were considered a normal way to work up an appetite for lunch, she might need other things besides money.)

She also told herself that it was good rather than bad that the two boatmen hadn't so much as raised an eyebrow over the injured. People who could keep their mouths shut when they were paid enough were always useful—more so if one was on the gray side of the law. *Which is precisely where I've put me!*

Five minutes on the way to the First Temple, the black sky opened and spewed out not only chilly rain but a howling wind. By then the boat was out in the middle of the "canal" (really an arm of the bay to the south of Bassar), and several hundred meters from the nearest land. With the wind churning up the waves to make the little craft lurch like a tractor with a flat tire, Alanni couldn't help wondering. How much water lay *under* them?

By the time the rain was coming in horizontally, the boatmen decided to take the storm seriously. Groping through visibility reduced to less than twenty meters, they ran the boat into the mouth of the real "canal," flanked on either side by three- and four-story buildings.

One of the boatmen looked dubiously up at the buildings. Out of the wind now, Alanni could speak instead of screaming.

"What's wrong now?"

"Oh, just lookin' to see if we maybe have that one down on top of us, 'fore the storm's over."

"Firm?"

"He don't know, lady. A blow like this—it's gone before anything falls over."

"Some, maybe. I've seen 'em this hard, they last–"

The argument over how long the storm might last gave Alanni a chance to crawl into the shelter amidships and examine the injured. The woman was conscious and pale with both shock and pain. She still had the strength to grip Alanni's hand and smile at her. The burned man was still out of it. A mercy, that. The Brother seemed to be meditating, which might not do the victims any good but at least couldn't do them much harm. Alanni left him alone.

The boatman who thought the storm was going to last had just finished convincing his partner—when the wind began to drop and the rain died. That started the argument all over again. By the time the boatman agreed to disagree and started the motor again, even the open water was doing no more than heaving gently.

Now if it will just stay this way . . .

Alanni knew of worse places to go swimming than a Bassar canal . . . a flooded greaseroot paddy at night in the worm-spawning season would be one pleasanter substitute. She couldn't think of many. As for her two helpless charges, maybe the Brother could help and probably the boatmen would. So far on Hellhole the probabilities hadn't been working much in her favor. She would believe in their doing so when she saw it.

The bay narrowed to what might have been a natural river channel with a little engineering work along its banks. Here the buildings were no more than two stories high but packed together. Some of them leaned crazily toward one another, like homebound drunks holding one another up.

Where they ran out of land, the Bassarites took to the water. Houses, huts, tacked-together shelters, and even a few tents sprouted from boats all along either side of the channel. Some of the boats looked like once-seaworthy craft now retired. Others were barge-like arrangements of randomly-chosen and assembled pieces that couldn't have sailed across a pond in a stiff breeze. Beside one quay, workmen were swarming over an obviously new craft, fitting a cabin amidships. This one was a good thirty meters long. Alanni saw the name *Chrysalis* roughly painted on the stern.

"How's the boatbuilding trade?" she asked the first boatman. "I've heard they want workers."

"You come here thinkin' that, you weren't thinkin'," the man said. "Plenty of jobs, and maybe eight people asking for each one. Me, I got a cousin in Kuru's yard. If you're friendly to me, I give your name to him?" His eyes tramped heavily up and down Alanni's body.

The second boatman threw back his head and did something halfway between sneezing and laughing. "That cousin of his—he works when he's sober on a day they need help. That doesn't come often."

The first boatman glared, then went grumbling back to the stern. He sat there in a sulk the rest of the way up the canal to the Brotherhood's dock.

The First Temple of the Brotherhood stood half a klom back from the canal and a hundred meters above it. Stone steps wound all the way up from the dock to the gate in the walls around the Temple. Alanni looked after the rapidly-disappearing boat and wondered how she and the Brother were going to haul their charges uphill.

"Huappppp! Duty!" The Brother had his good hand cupped around his mouth and was shouting in the manner of a browser herdsman trying to turn an enraged bull. "Duty!"

The shouts brought four women and a young man dressed the same as the Brother scurrying out of the hut to one side of the steps. The older man made a series of gestures that looked as if he was trying to scratch the itches of five people at once. The young man bowed and ran off up the stairs in a flurry of yellow skirts. The women bowed even more deeply and squatted on the dock around the two riot victims.

Alanni studied the women. All were young and looked both well-muscled and slightly underfed. *Just girls.* The subcutane around their eyes was a blue so pale it looked almost white on the darker skins. As for their attire—they were barefoot, bareheaded, and otherwise wore only knee-length shorts and abbreviated tops, both of which fastened up the back. The clothes were identical in fit (wretched), cut (baggy), and color (a gray so dingy Alanni couldn't decide whether they were dirty or not).

The tops and shorts looked to her as if they'd been designed while drunk by someone who'd heard a general description of a woman but never actually seen one, clothed or otherwise. At least Alanni decided this would do as a working hypothesis until she had more evidence.

She wasn't looking forward to being around the Brotherhood long enough to gather that "more evidence." Maybe these girls were servants . . . or members of the cult who were being . . . punished? Maybe they were undergoing an initiation.

And maybe their thin-flanked look, their bare feet and wretched clothes, their refusal to meet her eyes, all said something about the way the yellow-robed brethren treated females.

Alanni considered, while her lips went very tight. Of course her briefing hadn't damned the Brotherhood for playing sex-

and-power games. It hadn't said they did *not* play such games, either. In fact, it had been silent on the whole matter.

She wondered how much of the information for that briefing must have been supplied by Councillor Nortay. *It makes too damned much sense to think Nortay withheld what he knew on the Brotherhood's treatment of women, so I wouldn't learn what I had to deal with until it was too late. And it is too late. So shut up, you fobby voice of alleged common sense!*

(The voice said nothing. Alanni wondered if it agreed with the notion that Councillor Nortay was taking an exquisitely subtle revenge. It would certainly be like the wormspawn!)

Meanwhile, two hurt people were still lying on the dock and the sky was turning black. Again. *Are the gods of Arsehole always at a beer party, so they're always pissing on us?*

"Let's move these people under shelter," Alanni told the women.

One of them looked up nervously, then squeaked when another grabbed her hair and pulled her head down again. Otherwise they might have been four statues.

"I said, let's move these people under shelter," Alanni repeated more loudly.

They weren't deaf even if they might be mute. Was it that she wasn't one of the Brotherhood and so had no authority over them? She turned to the older Brother.

"Can you tell these women–?"

The Brother looked at her with something distinctly akin to distaste on his face, but made more quick signals with his good hand. The girls were just picking up the burned man when the younger Brother came hurrying down the stairs, followed by six more females.

Five were dressed identically to the first four and carried two stretchers. The last was older, solidly-built, nearly black, and carrying a medkit. Her subcutane and the younger Brother's were both greenish. So was her tunic. She didn't meet Alanni's eyes only because she went straight to the burned man, knelt beside him, pulled a tube of sterigel from her kit, and started squirting it on the burns. Alanni recognized the kind of daktari to whom the rest of the world wasn't quite real when a patient needed care.

She stepped back, relieved to see at least one woman in the Brotherhood who seemed to be other than a semi-slave. She was even more relieved to have someone competent taking charge of the injured.

Too relieved?

Certainly her faith in her own competence had taken a few knocks today. Probably more than on any single day since she had been a freshly-admitted academy cadet just learning the policer's trade—although there was that first time she and Tilno ever soared, or *tried* to soar . . .

She closed her eyes. *Stop it. You don't love Tilno and even if you did the only way back to him from this Light-forsaken Arsehole is through the Brotherhood's treasure room!*

I can still miss him even if I don't love him (defiantly). *And I can still miss sunlight and a dry wind, too.*

Maybe the Brotherhood's clothing for its women made a perverse kind of sense? At least in Bassar at this time of year, the weather was so damp one might as well have been taking a bath all the time, and whoever wore clothes in the bath?

That still doesn't explain those fastenings in the rear—and if there's any innocent purpose for them, I'm a–

"Elder Brother Luctan! This is an honor!"

A pleasantly deep voice replied. "Only sinful curiosity, I fear. It seemed to me that there was more than a simple matter of Duty here. It seems that I was correct."

Alanni felt fingers digging into her upper arm, forcing her around to face the second voice. She stamped on the impulse to vivisect the fingers' owner and let herself be turned.

Elder Brother Luctan stood a beautifully-proportioned 185 sems and balanced on his bare feet like a dancer. The subcutane around his eyes was also crimson, but stretched back to his ears and halfway down his cheeks. In spite of this exotic look, the simple Brotherhood robe he wore didn't conceal the healthy male animal.

Too healthy. *He looks like a holomeller-romance actor playing a cult priest.* Both the judgment and her haste in reaching it bothered Alanni. Before she could explore the matter any further, Luctan was speaking to her.

"Is it true that you have shown a sense of Duty rare in one who has not sought the Way?"

Alanni bowed her head, which looked becomingly humble. (It also dropped enough hair down over her face to hide most of its expression.) "I do not know what comes of seeking the Way. Indeed I would be lying shamefully if I said that I came to Hellhole seeking it. I sought–" what was the phrase pseudo-ascetics always loved? "–worldly wealth. What I found was a need to do work that it seemed I was the best person to do."

She summarized the day's events, or at least all the events other Brothers (or simple inquiries) could confirm. (Skyraft was none of Elder Brother Luctan Holomeller Star's business.) When she'd finished, she thought Luctan was trying to hide a smile.

A very good holomeller-romance actor playing a priest.

Luctan signaled to the doctor and they spoke so low that Alanni couldn't hear. She had time to notice that another man was standing close behind the Elder Brother.

Also the way he was standing. Graceful, but not like an actor or a dancer. More like a trained martial-arts adept, ready to move into action in any direction between one breath and the next.

In plain words, a bodyguard.

"Sister–"

"My name is Yimra Tewao, Elder Brother."

A precisely-timed frown wrinkled the elegant features. "Sister, our Healer says that you did well for those your sense of Duty caused you to help. Are you a Healer yourself?"

Here's a chance to be more than a slave–

And also to be in a real slimepit once they learn you've lied!

"No, Elder Brother. I—this Sister is no Healer. At least she has no training as one. What she knows is what she has learned, working in places where there was no Healer at all and it seemed that others would do more harm. Over the years, it seems that she has learned something."

The daktari nodded and the Elder Brother grinned. *If you are grinning because referring to myself in the third person is what you expect of a woman, one of these days I am going to remove both that grin and the equipment you use to grin with—very slowly. Although I do have a date with Councillor Nortay first.*

"Then would your sense of Duty allow you to enter the service of the Brotherhood? There is much healing to be done here in Bassar, as I am sure you know."

"This sister has seen as much," Alanni said, and bowed her head even lower, as if overcome by the honor of the offer.

She *had* to hide her face while she wrestled with her decision, for all the seconds she had to make it.

As a woman, she was probably going to have problems in the Brotherhood. Big fat problems with long claws and knotted hair and bad breath. That stuck out like Tilno's slicer and wouldn't lead to such agreeable experiences.

On the other hand, she was being invited right into the Brotherhood itself. Maybe even into the First Temple, where the Invisible Wisdom lay? She wouldn't have to waste time finding (a) a way to receive the invitation just handed to her on a platter or (b) the equipment to pull the snatch from the outside. Since saving time was important (save time = save Jay and Bouncy), wasn't this the best offer she could have hoped for?

(Not to mention the little problem of keeping herself alive in Bassar while she explored other approaches to the Invisible Wisdom. Even if she wasn't known to the policers now, it seemed remarkably easy to become known to them. Unfavorably known. After that—she remembered Shirpon's bullet-mangled head. And the policers wouldn't be the only enemies it would be hard not to make, and maybe not even the best-armed. *Bassar's a jungle, and you want to turn down an invitation into the fort?!)*

She tried to speak, found that dry lips wouldn't form words, coughed to cover that, and took a deep breath. "This woman knows only some of Duty. She has not yet learned Silence and Obedience."

"The Brotherhood demands nought else save that you learn with a free will and a ready heart," Luctan pronounced. "We would be foolish indeed if we call unfit all who have no fault save ignorance! The Dark Lord, Tarf al-Barahut, has greatly blessed us and through us all who seek His Way, by giving us the knowledge of how to teach. Blessed be the name of Tarf al-Barahut."

"Blessed be his name," everyone around her kneejerked, in a ragged chorus. Even the daktari joined in—while her eyes remained aimed at Alanni with an expression not wholly clinical.

I wonder if she's a lesbian with designs on my body as something other than as an assistant or a patient? If so . . . it's opportunity's knock! I go through training in Duty, Silence, and asskissing, and sleep my way into being her assistant. More status, more freedom of movement . . . and more chances for snatching the Invisible Wisdom. She gave her answer:

"Blessed be Tarf al-Barahut, who has caused the Brotherhood to be. Blessed be the Brotherhood, which has given this one a chance to learn the Way!"

"Blessed be our new Sister!" Luctan shouted, and the same ragged chorus followed. He bent down to kiss Alanni chastely on the forehead. She had a brief ghastly thought.

What if these nuts aren't *up to their tonsils in browser-dung?*

7

Alanni nodded to the girl who held the wooden post upright in the hole. She took a firm grip on the post while Alanni took one on her sledgehammer. She swung the hammer back, up, over, and down on the head of the post. Five good thumps and the post barely wiggled when the other woman tried to shift it. Two more, and Alanni nodded again, this time to the wiring party one post behind her on the bank of the new drainage ditch.

Alanni shouldered her sledgehammer and led her teammate down to the next hole and the post lying beside it.

All along the newly-dug ditch, teams of men and women were digging holes, driving posts, and stringing wire for the fence. With more expert supervision than the Elder Brothers seemed able to give, Alanni knew the work would have gone quite a lot faster. With proper machinery, she could have finished the whole job yesterday and with five helpers stead of thirty.

This, however, was not the way of the Brotherhood of Servants of Tarf al-Barahut when they taught their new recruits—the Children—Duty, Obedience, and Silence. Even if they could have provided the machinery, they preferred to use methods that kept as many of their new recruits working as hard as possible for as long as possible.

If you're too tired to think, you don't ask awkward questions. So went Alanni Keor's sour theory.

Maybe that was doing the Brotherhood an injustice. The ditch needed a fence to keep their sheep from falling into it. The ditch was needed to drain a waterlogged field on the farm surrounding the Second Temple, in the hills of the peninsula above Bassar. That field was needed to grow vegetables for the Temples, with leftovers donated to the hospitals in the city. Alanni knew that her sweat and aches weren't being entirely wasted.

Only problem is, if we try to drain every waterlogged field on Arsehole, the oceans will rise and drown everybody. (On the other hand, maybe that's not such a bad idea.)

Twenty days of Heller weather and the Brotherhood's hard work, scanty meals, and curious notions about Obedience (and females!) had made a few changes in Alanni.

Her figure was better. Her disposition was worse. Her vulva was sensitized unto soreness from being sliced by Brothers with more urge to merge than knowledge of how civilized folk screwed. Though she was perpetually hungry, she savored the growls of her stomach. They were about the only noise she could make without being reprimanded or punished.

She also knew a good deal more about the Brotherhood. Little was to the cult's credit. She knew very little about the location and security of the artifact called Invisible Wisdom.

This did not strike her as an outstanding record of accomplishment after twenty days-Heller. She only hoped that if Councillor Nortay heard the scrute on her situation, he'd give her credit for intentions and good faith, if not for work accomplished. (Hadn't there been a Homeworld religion that wound itself into snarls and schisms over the matter of faith versus works?)

At least things seemed likely to get better rather than worse. She could do the work of any two of the other Children of the Brotherhood. Nothing surprising in that; most of them looked as if they came from homes where a full meal was a major event. It did not unduly tax the intellects of even the most persistent stash-hounds among the Brotherhood to perceive that Sister "Yimra" was a welcome addition to the work gangs. A sledgehammer, yet!

Any hopes that this would spare her the attention of the stash-hounds were quickly smashed. Obedience was Obedience was Obedience. All her good work meant was it, plus a lot of opening her legs, would guarantee her a high mark—once she'd finished her Novitiate.

So, Alanni/Yimra gritted her teeth (quietly, because that was a disObedient noise) and took what she had to take. With her eyes and ears open as well as her legs.

Being in search of the Way did not seem to make the Brothers less talkative, particularly when they had their robes hoisted and their attention focused on a woman in similiar condition—and on all fours, usually. Between grunts and groans (usually theirs, unless she had to fake a response—and occasionally one did get to her—briefly), Alanni learned quite a lot.

Luctan's spring-heeled shadow/bodyguard/whatever was Tuke. The Elder Brother who'd met her in the terminal (and whose broken arm was healing nicely) was Chayim. Older, he seemed closer to having the sense to find the right place when he wanted to piss than most of the other Brothers, Elder or Younger. The Healer was Sister Miembra-daktari, and there remained no doubt that she was a lesbian with her eyes on Alanni for both professional and recreational purposes.

Alanni hoped that matters would work out the way Miembra wished. Oh, Alanni preferred men. She also preferred a position with status, particularly since one now would put her in the First Temple with more freedom of movement than most of the Brotherhood.

With that first step up, she didn't expect too much trouble in finding the Invisible Wisdom. Of course getting out of the Temple and away from the Fog Coast with it would be another matter.

However, one thing at a time, as the bisexual Galactic male said to the three Jarps.

The work on the ditch was finished by noon. The work gangs ate lunch in the shelter of a tent-fly tied to a triangle of trees. The rain was undaunted; it blew in anyway.

Lunch was coarse bread, an even coarser vegetable that bit back when Alanni bit into it, and fish stew. Hardly a banquet, but she was hungry enough to enjoy anything. Some of the other Children must not have eaten this well in all their lives, before joining the Brotherhood.

(That knowledge made Alanni a lot more tolerant of the apparently willing slavery of so many of them. A full belly had power to overcome a great many scruples in a starving woman.)

Seasoning the lunch was the usual sermon and prayers. Today's sermon was already familiar ground—how Tarf al-Barahut had appeared to Kayab bin-Tarf, Eldest Brother. Nothing in it about Kayab himself (though Alanni knew he'd been a professor of history and philosophy at Planetary University in Golden), and no details about his alleged vision.

Probably can't agree on a story to pass on to the gaping multitude.

Some of the Children really were gaping, too. Not Alanni. She'd heard details of more different religions than she could count without taking her shoes off—had she been wearing any. She had never heard any convincing arguments for abandoning her own rule: look at what the cultists do in this world and don't worry about the next (if any).

So far, except for Miembra-daktari and Elder Brother Chayim, the Brotherhood wasn't showing up too well. Not to mention that Alanni wasn't sure the Brotherhood could take much credit for Miembra. For her, being a physician was a religion she'd taken seriously long before she ever heard of the Brotherhood.

Alanni found that she was happier to think that there was something smelly about the Brotherhood. She knew why, too.

The worse the Brotherhood was, the clearer her conscience about lifting the Invisible Wisdom out of their hands.

So why are you worried about a clear conscience now? Haven't you been in the gray long enough to know there's no such thing?

Being in the gray never taught me that.

Then you're a slow learner.

Maybe.

Maybe, too, she'd have been happier to find that the Brotherhood was really doing indispensable work in Bassar. Light knew there was work enough for *somebody* to do—work that might make the difference between life and death for a lot of Bassarites.

By the time Alanni's thoughts had traveled that far the

sermon was over and it was time for prayers. She came as close to praying then as she could, but her almost-prayers were distinctly unorthodox.

She was praying for Councillor Nortay to die of a slow and painful infection from a love-bite by one of his mistresses.

Any—Something—that answers this prayer can have my allegiance for as long as—It—wants it.

After lunch, the work gangs marched off for the afternoon's jobs. The Children tramped uphill in single file, rigidly maintaining a five-meter interval and looking down at the ground. This was common sense as well as a principle of Obedience; the track was rough for bare feet. On the other hand, Alanni had seen more originality in cyber-bartenders.

At intervals Younger Brothers and Sisters (Alanni saw only two of the latter) stood, ready to enforce whatever needed enforcing with their Instruments of Obedience. These Instruments were thumb-thick, thirty-odd sems long, and roughly cut from cheap wood. It took a strong Brother or an unlucky Child to produce permanent injury with such a club. Serious pain was something else again. Anyone who didn't seek to avoid the Instruments as much as possible was in Alanni's opinion either mentally deficient or fond of being hurt. Not being either, she was careful.

She was also grateful that the Brotherhood was apparently too cheap or too confident of the docility of its slaves to equip the "policers" with slavewands, Soothe, stoppers, or something even more potent.

At least officially, Alanni amended reflectively.

Just ahead of her walked a young woman named Shamat. She had obviously run into something a good deal more lethal than the Instruments of Obedience, and more than once. She looked no more than sixteen, with close-cropped dark brown hair and skin that might have had a lovely translucent quality if it hadn't been covered with dirt and scars. Scars marked her arms, shoulders, and legs, as well as other places that showed only in the bath. Some inside still showed in her eyes. For all this, Shamat was as tough as plasteel and next to Alanni the hardest worker among the Children. Whatever the Brotherhood had done to her hadn't turned her against them—and of course, Alanni didn't know how long Shamat had been with them. Some of those scars could date back before her joining—although in that case, how had she gained them?

Alanni had the feeling that Shamat might be worth some private conversation. She sighed. That opportunity wouldn't be coming soon, at least without dire penalities for disObedience.

Wait until I'm helping Miembra. Then maybe I can call Shamat in for an "examination" and ask a few questions in return for whatever she might call a favor.

Alanni tramped on up the hillside track, trying not to sway her hips or wiggle her rump. Tight shorts did nothing to hide such feminine movements, although she had fewer of them to hide now. She'd lost not only the three kilos she kept on to provide jiggle but five kilos more in addition. She hadn't been so lean and hungry since she'd left the Academy.

Halfway uphill she saw a Younger Brother waving his Instrument at her. He held it at such an angle that for a moment it looked as if his own instrument had suddenly grown to prodigious size. While Alanni suspected that his signal was indeed related to the state of his personal instrument, she doubted it had suddenly grown *that* much. She smiled (since giggling was disObedience).

Smiling was disObedience too, in the eyes of some of the Brothers—though not in the eyes of Younger Brother Jirish. He was polite as a man could be when he and the woman weren't allowed to talk and the woman wasn't allowed to say "No" even if she felt like a dead worm three days in the sun.

Alanni knelt in the moss and dead leaves by the track and waited for the tap of the Instrument permitting her to look up. It came. She did, and Jirish's look said the rest. She rose and followed him off into the trees, until they were out of sight of the track and the Children on it. They might not be out of hearing, but one thing Alanni never worried about in such trysts was whether he or she made very much noise.

Jirish's almost-civilized manners took over. He unfastened her shorts and softly patted her bare rear. Alanni stepped out of the shorts and went down on hands and knees, one shoulder braced against a tree. The rough flaky bark gouged her bare shoulder and gave off a pungent scent like burning leather. It was better than having twigs and stones gouging her bare bottom.

Jirish thrust into her so slowly that if he'd done only a little more fondling beforehand Alanni might have suspected him of sophistication. He wasn't so slow, once he was settled comfortably in place. She needed all the help the tree gave her to keep from being pushed forward, face down in the moss and mold.

Jirish was one with so many of the Younger Brothers. Not vicious or cruel, just ignorant and with no one to teach or restrain him until he'd learned. He was also weak. Weak enough to take advantage of whatever chance he found for slicing hurriedly, without thinking of his partner's opinion.

Weakness can be a worse vice than ignorance, though! Better not trust Jirish and the ones like him too much or too soon.

Uh . . . not bad movements on the man!—scratch that: boy . . .

She kept herself braced for those movements in and out of her, gently paddling her buttocks with his thighs, and let her mind fill with exquisitely detailed images: teaching him and two other Younger Brothers about civilized trysting/slicing/soaring. The picture included Jirish where he was now, with another brother under her, playing nicely with her dangling breasts. A third was stroking her hair and back as if he were giving her an old-fashioned back rub. The kind she had not felt in much too long . . .

Meanwhile Jirish pushed in and out of her warm clutch and began to gasp as he felt its movements, its growing humidity. Had he held his own for just a little longer, he would have encountered something surely brand new to him: a fully aroused woman.

He didn't. Alternating bouts of semi-celibacy and semi-rape did nothing to teach civilized slicing. The gasping man behind her began pounding harder and harder, so that the paddling of her animalistically-upturned buttocks by his surging body grew more and more like real paddling. She braced herself, listened to the slapping sounds, wished she dared reach up and pinch her nipple a bit, at least. She didn't dare. She had to keep braced. Now he was starting to snort. She felt that final big swelling of his ensocketed slicer and strove to appreciate it, knowing that Brother Jirish had just about had it.

About the time she began to sigh a bit, her Brotherly *user* groaned, gasped, emitted a distinctly unholy snort, and slammed his hips against her backside hard, several times.

"Uh!" Then he sighed and actually bent over—trying to kiss the back of her neck, she realized, and arched it a little for him . . .

And she was signaled to rise and rearrange her attire. All her red-"masked" *user* had to do was drop his damned yellow robe. Meanwhile the usee was so amazed by his last gesture that they were halfway back to the track before she was aware of being frustrated and annoyed—as usual.

Something might definitely be made of Jirish—other than a purse or landfill, that is. As for most of the rest of these flaining fobbers—why isn't inducing terminal frustration a capital offense? (Because, she answered her own mental question, if it were they'd all be doomed!)

The frustration was eating at her by the time they were back on the track. She was seriously trying to picture a three-way consisting of her, Luctan, and Eldest Brother Kayab bin-Tarf. That was a completely lunatic concept, and she almost chuckled. Luctan *might* be dedicated; he certainly wasn't wired correctly. As for Kayab, none save the Elder Brothers were allowed to interrupt him at his meditations. And that only once a day on matters of urgency!

As Alanni came morosely in sight of the top of the hill, it began to rain. Again.

8

Both work sites on top of the hill were already so muddy that the extra rain made little difference. Alanni drew the easier site, on the hill's jutting crest. The building there was no more than frame and sheeting, but it was finished enough to keep out the rain. Shamat was sent to the other site, to weed a field ankle-deep in slimy mud.

Another drainage ditch curled away from the fields, deeper than Alanni's height and fenced on both sides. As her party turned toward the house, she saw two men standing by the fence.

Elder Brother Luctan stood with his back to the ditch. He looked almost military despite the robe, with his hands clasped behind him. His bodyguard Tuke stood beside him, not seeming so light-footed as usual on the soggy ground, but still trying to look in all directions at once. Flat, nasty eyes he had for looking, Alanni noticed. They looked sinister and as if they were trying to conceal themselves within the dye-mask of crimson. An ever observant man, she thought . . . and not a pleasant one, Tuke.

Luctan became aware that Tuke's eyes had focused on a single target, rather than scanning the whole hilltop for threats. Tuke always looked as if he hoped to see a threat or three, Luctan mused.

"Yes, Brother Tuke?"

Tuke stepped close so no one could overhear. "The one who calls herself Yimra Tewao, Elder Brother . . ."

"What about her, that you have not said before?"

"She looks at the hilltop as I do, Elder Brother. She also has the way of one who looks about before a battle."

"You return to your old fear, that she is—one of Those Who Are Not What They Seem?"

"Yes. Have I been forbidden to speak of it, Elder Brother Luctan?"

"You have not. You may be, if you continue to see threats where they are not."

"Where they *may* not be, respected Elder Brother. That is not the same thing."

"It will take a very great and certain threat to turn me from my plan. Miembra is too valuable to the Brotherhood for me to sacrifice such a chance of making her grateful to us, both as a Healer and as a woman. Sister Yimra will finish twenty days more as a Child, then go to Miembra."

Tuke made a noise like an overripe hornfruit falling onto a hard rock. "She can do more injury in the First Temple than elsewhere."

"If it is in her to do us an injury at all."

"It is, Elder Brother Luctan. I swear it by the Dark Lord and by–" He seemed to catch himself just before swearing something that might have revealed too much of his past.

The Elder Brother knew that Tuke went so far only when he was uneasy. Still, what Luctan had said was just as true.

"It is also dangerous to the Brotherhood if we become unable to do the work that makes us accepted. Without Miembra and half a dozen others like her who give much for small reward, we would be much less acceptable, Tuke. So much less, in fact, that some would cease to be our friends and a few would become our open enemies." He lowered his voice to a whisper. "How many tickets to Bleak can *you* afford, Brother Tuke?"

Tuke shrugged. "My Obedience is to your will, Elder Brother Luctan. I cannot however make my eyes and ears your slaves."

"I do not ask that you do so, Brother Tuke. Only—do not trust them so much that they lead you astray and confound the work of the Brotherhood." Luctan's full yellow sleeves flapped with his gesture of dismissal. After a moment Tuke bowed and turned away.

Luctan still followed the lean, light-footed figure's progress up to the doorway of the house. He believed in Tuke's strange knowledge more than he believed in any gods; he owed his life and much of his prosperity to it. He still did not trust what Tuke might do with that knowledge.

Tuke trusted no one except Luctan, and nothing except his own skill at dealing death—or making people beg for it.

The gurgling scream jerked Alanni's head around. What she saw below made her drop her end of the pallet of sheeting. The man at the other end of the pallet glared but did not quite dare the disObedience of breaking Silence.

The Younger Brother who'd been handing out tools to the workers in the field lay on his back in the mud. A pair of pruning shears jutted from a throat gushing blood. A puddle of rust-colored mud was spreading around him. The Children in the field stared as if the body on the ground warned of the impending end of the Universe.

One tool—a sharp blade on a meter-long handle—was in Shamat's hands.

Shamat was running straight at Elder Brother Luctan, who still stood with his back to Alanni. She saw clearly the clumsy, uncertain way he prepared to meet Shamat's attack.

Shamat knows her business and Luctan doesn't, in spite of his size and muscles.

Shamat feinted to draw Luctan's arms into a guarding position, then struck savagely. In a bright yellow swirl of robes, the Elder Brother turned faster than Alanni had expected. He was hampered by the fence directly behind him but managed to take the sharp blade in his shoulder instead of his chest.

Five meters to Alanni's right the crest of the hill ended in a vertical drop, nearly overhanging the drainage ditch. Alanni measured the jump in one look, sought Tuke with another, didn't find him, and let out a martial-artist's yell.

At the same time she sprinted to the drop and leaped off.

She was in midair before she wondered why she was doing this . . .

Then she landed—hard, going down, rolling, demolishing her shorts but ignoring it as she churned to her feet and rushed at Luctan and Shamat. Before she reached them she had a moment to consider her actions.

Luctan's no prize. If Shamat kills him, there'll be chaos in the Brotherhood. There'll also be a lot more security on the Children—Younger Brothers carrying stoppers and so on. My job will be easier if Luctan is saved. Saving him is part of my job!

For once she'd have been at least moderately happy to see Tuke. She saw Shamat, her face a mask of sheer rage as she swung her weapon, muscles standing out on her thin arms. She saw Luctan too. In addition to his saffron robes, he now wore a good deal of blood and a this-can't-be-happening-to-me expression.

Alanni saw nothing else, particularly no Younger Brothers who looked as if they were even considering intervention.

So much for their Obedience. What will come of a Child-Sister proving she's more loyal than they are?

Then her time for thinking ran out; Shamat was coming at her.

Her nasty-bladed tool slashed down. Alanni went in under it and grabbed it, planning to throw Shamat hard enough to stun her. The first part of the plan was easy. Shamat was no heavier than a girl of twelve and she flew nicely.

She also landed with the same trained springiness as Alanni, rose, and attacked again. Alanni threw the tool into the ditch—better barehanded than using a weapon whose balance she didn't know—and met the charge.

Shamat showed expertise by trying to take out Alanni's right knee. Alanni rode the blow up on to her hip, went down, and tried to throw her opponent with a leg hold. Shamat let herself be thrown all right—and managed to land on top of her attacker, fingers curved into claws for mutilating every part of the other woman she could reach.

Her hands closed around Alanni's throat and started to squeeze.

Alanni brought her hands sharply against Shamat's ears. Shamat gasped and loosened her hold just enough to let the woman from Eagle bring both knees up into her opponent's stomach. Shamat flew over Alanni's head and *squished* into the mud.

Alanni took a little while to realize that she was alive and that the other woman was out of the fight.

By the time Alanni was staggering to her feet, both Luctan and Tuke were standing over her. Several Younger Brothers including Jirish stood behind them. At a safe distance, the Children gaped, except for those who showed exaggerated innocence or horror.

Alanni tried to keep her face blank under the Brothers' gaze. The fight had completed the demolition of her clothing. She wore only a liberal coating of mud and several trickles of blood. Her panting only served to call attention to bare breasts.

The exposure of her body bothered her a good deal less than the exposure of her fighting skills. She'd acted by pure reflex and she still thought she'd done right (as much as she was presently capable of thinking at all). She had also demonstrated knowledge of things about fighting that her cover-story background shouldn't have taught her.

Elder Brother Luctan spoke. Although he was swaying slightly, his eyes were entirely focused on Alanni. "You have shown high Duty and Obedience, Child-Sister Yimra. Break your Silence and tell me—tell me how?"

Alanni took a deep breath, hoping her hesitations would be taken for nervousness at speaking to Luctan or the aftermath of the fight. "When I worked, Elder Brother—often there were no policers—in the camps. A woman had to be her own defender. If—if she does this often enough, she learns much."

"You were not trained in the fighting arts."

"Only by—a woman who was—a friend, Elder Brother. Otherwise it was all—experience."

Luctan lifted his eyes to Heaven so abruptly that Alanni thought for a moment he was going to faint, and set herself to catch him. He was not falling. Instead:

"Tarf al-Barahut, hear us bless You for your wisdom in sending this woman to the Brotherhood to stand against disObedience."

"Bless You, Tarf al-Barahut," echoed Tuke, and all the Younger Brothers and Children took up the cry.

The loud chant pounded on Alanni's head like a club until she wanted to run. At least clap her hands over her ears! Instead she planted her feet more firmly in the mud and watched Tuke. If anyone refused to swallow her story and made trouble, it would be he.

Tuke did nothing other than shout blessings and send a messenger for Miembra-daktari. When the shouting died, he led Luctan over to the nearest patch of almost-dry ground and bandaged his wounds. When he'd finished that, he bound Shamat hand and foot with strips of her garments. Both Brothers ignored Alanni, who assumed she had been dismissed. She began to wonder about where to find some fresh clothes . . .

"Child-Sister Yimra!"

Still naked, Alanni knelt at Luctan's feet. "Yes, Elder Brother?"

"You deserve more reward than merely our thanks and our *request* for the blessing of Tarf al-Barahut. It is in my mind to make you handmaid to the Eldest Brother, Kayab bin-Tarf. Such a good and Obedient handmaid as you are would be a great help to him in his meditations in search of the Way."

"Elder Brother, I–I–"

"Am not worthy? The belief does you honor in the sight of the Tarf al-Barahut and also of your Brothers and Sisters. But it is not true. Would you disObediently lie to us all?"

Alanni shook her head.

"I did not think so, Child-Sister," Luctan said, with a tight smile. "And if you fear that you will not also be able to serve Healer Miembra, put that fear aside. The work of handmaid to Kayab bin-Tarf is no great burden for one so strong as you. Miembra's clinic is close to Kayab's chamber. If you find time to give Healer Miembra service, she will be happy to receive it."

I'll just bet, Alanni thought. She couldn't be quite as cynical about the rest. An easy job in the First Temple, within reach of the Invisible Wisdom . . . or at the very least, people who might know where it was!

Alanni corrected herself. A job that *might* be easy. *If* Kayab wasn't senile, insane, perverted, or fobby in some other way certain to make the life of his "handmaid" difficult. Of course, if he was only a little cracked, it might be easier to slip out at night and learn her way around the First Temple . . .

There might be something to salvage from anything short of his being a homicidal maniac!

"I am honored by the trust of the Elder Brother and the Brotherhood."

"You are worthy of it, Sister."

Luctan staggered to his feet, put both hands on her shoulders, and kissed her on the cheek. It was a much less brotherly kiss than the other one Alanni had from him. She sensed sexual tension lurking not far inside Luctan—and this in spite of his wounds!

Does he flash on violence? If they didn't check that circuit before they let him out of the factory–

If so, the worst problem Kayab bin-Tarf might have didn't bother her as much as Elder Brother Luctan's. Luctan and Tuke together were an even nastier combination. Her job here was to make them want to do their worst to her, and what that worst might be . . .

Miembra-daktari and her assistants were all safely out of hearing when Luctan summoned Tuke to his bedside.

"Brother Tuke . . ."

"Elder Brother?"

"It would seem that you saw more clearly than I, in the matter of Child-Sister Yimra."

Luctan was pleased to see the other man looking slightly confused. "Then why–?" Tuke began.

"Then why did I send her to Kayab? She so greatly deserved a reward that it would have caused much talk had I not given her one. Would you have that? Kayab is without power to do us harm, no matter who we send him. The matter for concern now is that neither Yimra nor others like her can find an ally or learn much from Shamat."

"She might not know much," Tuke said. "I should judge her hardly more than a trained fighting slave, quite expendable." He shrugged, brows slightly raised, walnut eyes cold and glittery as frozen marbles back there in their blood-red mask of subcutane.

"Also fit to be trained by you, if she is spared?"

Tuke smiled—while those dark, dark eyes remained cold and veiled. The chance to find pupils in the arts of fighting was one of the few things that could make him smile even that much.

"I admit this sinful weakness," he said in an equable tone.

"That is as well," Luctan said, nodding. "I fear, though, you have been wrong before about what people know or do not know. Shamat must be put where no one will be able to talk to her."

"Ah."

"Yes. Do not be in too much haste, either. She must–"

"Die slowly for her disObedience? Surely you do not think I have lost my skills, Elder Brother?"

Luctan sat up, wincing at the pain the effort gave him. "I do not. Quite the contrary. I think you are too fond of using those skills to be a good judge of when *not* to use them, *Brother* Tuke. When I said not to be in haste over finishing Shamat, I meant this: wait for an opportunity to make it look like suicide. *Exactly* like suicide, even to the best-trained eye."

"Such as Yimra's?"

Elder Brother Luctan met Tuke's steady, cold gaze. "If she has such a well-trained hand, why should her eye not be the same?"

"Just so, Elder Brother Luctan."

9

Brother Luctan shoved Alanni forward, his hand on her backside, as he knocked on Eldest Brother Kayab's door.

"Eldest Brother, it is Elder Brother Luctan. May I call you from your meditations to meet your new handmaid?" His tone would have sounded thoroughly respectful to anyone who hadn't noticed that the man was an actor. Alanni had given up trying to guess his real thoughts. Certainly they weren't religious.

She'd never even tried with the beautifully-built Brother Tuke, who stood close behind them, as impassive as ever. On his face, the subcutaned Brotherhood band was pure Sinister. The man gave away nothing if one watched him as if casually. Nothing happened if one watched him closely, either, except that he became suspicious. A suspicious Tuke was a deadly dangerous Tuke, since Alanni was tolerably certain he was more than her match in combat.

The solutions for Tuke were two and two only: ignore him or kill him.

The first was difficult at best. As to the second . . . Tuke had the look of a man who'd take a lot of killing.

The heavy polished-wood door swung open. Alanni knelt Obediently without waiting for the pressure of Luctan's hand on her shoulder. Her gray shorts had been replaced by a knee-length reelsilk skirt the color of cheap red wine, and she wore an abbreviated leaf-green jacket rather than the still briefer top. She still wore nothing under either one. Furthermore, the flainin' skirt was so snug that if she moved too fast she might make her first appearance before Eldest Brother

Kayab with it split all the way up to her depilated crotch. Surely that would be considered disObedience!

In this absurd kneeling posture, Alanni's eyes were on a level with the doorknob. She noticed that the door seemed to have no lock on the inside. A curious omission, surely, for a man so devoted to his meditations?

She stopped guessing as Eldest Brother Kayab appeared in the doorway. His lean 175 sems were clad only in a white loincloth and a single earring of prass and coral. The only notes of color on his pale chocolate skin were gray eyebrows and black triangles of subcutane under each eye. His head was so large for his body that he would have looked topheavy if he hadn't been completely bald.

Alanni remembered that staring this way at the Eldest Brother was probably disObedience, at least before one had been properly introduced. She bowed her head until her chin almost touched her breastbone, and she held that position while Luctan explained why Child-Sister Yimra Tewao was worthy to be handmaid to the Eldest Brother.

The explanation took quite a while. It did *not* include asking Eldest Brother Kayab whether he approved of the supposed Yimra Tewao. Nor did it mention the possibility of his asking for someone else if she turned out to be unsatisfactory.

Eldest Brother Kayab seemed to have no more choice in the matter of handmaids than Alanni had enjoyed in the matter of sexual activity during her Initiation. That seemed so inherently improbable that Alanni would have rejected it on the spot except for one thing.

She'd won two promotions by following up "inherently improbable" theories about crimes, until she had evidence to prove they weren't improbable at all.

Alanni Keor was a professional skeptic, which she defined as refusing either to believe *or* doubt without evidence. Since in this case there wasn't any evidence . . .

Finally Luctan finished consigning Yimra/Alanni to the service of Eldest Brother Kayab, rather like a merchant consigning a shipment to a freight warehouse. Kayab finally broke his silence to tell "Yimra" to rise and enter his chamber. She obeyed, and the door closed behind her. A moment later she heard the faint but unmistakable sound of a mechanical lock's being set—from the outside.

Alanni studied the room with an eye trained to extract the scrute about someone from how it lived. After a moment she had to strangle a sigh of relief. This didn't seem the room of a man with his brain fragged by thinking he'd had a personal message from the Higher Authorities!

The polished wood of the floor gleamed with the hue of fresh lemons: walls and ceiling were white plascrete. Green curtains covered with intertwined geometrical figures set off the sleeping space at the far end of the room. The curtains were half-drawn, and through the gap Alanni saw a low, wide bed tightly made with clean sheets. (Only a masochist would use blankets on Hellhole.) Beyond the bed she saw the door to the sitter.

In this half of the room–

"Forgive me for not giving you more of my attention," a soft voice said, from behind her. "I was truly meditating when the Dark Lord moved Luctan to bring you."

Alanni was already falling to her knees when she realized that both words and tone had been almost apologetic. It was too late to stop. She landed with a thump. Also a *rrrrripppppp!* as her sluttish skirt split all the way up, to become a lot more sluttish. Also cooler.

She mentally cursed her Brotherhood-corrupted Obedience reflex and the stinking rotten quality of their clothing. Still she didn't dare look up. Eldest Brother Kayab spoke again.

"As I said, I was meditating when the Dark Lord's spirit moved Luctan to bring you." *(And why*, Alanni thought, *do I suspect that his words are hiding something, just as I suspect Luctan?)* "It did not occur to me that he might not have instructed you in your duties. And do feel free to raise your eyes to me."

By the time this last command came, Alanni had realized that Kayab actually seemed to be *apologizing* for neglecting her. This was so incredible that for moment her head spun too fast for her to raise it. Then she obeyed, and nearly had another head-spin when she saw Eldest Brother Kayab smiling down at her. Of course, he had a remarkably good view of her cleavage, but somehow he didn't look as if that was the reason for his smile.

"How may this Sister best serve you, Eldest Brother?"

Alanni did not stand up, partly because he hadn't given permission and partly because with her ripped skirt she would look as if she had only one kind of service in mind. *No doubt that will come in time, unless he's not interested in women!*

She also thought she'd have heard some mention or hint, if Kayab preferred boys or female fangfaces.

"First, clean this part of the chamber. I have been without a handmaid for twenty days. Although I have done my best, I fear uncleanliness has advanced. Then prepare a meal from what is in the larder there." He pointed toward the door to the . . . sitter? "There is nothing in it unwholesome for me. Otherwise, leave me to my meditations. Oh, and do not try to rearrange my bookshelves." He started to turn away, then without turning back added:

"If you wish, you may also prepare a bed for yourself at the foot of mine. You may use cushions from the couch and the spare sheets."

It was just as well that Kayab turned away then, without another word. Alanni couldn't have replied to save herself from being slowly dismembered by Tuke. Her chin was down on her breastbone again, this time solely through the force of gravity.

Is he really saying that I don't have to play hust for him?

He might be. If he is, don't look at the horns of a free browser.

Alanni wanted very badly to believe it. Both her stash and her tolerance for being used were wearing out. But–

There's no reason at all why Kayab has to be a stash-hunter himself, just because he lets the Brothers do it. A lot of people allow vices they don't practice.

Firm, but he sounds as if he wants to be . . . kind—to me.

"Sounds" is the word, she warned herself.

She had to admit the sense in that little qualifier. Kayab certainly sounded civilized, but she'd been among the barbarians so long she was ready to be grateful for almost anything. She was also ready to be a poor judge of real civilization.

She decided that it would be wise to continue skeptical, since nothing really deserved the name "evidence"—and start cleaning the room.

By the time Alanni had finished her cleaning and cooking, she was more confused rather than less. What Kayab called "uncleanliness" would have passed a white-glove inspection in academy barracks.

A bit obsessive on the subject, isn't he?

Obviously he had also been doing a lot of his own cleaning during those twenty days without a handmaid. Alanni had cleaned up at most two days' worth of dust, rather than twenty. She had already learned that these silly religiosi "did not believe in" such work- and mess-saving devices as ionic dust collectors. Why oh *why* did "religious" so often mean "uncivilized?"

She wondered briefly whether Kayab's apparent obsession with cleanliness was a fellow traveler of his (apparent) lack of interest in soaring. The two sometimes went together, as Alanni had reason to know. (The best-looking man she'd ever asked to tryst and soar with her had proven that sort of . . . person. *Wonder what ever did happen to Pinchar, anyway?*

She filed the hypothesis under "Insufficient Evidence" and went on working.

The shelves Kayab didn't want rearranged were certainly evidence of something, although Alanni could not be sure what. Eclectic tastes in reading and no interest in pop entertainment booktapes, at least. Or maybe he just had an orderly mind and knew where everything was. Out of more than a thousand films and tapes (the shelves covered one whole wall), Alanni saw not a single popular piece of work. A pile of material on geology, physics, and history, yes. Anything *fun*, no. And nothing but a flatscreen twenty sems on a side for reading all this mind-improvement.

About what might be expected of an ex-professor, she mused. Not what she'd have expected of one who had withdrawn from the active management of the religion he had founded to a life of "meditation." No, erase the quotation marks. *He probably does meditate a lot, to keep from going fobby through being locked up in here!*

That's assuming too much.

Is it?—with the only lock on the outside of the door?

This job is throwing up questions faster'n I can find answers!

Is that so surprising? And who had her gear Poofed so that she can't manage a straight in-and-out snatch-job on the Invisible Wisdom, hmm?

Alanni conceded the point to her own not-so-still inner voice. She had also stopped feeling so guilty about the destruction of her equipment, since she'd seen the First Temple from the inside. Even if she had learned where the I.W. lay, she'd have had to come inside to be sure of snatching it. And that would have been only after losing the Light knew how many days digging out the scrute!

Right now she was probably ahead of where she'd have been otherwise.

None of which solves the mystery of Eldest Brother Kayab bin-Tarf, she thought, and kept looking for a pin for her ruined "dress."

The larder wasn't really in the sitter—the bathroom. It was in an alcove on one side of the small anteroom, with the sitter opening off the other side. The larder showed Alanni that Kayab had at least one vice that she was going to have to endure. He was a vegetarian. (Alanni was an aggressive omnivore, a carnivorously-leaning one, and more so than usual after nearly fifty days-Hellhole on the Children's diet of the Brotherhood. To her vegetarianism was definitely a *vice,* not to mention sick.)

Of more interest than Kayab's taste in fruits, nuts, and flakes was a small plass door in the (wooden) rear wall of the storeroom. Not much to Alanni's surprise, it was sealed from the other side. Still, it might be breakable and it might lead . . . somewhere interesting.

If both were true, it might also give her an escape route. *If* it could also be opened without leaving any traces, she might even be able to come and go as she pleased when Kayab was asleep. (She was now quite sure that he wasn't so fobby that she could just act as if he wasn't there.)

A lot of "ifs" and "mights."

Alanni prepared his meal of oatcakes, dried fruit reconstituted in dried milk, and shelled nightmare nuts. He ate with an abstracted air, his eyes so firmly fixed on the viewscreen that he sometimes spilled food down his chest. Alanni wiped him off each time, stealing glances at the screen as she did.

The film he was reading did not lead to comforting thoughts for anyone who'd seen how low-lying Bassar was. It was a study of *tsunamis*—earthquake-caused waves that could rise fifty meters or more when they hit land.

Definitely not fobby, although it's hard to see what he's doing with all the scrute, shut up here like a prisoner.

Like a prisoner? Maybe he really is one!

Alanni realized that this thought had been hovering on the fringes of her mind half the day. Now it stood full-blown and smirking in front of her and refusing to be filed away under "Insufficient Evidence"—even if that was where it belonged.

She had to do what she hated to do with an idea—keep herself too busy to think about it until it went away. By the time she'd cleaned up after Kayab's dinner, prepared and eaten her own, and cleaned the kitchen, the idea was fast asleep.

So was Kayab, as Alanni discovered when she tiptoed into the bedroom to do the expected. He was not only asleep but snoring like a mired tractor.

The handmaid looked yearningly at the wide soft bed. And decided in favor of caution, at least for tonight. She tiptoed back the way she'd come and made her pallet as Kayab had directed. The cushions of the couch and the spare sheets fitted handily at the foot of the Eldest Brother's bed.

She was more comfortable here than she had been in any other bed since she had left Eagle. That didn't make it any easier for her to get to sleep. Of course Kayab's snoring was one deterrent. Too, there was the fact that for the first time since entering the Brotherhood she hadn't spent the day in grinding physical labor—with intervals of holding (relatively) still for skewering sexual use.

Finally, what she'd seen of Kayab's situation and what she'd been told were separated by a distance so great that it could be measured only in astronomical units. She took it for granted that the official Brotherhood line was just that. A line. A lie. What was the truth, according to Eldest Brother Kayab himself?

She had a feeling that the answer to that question might have some connection with her getting off Hellhole with a whole skin, let alone with the Invisible Wisdom.

10

Alanni awoke to see Kayab's bed empty. Learned fear of punishment for disObedience ripped through her. That unworthy fear was followed by self-loathing for being so intimidated by these bugs of the Brotherhood. She hurried out into the sitting room and knelt before the Eldest Brother.

He was naked and in the lotus position. Breathing deeply, sawing the air in arm and hand exercises, his black "masked" almond eyes aimed at a point in the middle of the ceiling. It didn't take Alanni long to realize that nothing short of hitting him over the head would attract his attention.

That would not only be disObedience, it would be disCourtesy, which was much worse by Alanni's standards. *It might also get me disMembered.*

She left Kayab to his morning routine and daringly treated herself to a real luxury: washing all over with a sponge dipped in hot water. Though she didn't quite dare to turn on the shower or fill the tub, she was going to be clean if it killed her. (Kayab probably would not go so far as that—she hadn't even seen an Instrument of Obedience in his quarters. As for his calling someone else in to punish her . . . well, assuming he could do that at all, Alanni thought she could make it worth his while not to.)

By the time she had finished both her bath and preparing breakfast, Kayab was no longer sitting in lotus position or indeed at all. He was performing some complicated calisthenics in a style Alanni didn't recognize. On the other hand, she certainly did recognize a man who kept himself in excellent physical trim when she saw one.

And why shouldn't he, just because he's a scholarly religious recluse?

No reason at all, except it's a big surprise, and makes him even harder to read.

This time Kayab saw her. She knelt.

"Sister Yimra, if you wish to take proper care of your body, you may join me." He swallowed, then added, "It is best that you be unclothed."

Alanni would have removed not only the clothes from her body but the skin from her bones for a chance at a proper workout. Slave's work did nothing to sharpen the coordination and reflexes she was sure to need before she was out of reach of the Brotherhood. She unbuttoned the jacket, threw it away, and sent what was left of the skirt after it.

Kayab looked away from her nudity as she started her routine. She put that down to his being a man for other men, after all, and forgot about it in the pleasures of feeling muscles and tendons stretching into familiar shapes. She didn't look back at Kayab until she'd worked up a good sweat.

He was staring at her so hard that for a moment she feared that she had revealed too much of her unarmed-combat skills. Then her gaze leaped down his body. She swallowed a laugh—at herself and her assumptions about this surprise-filled man.

Kayab was standing at attention to honor her nudity. Respectfully, even gallantly at attention, with nothing lacking in either quantity or quality that Alanni could see.

She not only swallowed the laugh but ruthlessly beat it to death. Here was a man who wanted her but was *too nervous* to ask! Laughing at him would be—something she'd think twice before doing to Luctan himself. (Although maybe not to Councillor Nortay. If he had to worry about his ability to rise to the occasion, he might have less time to prosecute old feuds at the expense of innocent people.)

Alanni went to Kayab and knelt close enough that she could lay her head against his stomach. It was a distinctly agreeable stomach for the laying-on of heads—firm without being unyielding, the skin lightly furred with fine hair and exhaling healthy man-scent of a sort she hadn't smelled in so damned long–!

She stopped herself just short of lowering her mouth to Kayab's saluting gun. He was in good working order without that, and if he'd really managed to survive most of a normal life without learning how to *ask* a woman—well, it could be as bad as laughing at him.

She flowed to her feet and pressed herself against him, body to body from shoulders to knees. When she stood on tiptoe, her nipples brushed his. She stifled a gasp as she felt hers tightening, and knew they were hardening. Then the Eldest Brother's lips came down on hers in manner distinctly un-Brotherly. His lips were closed, but not for long. He needed to breathe, and when he did she put her tongue out and in. Meanwhile, her nipples having become bullets, she raked his chest with them in a way that sent shivers through man and woman alike.

She knew it was time to take him by the hand and lead him to the bed so gently that he would think he was leading her . . .

The gliding trek to the bed was the last time she needed to be subtle. This man might not know how to ask, but he knew well enough what to do when the answer was "yes." Nor did his salute fail him at the last moment or any other. (His partner's state of agitation was such that if his slicer had proven incapable of slicing his remaining lifespan might have been measured in seconds.)

She was half-soaring before he seated himself fully inside her, at the mere thought of a chance for civilized slicing again. This darling man even propped himself on his forearms to keep his main weight off her!

Then she wanted to drag him even farther inside her, draw his lips on to her aching nipples and—she wanted so much that she realized (vaguely, sighing and soaring) that even two trained Jarp contortionists couldn't have provided it. She ceased wanting firebeans in her brandy and clamped her hands on his neat firm buttocks to do the best she could with what she had to hand (and in stash, and on belly).

His salute did not fail either of them. She sighed, groaned, whimpered, stifled a scream, then sighed again, all in rapid succession. Even while the climactic ripple went through her body he kept right on moving, riding it, sluicing, pumping away, neither energy nor enthusiasm diminished, nor attention to her, nor anything else . . . And then he was groaning bullishly, straining.

Just to finish the occasion in proper style after his climax, he did not immediately roll off her when he was through with *his* groaning and sighing. Instead he pillowed his shining head on her breasts—a little too hard now for his comfort, Alanni suspected. She would also have liked his lips where they were now, much sooner.

Neither of them quite fell asleep, which was just as well. They had barely untangled themselves and stood up—Alanni not too steadily—when someone knocked on the door.

"Eldest Brother Kayab, Miembra-daktari craves audience, if the Eldest Brother's meditations permit him to grant it."

Alanni nearly giggled at the strained note the effort of seeming humble put into Miembra's normally crisp voice. She also snatched up her clothes and ran into the bathroom to pull them on out of Miembra's sight.

Miembra would probably think jealousy of Kayab either disObedient or silly, once she knew Alanni. Right now she didn't know her future assistant. The less she was slapped in the face with Alanni's other bedroom activities, the better Alanni's chances of using her work with Miembra to help her do her *real* job here.

Kayab might give you more, if you can win him to your side.

He might if I could, but what if he doesn't or I can't?

Kayab's still a mystery. Miembra already knows that I can be useful.

She also suspected that in total crisis—say, Luctan's wanting to turn Tuke loose on her—Miembra would be a better defender than Kayab. Oh sure, Kayab was the Eldest Brother, but . . . . He wasn't likely to be as indispensable to the Brotherhood's public reputation as Miembra-daktari.

The young man who would call himself Ugru while he was on Hellhole had just stepped out of the terminal when the madman began speaking. Or at least he looked and sounded fobby!

He wore only ragged shorts and a beard that covered more of his scarred, filthy brown skin than the shorts. It reached as far as his fifth rib—which Ugru knew precisely, because he could count the man's ribs. The fellow was shouting something about "vengeance on the Pishoe Corporation," and that made Ugru stop and listen.

His briefing had mentioned the Pishoe Corporation. It had been organized three Hellholer years ago, to settle the inland regions of the Fog Coast continent. "The victory of optimism over experience," Ugru's briefer had said. "Rather like a Jarp who still hopes to bugger a normal human male."

The briefer went on to explain that PishoeCorp actually had sent a respectable number of settlers into the interior. They'd also accepted deposits on homesteading outfits from many more. The deposits varied in amount, with at least one so cheap that all but the poorest in Bassar could borrow the money to put it down.

Now, it seemed, there was no more PishoeCorp. It had dissolved, and along with it both the settlers' and the depositers' hopes. The settlers would be thrown back into the warrens of Bassar and the depositers would never leave them. Both would have the bankers hounding them for money they could never hope to repay—and on Hellhole "indenture" (translation: slavery) for debt was at least winked at, if not openly encouraged as a way of periodically pruning the ranks of the poor.

At least this was the picture Ugru pieced together from memories of his briefing and hints from the bearded shouter. Ugru felt that he must have heard more incoherent and hysterical speakers, but couldn't remember precisely when or where.

That didn't seem to matter, here. Ugru was no longer the only person listening to the bearded man. The square inland from the terminal was slowly filling with people. A circle of listeners was spreading around the man like an oil slick on water, until Ugru could barely see his waving hands above the close-packed heads.

The man must also have noticed that he was disappearing from the view of his audience. He jumped up on to the roof of a parked hovercar, without missing a word of his harangue. He couldn't gesture as wildly on the slick metal, but he didn't need to. The hysterical certainty in his voice was seeping into the crowd and beginning to turn it into a mob.

"The home of these PishoeCorp robbers in Bassar is Jaglan House! Those who have lost in the robbery, follow me! Those who wish to see justice done, follow me! Those who wish to defend their comrades against the policers who defend the robbers, follow *me*! Those who do not follow me, they are no better than the policers themselves and they will meet the same fate!"

There were only a few certainties in Ugru's life—his dedication to his arts, his loyalty to his master and his clan, and his taste for good saki. Now he added another certainty to his list—the certainty that he wasn't going to follow this man to a public sitter, let alone to the storming of Jaglan House.

Most of the men and women in the crowd looked as if they hadn't been able to afford a decent meal or change of clothing in years, let alone a deposit on an inland homestead. Some of them gave Ugru the distinct impression of not having bathed in as long. Except possibly in Bassar's canals.

Or maybe the policers of Bassar were looking for an excuse to remind the people who was *really* on top. Ugru had heard tales of the riot in the terminal, but that had been nearly two Heller months ago. The street mob had a short memory—or so any policer with a yen to break heads could always persuade himself.

Either way, the madman stank to the very Shrine itself of a police provocation. He'd lead the mob into a trap where the policers could run wild, then conveniently vanish.

Ugru hadn't any intention of being a hero. These would-be rioters weren't his people. Their fate wasn't his concern; turning it aside wasn't part of his job.

It also wasn't part of his job here on Hellhole to become known to the policers. If he went with the mob he would need much luck to avoid that fate. To Ugru, relying on luck was contemptible.

On the other hand, in order to escape from this square he would need to use his art of being invisible in a crowd. If he was seen leaving, someone might decide he should be the first victim. Oh, he might fight his way clear, but before he did he would have revealed all his arts.

That also would bring him to the notice of BMP—Bassar Municipal Protectors—the local policers.

Best to use his art, and hope there was no other adept here to see him, recognize him for what he was, and give the alarm.

Ugru started to bring his breathing under control, then the rest of his body. He would make no sound that anyone could pick out from the noise of the crowd. He would be able to stand beside a man and still not be heard. Slowly he flexed each arm and leg, each finger and toe, so that no faint *pop* from joints would break his blending into the world around him–

"Aiyyyyyycccchhhhhhh!"

The shout jerked him back to full awareness. Training in serenity couldn't suppress mental cursing at the time lost or at his own weakness. He looked up.

The mob leader wasn't standing atop the hovercar any more. He was lying face-down on the roof, with a tan-clad policer's boot in the small of his back. The policer was cuffing the man's wrists securely.

The crowd had fallen silent at seeing its leader (?) downed. Now curses and wordless growls broke the silence. The nipper seemed to be all alone. Surely he couldn't do much if they all tried–

The BMP officer drew a chemical-explosive projectile pistol with one hand and a can of Soothe with the other. Ugru noted that his tan uniform needed cleaning and that he himself could stand to lose some weight. He still balanced lightly on the precarious footing of the car's roof.

"Stop being fools!" the policer shouted. "This man didn't care what happened to to PishoeCorp or to you either. All he wanted was to feel big for a day. The more of you were stamped or shot by us nippers, the happier he'd be. Does anybody here really want to die following a man like that?"

He had them now, Ugru saw. The growls and curses were fading.

"Don't think you can rescue this bug, either. Not except over my dead body, and I won't be easy to kill. Anybody want to find that out the hard way? I'll be good for a dozen lessons or so."

Nobody seemed eager for this supplement to its education. Ugru smiled. The nipper could teach some *senseis* how to establish psychological dominance over an opponent! Appeal to pride, then appeal to the sense of self-preservation. What next?

"Firm," the policer went on. "I didn't think I was dealing with fools, except for this one here." He not-too-gently prodded the mob's ex-leader with a toe. "Now, I'd like a couple of people willing to be known to us of the BMP as respectable citizens, to help me tote this bug down to the station. You, friend? Thanks. And you? Two more, I think. Fine."

The four men lifted the mob leader off the roof of the car and held him between them like a frozen carcass. The policer looked down on the man as he might have looked down on a manure pile.

"If I'd come as close to being a mass-murderer as you have, I wouldn't sleep easy tonight." He looked back at the crowd. "Some fobber has probably already called my friends. So I think you'd all better think of business elsewhere. AND DON'T ALL RUN OFF AT ONCE!" he bellowed, as the crowd showed signs of doing just that.

"Do you want to trample the children and the old ones? Everybody just freeze until the people with children and the old ones are clear. *Then* walk, do *not* run, to the nearest street out of here."

While the nipper was damping the panic, Ugru had been studying the people around him. One gray-haired woman was standing with her arms protectively around a girl about four years old. Ugru elbowed his way to them and took the woman by one arm.

"Come along, mother. Let's go home."

The little girl stared at the stranger looming over her and started to squall. The woman had the sense to clamp a hand over her mouth. "Firm, my son. This is no place for old bones or small ones."

Ugru cleared a path for the woman and the girl with judicious use of elbows, knees, booted feet on people's sandaled toes, and occasional flourishes of his carrysak. The old woman and the girl stayed with him all the way out of the crowd, on to the next corner.

Once around the corner, Ugru allowed himself an unartistic

sigh of relief. He would not have done so merely over his own survival. Seeing so many people saved from an ugly death was another matter.

"Thank you," he told the woman. He was fishing around in his pocket for some money, but she shook her head.

"May the Dark Lord bless you," she said, and took the girl by the hand, and hurried off as fast as her thin legs would carry her.

Ugru waited in a doorway while the able-bodied adults from the crowd streamed past. He waited a little longer, to be sure that genius of a policer and his hastily-recruited deputies were out of sight. Then he walked back to the square.

It was now the same as when he'd first seen it—a gray rectangle of plascrete lightly patterned with scummy puddles, cracks, and bits of garbage now trodden into paste. Not a worthy place for one of the finest battles Ugru had ever seen fought. If that policer could not have comrades worthy of him, at least he should not have to fight his battles in places where the gods themselves might never see his virtues!

The jerky wailing of an approaching siren told Ugru that the policer's warning had been the truth. His briefing had told Ugru that few of Bassar's "protectors" were people worth meeting. Least of all did he want to meet them as the last person at the site of a near-riot, with baggage that might not stand close inspection.

He was out of sight of the square before the sirens gave way to shouting voices, and he kept right on going. It was time to find lodgings for tonight, and for as many nights more as he needed to study his opponents and choose his tactics. He wished to tread the fine line between places where he might be noticed and places where he might be murdered in his sleep.

His briefing had listed some seven or eight hotels not obviously in either category. After two hours in Bassar, it was Ugru's opinion that a briefing was less than ever a substitute for looking himself.

He shifted his carrysak to his right hand and moved out down the street at a trot.

11

The door chime of Miembra's clinic *tinngggged*. Alanni scurried across the waiting room to answer it. As she pressed the opener button, she also pulled her face into a properly Obedient expression. No telling who was coming with Shamat. Some of the Brothers insisted on the Brotherhood's Three Principles (at least from women) even in the daktari's clinic. At least Alanni could cover her now-obscene skirt with a pale green smock here!

Besides, if *anyone* saw how much she was anticipating the chance to be alone with Shamat—well, that would pull all the dampers out of the pile and toss them away. Even Miembra might notice. (She was as horny as a Jarp when she was horny, which was often. She was *never* stupid. Any woman who'd carved out Miembra's niche of independence in the Brotherhood couldn't be.)

The door slid open. Two Younger Brothers stood there, wearing the vomit-gray coveralls of those assigned as Overseers of Obedience.

(Translation: prison guards and torturers. From what she'd heard of their duties, Alanni was surprised that the Overseers' coveralls weren't dark red, to hide the bloodstains.)

They had Shamat held firmly and nearly held up between them. She wore only shorts. From the bruises on the skin stretched tight over Shamat's ribs, Alanni wasn't surprised that the woman could barely stand.

Behind Shamat and her guards stood Ipparo, the foodstand owner Alanni had rescued after he'd been burned in the riot. Most of his face was hidden by bandages. (Burnpak and other modern treatments were another amenity in short supply on the Fog Coast.) So he was now well enough to walk to Miembra's clinic? Alanni hadn't heard this, but she supposed it was good news. Ipparo was lucky to be alive at all, although sometimes she wondered if he thought so.

Without major regen work he'd be blind in one eye and probably in both within a few years. His scars would frighten children into fits, and his speech would always be slurred from the damage to his lips and tongue.

Hellhole possessed no facilities for that kind of regen. At least none nearer than Golden, Alanni corrected herself, and those were notoriously closed to people from the Fog Coast (unless they were so well-off that one wondered what they were doing sloshing around on the Fog Coast in the first place).

Ipparo was the kind of case who sometimes made Alanni ask herself "What's the use of anything?" That he was only one of ten thousand like him on the Fog Coast didn't help. Trained and tough as she was, the parade of misery Alanni had to face as Miembra's assistant sometimes downed her.

Apart from that, it also kept her far too busy to use the freedom of movement that came with the job to look for the Invisible Wisdom. By the time she was finished at the clinic, she had to go straight back to Kayab's room. By the time she'd finished her duties to Kayab both in bed and out, it was morning and time to go back to fight the hopeless battle.

She had neither thought nor hope of consolation for her second problem. She hadn't expected to find any help with the first either, but Miembra's persistence was the sort that could have done anything short of converting a Jarp to celibacy. (Which she wouldn't have tried anyway. Miembra-daktari wouldn't have urged celibacy on her worst enemy. Castration, perhaps, but not celibacy.)

As she'd said to Alanni, halfway through one non-celibate afternoon (for once there was a shortage of patients):

"So maybe I can only save ten percent of the people who need help. Everybody's still important to itself, and in Bassar, ten percent of the people who need help is a *lot*."

"Have I said anything to make you doubt I believe that, Elder Sister Miembra?"

"You haven't. But you're new at this work. You haven't had time to *learn* all you have to know if you're to do the work of the Brotherhood for as long as it will need doing in Bassar."

Does she really not know the "work" the Brothers mostly do? Or does she let them get away with it as long as they support her real work? Is she an idiot or a weird mix of cynic and idealist?

Alanni didn't get any further with her questions that day. Miembra started kissing her, nipples first, then working down. (Miembra's lips were talented, and her tongue deserved to have poems written about it.)

That was ten days ago, and she still didn't know the answer, or even if there was one.

Back to the matters at hand. "Thank you, Brothers," Alanni said politely to the Overseers. "Miembra-daktari and I will do everything else that must be done."

"It would be best if we stayed with the disObedient one," said the left-hand Overseer. The rightward one nodded.

Alanni had to swallow anger at their not even giving Shamat her name before she could say anything. By then Miembra was standing in the doorway to her office. A woman with a high forehead giving way to a widow's peak, and eyes so deepset they seemed prisoners of her skull.

"You don't need to guard one of my patients," she said briskly. "I'll call you when I'm through with Shamat."

"Daktari-Sister, the disObedient one is dangerous," said the right-hand Overseer. His cohort nodded.

"Not half as dangerous as I will be if you don't Obey me," Miembra said, less briskly. She had her sleeves rolled halfway up her well-muscled black arms and generally looked a match for anyone in the Brotherhood, short of Tuke.

"Please," said Ipparo. "I—rill—wash—de udder—one." Alanni had to strain to make sense of what his burn-twisted lips were trying to say. She wanted to hug him.

"You can hardly watch out for yourself," she said.

"I—do—bekker—an—deeze," Ipparo said, with a vague gesture in the direction of the two Overseers.

"The man's right, you know," Miembra said. "So why don't you two slok off?"

The two Overseers weren't ready for a test of their authority against Miembra's. Not over trivia. They redshifted.

Miembra let out a sigh that would have blown the Overseers several meters had they remained within range. "Yimra, take these two into the examining room. Give Shamat a trank and a bath if she can't take it herself. I'll go prepare the scope and sponges for Ipparo."

Shamat could not stop shivering. She said nothing as Alanni stripped and tranked her. Her eyes couldn't seem to focus on anything, except once. When they did, the look in them made Alanni turn away and hope they'd unfocus before she had to look back.

Then Alanni saw the bruises and worse that Shamat's shorts had hidden, and understood the woman's eyes. "Can you take a bath by yourself?" she asked.

Shamat said nothing.

"You can trust me now, Shamat. You aren't trying to kill me or anyone else. So why should I do you any harm, even if Miembra would let me?"

Slowly Shamat nodded. Alanni smiled, partly to reassure the woman and partly in relief at discovering that Shamat's mind wasn't completely gone. How much of her memory was left was another question.

Shamat rose and shuffled toward the bathroom, wincing at every other step. Alanni watched her go in and close the door, meanwhile inventing new and exotic punishments for the people who'd worked Shamat over so brutally. A dose of their own medicine would be much too good for them.

A nice castration all around, Alanni thought. *A slow castration.*

"Will you be all right while I find a robe for Shamat?" she asked Ipparo.

He nodded slowly, but his gaze wasn't focused on her. It seemed to be roaming vaguely around the room, and there was something *odd* about his visible eye, too . . .

Poor man's probably ready to pass out from the effort of helping Shamat, Alanni thought. *I'd better hurry with that robe.*

By the clock on the examining room wall, Alanni had been

gone exactly three minutes when she came back and found the room empty. She frowned.

Ipparo probably went into the bathroom to help Shamat. Light bless him for it, but he hasn't any reason to Poof himself helping her. She listened at the bathroom door for the sound of running water, heard nothing, and pushed it open.

Shamat lay in the tub, one thin scarred leg dangling over the edge, her head thrown back and one hand clasping her belly.

Her other hand held a spray injector. An *empty* injector, and Alanni recognized the markings on it. An injectorload of that would produce almost instant heart failure.

Still Alanni bent over her to feel for a pulse. She looked into the staring black eyes, listened for even the shallowest breath. Then she straightened up and slammed her fist into the wall over the bathtub so hard that she broke the skin on her knuckles.

She was sucking the blood off them when Miembra came in. Alanni would have given a lot for the chance to have hysterics for about ten minutes, but professional reflexes took over. She reported what she'd done and found to Miembra as if she'd been reporting to Prefect Kilwar.

She went on rubbing her knuckles until Miembra gently unclasped her hand. She kissed her assistant before she scoped and sprayed the damage.

"You were lucky not to break something, Yimra."

"I wish I had," Alanni muttered. "I'd still be better off than Shamat."

"What good would you be to either me or Kayab with a broken hand? We both need you. Shamat—she is past needing anything except quick burning. Nor could you have known that she was as she was. It's hard to prevent suicide in one who says nothing, only goes ahead and does it."

If it was suicide. Alanni's professional reflexes were still working. *I can't imagine anybody coming in from outside, and I can't see how Ipparo could have done it even if he had any reason–*

Wait a minute. That "something funny" about Ipparo's eye. The one I saw was black—obsidian black.

Ipparo has medium brown eyes.

Someone disguised as Ipparo, so he could kill Shamat and make it seem that–?

"Tuke!"

"Yes, Elder Brother Tuke will have to be informed," said Miembra gently. "I do not like him either, but he does exercise authority over the Overseers. I will not let him punish you, for a suicide you could not have predicted or prevented."

Was that an ever-so-slight emphasis on the word "suicide"?

Probably. She's giving a gentle hint. Miembra's not an idiot.

She isn't, but I'll feel like one if I let this murder pass.

Isn't that better than feeling dead?

It was. Alanni didn't have much doubt, either, that she would end up dead if she pushed the matter of Shamat's death any further. *Now.*

She couldn't do anything by going the fingerprints-on-the-injector route except reveal knowledge she shouldn't have. Miembra might keep her mouth shut, but Miembra also wasn't going to butt heads with Tuke over Shamat. She might not even do it to protect Yimra/Alanni.

Try to send the scrute about Shamat out of the Temple? Where to send it? This sort of thing wouldn't be going on if the Bassar policers hadn't been in the habit of turning a blind eye to the Brotherhood. Even if they hadn't acquired that habit, Alanni had little confidence (to understate her sentiments considerably) in BMP's ability to handle this sort of of bungle competently and discreetly.

Better off sending the scrute to Bleak. The Bleakers couldn't do much less to help and they'd have no way of telling Brotherless Tuke.

Alanni shuddered in bitterness, frustration, and something that wasn't quite fear but was a little more than mere apprehension over Tuke. Seeing the shudder, Miembra put her arms around her and held Alanni comfortably close in an almost motherly embrace.

Miembra couldn't be more than five years-ess older than she was, but right now Alanni felt that a little mothering was exactly what the daktari not only ordered but was providing.

• • •

Brother Tuke didn't remove the bandages disguising him as Ipparo until he was safely back in his basement *dojo*. No one could be trusted to see the metamorphosis from patient into Brother.

Tuke would have trusted nobody except himself with any important work, if he'd had either a reliable clone or the ability to teleport. Since both were impossible for him, he sometimes had to use other men's hands and senses for important tasks.

However, he was confident that the two men who'd removed the real Ipparo from the hospital would hold their tongues. Both had fled to the Brotherhood after careers in the slums of Bassar that even the corrupt policers of the Fog Coast would take seriously. Neither could risk being cast back into the streets with the nippers told where to look for them.

It would seem that Ipparo had wandered away from his bed and vanished. Under the First Temple, kloms of rooms and tunnels stretched and roamed. A badly hurt man might easily lose his way completely, wander until he was too weak even to call out, then die alone. Certainly no one who found the body would be able to prove anything else.

Correction. No one would be able to prove anything without Miembra-daktari's help, which she wouldn't give. After all, Shamat had "committed suicide" while under her care. Her own position wasn't strong enough to let her voice too many suspicions. What there was of her position, the tough-minded physician wanted to keep.

Tuke smiled grimly. At last he had succeeded in shaming the untouchable Miembra, yet in a way that would give her no cause to leave the service of the Brotherhood. Elder Brother Luctan could hardly complain about anything. (Except maybe Tuke's doing the whole job without telling him, and Tuke had become selectively deaf to Luctan's fussing and fuming on that point.) The ever-so-precious physician would go on helping the Brotherhood appear as Luctan wished it to.

Tuke leaped, spun in midair, landed spring-kneed, and launched a sidekick at an imaginary opponent.

If the day ever came when Miembra was no longer indispensable to the Brotherhood, she would not have a shred of pride when he finished with her, and only a little more skin.

She will die breastless and screaming.

This he swore, on the tombs of his ancestors. And Brother Tuke smiled.

After a few more minutes' exercises, he felt calm enough to play back the tape from the hidden pickup in Miembra's examining room. It told him nothing, or at least nothing interesting, and ended in sighs and moaning as Miembra and Kayab's handmaid soared. Tuke's interest in such sludge being non-existent, he turned the tape off.

Yimra Tewao was another woman Tuke would like to be alone with for a day or two. Why Luctan had rewarded her as he had, so that it was hard to make her just disappear–!

It was an offense against his honor that the fighting skill of another should have saved Brother Luctan. It might be more than that. Tuke could not believe that Tewao was what she seemed. Yet if she was, and Brother Luctan became impatient with Tuke, now there was someone to take his place.

That had not been true before. For a moment Tuke was afraid. He stared at a wall the color of necrosis.

The moment passed quickly, but not before Tuke swore, again on the tombs of his ancestors, that Yimra Tewao would pay for putting him in fear.

12

Yesterday's riot had been on one of the rare dry and sunny days in Bassar. The fires set had gobbled up everything burnable in the whole neighborhood before the canals stopped them. Ugru suspected that without the canals half the city might have gone. Certainly the policers had been worse than useless, and the firemen gallant but hopelessly understrength and underequipped.

Bassar Municipal "Protectors," my left testicle! (Which Ugru suspected was of more use than the BMP, although he knew of no living tangible evidence of this.)

Most of the people on the path up to the First Temple of the Brotherhood seemed to be initiates—Children, Ugru remembered they were called—carrying casualties on stretchers. He saw a good many walking wounded also, but practically no one able-bodied.

He was not surprised at such ugliness. Serious as the situation in Bassar was now, it wasn't bad enough to drive the homeless into the countryside. There the "government" (Ugru snorted) would have to notice their existence, which did *not* mean it would have to feed or clothe them. (At least not until they reached the labor camps or whatever equivalent the oligarchs of Hellhole would use to "solve" the refugee problem.)

So . . . all the homeless who didn't need medical attention they couldn't find in Bassar anyhow were crowded in with relatives or friends, squatting in abandoned buildings, or simply camped in the streets. Sometimes the BMP tried to clear the camps away. Most of the time the men in tan turned a blind eye, both to the homeless and to the animal-men who preyed on them.

It was when he had to stand by and watch a girl only just become a woman raped to death that Ugru decided. He had to leave Bassar and seek the Brotherhood. There was nothing he could do to help in the city, and plenty of opportunity to be killed. The oaths of his art meant much, but so did his oaths to his master.

Ugru joined the line of stretcher-bearers on the path. He walked slowly, in order to be able to observe while seeming to keep his eyes humbly on the ground.

The First Temple hardly matched the description in his briefing. It seemed to sprawl all across the hilltop and also to have added at least one story. A closer look told Ugru that both roofs and the ground outside the walls had sprouted tents. Even if they were taking only the hurt or sick, the Brotherhood was up to its chin in people.

It was against Ugru's principles, if not his oath, to take advantage of such suffering as he saw all around him. Still, he couldn't deny it—his work would be much easier because the Brotherhood was too busy to afford to turn away able-bodied recruits—or even examine them very closely.

At the gate in the walls, the stretcher-bearers handed their burdens over to new teams, then knelt before a small yellow tent to receive new orders. Most of them were sent back down the hill for a new casualty. Ugru pushed his way through the kneelers—mostly women, he saw, and many looking half-starved. It was about what he had expected.

Before anyone could stop him, he thrust head and shoulders into the tent.

The old man at the table there started, then stared bleary-eyed at the intruder. He was a small thin man starved still thinner, and so pale with exhaustion that the crimson circles of subcutane around his red and swollen eyes stood out like beacons. The yellowish light creeping through the tent cloth gave him the appearance of a dried autumn leaf, about to fall.

"If you are in need of healing, go to the hospital. This is the office of Duty to the–"

"I beg your pardon, Elder Brother," Ugru said with special care for politeness. "I have no need of healing. I came to join the Brotherhood, and through it to give my strength to those in need."

For a moment the man looked as if he was going to weep. Just as Ugru started to look away, the red-mask coughed, blew his nose on a ragged saffron sleeve, and stood up.

"May the Dark Lord and the gods of your birth-world bless your wish, Brother," he said, with desperate sincerity. He studied Ugru closely, focusing his eyes with difficulty.

"Your birth world might be Terasaki, yes?"

"That is so."

"May I ask your clan?"

"I have sworn not to name it. I was wrongfully accused of disgracing them and cast out. Because they thought they were shamed by what I had not done, they will gain no honor from what I do."

The red-"masked" man nodded. "The Dark Lord does not ask that you reveal all your secrets. Only that you work well in this time of troubles, and practice Silence, Duty, and Obedience." He sighed and slumped down into his chair, as if the formality had drained the last of his strength.

"There is no time to give you a proper Initiation. There is simply too much work to be done. I trust you are not disappointed?"

Ugru shook his head. "Let me do my work well, that the Dark Lord sees and approves. I ask nothing more."

"Again I bless you. Do you have healing skills?"

Ugru's "Yes" would have satisfied any lie detector. When one had learned human physiology for the purpose of more efficient killing, one had also acquired the knowledge that could be applied to healing. The old Brother closed his eyes—about the only gesture of happiness he seemed to have the strength for.

"Then go to the hospital and ask for Miembra-daktari or her assistant Yimra Tewao. Tell them that Brother Chayim bids them put you to work, to do whatever you can."

"Miembra or Tewao. I thank you, Elder Brother Chayim, as do my ancestors who know I was wronged."

Ugru bowed as low as he would have to his father or his master, and hurried off. He did not stop to ask directions. If he became lost, that would be just one more excuse for exploring the Temple grounds.

It was too soon to be complacent, but fortune seemed to be with him. He would be spared the sacrifice of his carrysak and a search of his person and clothing. Little of what he carried revealed its true purpose openly, but he could not be sure that *ninjitsu* was a blank film to all among the Brotherhood.

He would also be spared the degradation of having to use the Child-Sisters or be used by the full Sisters. Ugru knew that he was handsome even without the grace of movement and the supple muscles given by his art. He'd never had to behave dishonorably toward a woman, and he would be happiest if the necessity did not arise now.

Luctan listened to the entire tape, then shrugged. "What is your purpose in bringing this to me, Brother Tuke?"

For once Tuke seemed to hesitate before answering. And was that a look of anger on his normally-plasteel blank face? Or sweat visible against the crimson squares of subcutane around his eyes?

"Have you seen this man who calls himself 'Ugru'?" Tuke finally replied.

"I have not, Brother Tuke."

"Your pardon, Elder Brother Luctan," Tuke said, reminded that he'd left off his superior's title. "I have. I have never seen a man more likely to be other than what he seems. There is *ninjitsu* in every line of his body."

Luctan nodded. "I bow to your superior knowledge of the matter." He hoped he hadn't sounded too sarcastic. Lord, was he tired! He'd spent much of the day visiting the hurt and the sick, work normally done by those Elder Brothers who still believed in the Brotherhood. Better done, too—the transparent sincerity of these bovine idiots was awesome even for Luctan to behold. It was even more inspiring for the patients.

Now, however, the Elder Brother who was public leader of the Brotherhood of Servants of Tarf al-Barahut had to let himself be seen. Otherwise there would sooner or later be a cry for Eldest Brother Kayab bin-Tarf to show himself.

That could not be permitted.

"Thank you, Elder Brother. I rejoice in your trust," Tuke

said. It was impossible to tell what lay behind those words. ''It is made worse by Ugru's serving Miembra, along with Yimra Tewao.''

''You believe they might be a team finally united, and now ready to move against us?''

''Would they not be formidable if they were, Elder Brother?''

Luctan lifted his eyebrows. ''Even to you, Tuke?''

''Even to me, if they had trained together. I wish to learn what Elder Brother Chayim was thinking, when he caused them to be united in Miembra's service.''

Luctan suspected that the old man had been almost too tired to think of his own name, let alone plot against the Brotherhood. He shook his head.

''We have yet to find one of these . . . outsiders, who knew of anyone else in the Brotherhood serving the same master. That makes it–''

''Perhaps they were not told of the others—Elder Brother,'' Tuke added hastily, as Luctan's face hardened.

''You presume close to disObedience by interrupting.''

''Your pardon, Elder Brother Luctan.''

''Granted. You may be right about the partners not being informed of each other's existence. But then what is the advantage of sending more than one, if they cannot help each other?''

Tuke's face remained set in a mold just short of defiance, but Luctan ignored it and continued. ''No, I think the danger Ugru presents is not great enough to risk giving further offense to Miembra-daktari.''

''She would not dare leave us now, when there is so much of her work to do, would she?''

Luctan succeeded in not looking pityingly at Tuke. ''There is so much work that she can go anywhere in Bassar and people will come to her. People will also believe what she says against the Brotherhood, even to protecting her against us if they think she is in danger.'' Again he raised his brows, and studied Tuke's face for reaction. The sweat was definitely there. What else, less visible?

''The Bassar mob?'' Tuke looked ready to spit.

''Ten men who think Miembra is worth dying for can protect her even from such as you, Brother Tuke.''

Tuke flipped five at Luctan, who continued in a voice he tried to keep from grating. "Also, you are forbidden to so much as *speak* to Elder Brother Chayim."

"Why?"

The defiance in the voice was so open that Luctan was tempted to reply, "Because I command it. Are you determined on disObedience?" He resisted. It was just barely possible to keep the peace between him and Tuke with a civil answer.

"Brother Chayim is about the least likely man of anyone in the Brotherhood to be part of a plot. He is also one of our best men for making us seem to the world as we wish to seem. Finally, he is getting more work out of the Children than anybody else could. He is probably more useful to the Brotherhood right now than you or I!"

"Do you fear that I will defy you, Elder Brother Luctan?"

Up went Luctan's brows. Again he swallowed a reply along the lines of "Do Jarps slice?" He shook his head. "You have never disObeyed me. You have often done things I would have ordered you not to do if I'd heard of your intentions beforehand. Your elimination of Shamat, for example. Why in the name of all the gods of the Galaxy did you have to use it to wage your feud with Miembra?"

Tuke looked as if the answer should be evident to anyone above the mental level of a child of five, before bowing his head. "I will Obey, Elder Brother Luctan."

"Very good. I also order you to make whatever arrangements you think necessary for the greater security of the Red-Grade Rooms in the First Temple. See to it that they are more secure than they are now, but with fewer Brothers needed to watch them. We cannot take too many hands away from our public work even if all the *ninja* clans of Terasaki descend on us!"

Tuke was just able to manage something vaguely resembling a smile. "I will Obey, Elder Brother. It will not be cheap and much of what we would truly need may not be easy to find–"

"Whatever you need of time and money will be yours, within reason." Luctan started to make a gesture of dismissal.

He reconsidered and aborted it. Instead he returned Tuke's almost-smile.

"Do not fear that I turn against you, Brother Tuke. You are as direct as a laser and you cannot be otherwise. Nor would I honor you as I do if you were. Do not fear, I say. That the time to give you Miembra and the rest is not now, does not mean that it shall not come."

Tuke redshifted, and Luctan sank into the softest chair in the room. He wished there was one to swallow him up like the Maelstrom, then spit him out on a *very* distant planet. He would like to live there for a century or so, being waited on hand and foot and crotch by beautiful nude women. *Women, not these silly religion-blinded girls,* he mused. And about half of them true masochists . . . For a moment he smiled.

A century or so of such recreation might be enough time to get the Brotherhood out of his system.

Failing that, he could at least give some thought to removing the increasingly fobby Brother Tuke. He did, all traces of smile leaving his face. This newcomer Ugru seemed a platinum-plated gold-cored opportunity to solve the Tuke problem. If the Brotherhood could find the price of Ugru's loyalty, he might take Tuke's place.

His first job after that, of course, would be to remove his predecessor.

His second would be to . . . placidate Sister "Yimra Tewao." (Oh yes, Luctan was entirely familiar with that one of several euphemisms for "kill.") If they were partners, Ugru would either betray himself or expose her. Then—well, a man with a plasmer or a stopper set on Three could placidate the best ninja in the Galaxy if it wasn't expecting the attack. Poof!

If "Ugru" and "Yimra" were not partners, the former would be instructed to take his time with the latter. Stretch it out, give her lots of opportunity to babble. Tuke's pickups had no doubt recorded most of what she had said to Kayab, but there would always be holes worth the trouble of filling them in.

Luctan did not believe in incomplete data, particularly when methods of completing it promised to be an experience he would remember with pleasure for many years.

13

Younger Brother Jirish unlocked Kayab's door and held it open for Alanni. She bowed her thanks. She even walked steadily and stood straight until the door closed behind her.

Once it had, she went limp as a worm tossed into boiling water. She nearly fell to the floor. As a matter of fact, that would have been fine, if she hadn't wanted a shower so badly. Somewhere she remembered a man named Kayab bin-Tarf, who had to give her permission to take a shower. She couldn't remember exactly why this was so.

She couldn't remember much of anything, in fact. At least not much besides the endless march of the maimed, the burned, the terror-stricken, the lost, the sick–

She ran for the bathroom, but not for the shower. Since she hadn't eaten anything since breakfast, she didn't have to spend long with her head bent over the sitter. When her stomach stopped heaving, she felt clearer-headed. Wonderful . . . that merely meant awareness of more aches and pains and foul smells. She stripped off her clothes as if she had Tilno waiting for her, not caring how many pieces they landed in. Then she stumbled into the shower and turned it on.

One good thing about this fobby mudball of an Arsehole, the Light be thanked. Nobody who can reach a bath ever has to stay dirty long. It's not short of water.

The number of lovers who'd felt better than the first touch of hot water on her skin—she could count them on one hand and *maybe* need a finger of the other.

She would have liked to peel off her scalp and hair as well as her clothes. Nothing else would completely wipe away the stink of blood, pus, vomit (and what in the Light's name did people in Bassar eat that made them vomit purple?).

Instead she picked up the skweezpak of soap and started working up a lather in her hair.

She'd just lathered her scalp to the point at which she didn't dare open her eyes when she heard someone calling her name. A male voice, close by. Then she heard the sound of the shower door opening.

She knew how down she was when she realized she didn't care if it was Kayab or Tuke or a madman with a knife ready to stick between her ribs. As long as the soap was in her eyes she wouldn't see it coming.

Maybe it will Poof the memories of a city coming apart.

"Yimra?"

It was Kayab's voice calling her name, without the "Sister." Had she started hallucinating, or did he really sound worried?

"Eldest Brother?"

"Firm. Are you well?"

"Neg."

"Is–is there anything I can do?"

"Pos. Let me rinse my hair."

"Firm."

The shower door closed. Alanni thrust her head under the water and clawed at her hair until all of the soap and some of the stink and filth were out of it. Then she turned off the shower.

As she did, the door opened again. Kayab stood there, nude. Alanni looked down and learned she still had the strength to smile. Kayab did want to stick something into her, but it wasn't a knife. Nor was its destination anywhere close to her ribs.

Unfortunately neither that nor the sight of his well-toned body could change the fact that she was about as eager to soar as one of those corpses lying on the ground outside the hospital in the evening rain until somebody could organize a proper burial party.

Right now, my flash point is so high Tilno couldn't find it.

She rested her head against the plas of the shower stall and held on to the water dial with one hand. Oh, she'd handled disasters before, but not ones like this, with the odds so hopelessly against being able to do anything for most of the victims.

She knew she was out of practice. Maybe her nerve was gone? She still couldn't forget that the last time she'd handled a disaster, it had been as Captain Alanni Keor, T-SP. She'd been one of the two senior officers in command of a force of policers and medics who considerably outnumbered the victims of the hover-bullet train.

Anybody who hadn't been saved then—well, it was because it was in such a shape that nothing short of cloning would do any good.

"Sister Yimra? Should I summon Miembra-daktari?"

Alanni started to laugh at the idea of Miembra's having any strength to spare for her. Then she clenched her fists until the pain of nails gouging her palms wiped the desire to laugh.

If she started laughing now, she might not be able to stop.

Kayab stared at her. He still wore nothing but a concerned look, but at least he was no longer at the salute.

No, I shouldn't really take consolation from that. I wonder how much of his present trouble stems from his stem not flowering when he wanted it to?

Then Kayab was toweling her dry—*he* drying *her,* and somehow she wasn't worried at all about the disObedience because she had to Obey Kayab and *nobody* could force him to Obey except the Dark Lord–

–and the people who are keeping him prisoner here, while they run the Brotherhood for their own fun and profit.

Or ruin it.

The words thumped into her mind one at a time, like police flyers making sloppy landings at the Academy field. She felt each thump as if somebody was actually punching her.

She still felt better, all at once.

Those words were the only way to make sense of all she'd seen here in Kayab's . . . cell. "Reaching a working hypothesis is the most necessary step to solving any mystery," her Basic Criminology program had always said.

That assumes you can take any action on the basis of the hypothesis.

Why can't you? With all the confusion in the Temple–

"Sister Yimra?"

He was holding out a robe—one of *his* robes. Alanni slipped into it, wondering if the Dark Lord would have anything to say about the impiety of the handmaid wearing his Chosen's clothes.

"Sister Yimra," he repeated. "You are not well."

He reached past her and turned the water dial on full. For a moment Alanni thought he was going to take his own shower in order to be presentable when he summoned Miembra for her.

Then she realized that he was speaking again, so low that she could not hear him over the roar of the shower.

So low that no listening devices could hear him, either.

She tapped his ear, then his mouth. He raised his voice just enough so that she could hear half the words and lip-read the rest.

"It has started?"

"What is 'it'?"

"The end of Bassar."

She blinked at proof that he was aware; very much aware.

"This was the fifth riot in the last month, and the worst. I—yes, it has started. How did you know?"

"One knows when one's . . . attendants, are ready to fall over. Not just you, but those who came earlier today. Even Luctan. Also, I smelled the smoke."

Alanni nodded. She'd had so many stenches in her nose today that she probably wouldn't have noticed if Kayab had set his bedroom on fire!

"Yimra—who are you?"

Alanni jumped as if he'd suddenly turned a cold shower on her. She saw only curiosity and something else harder to identify.

Maybe—just maybe—it was the dawning hope of a prisoner who saw a way out of his prison.

Well, if we work together, why not? And if I tell him—something of the truth—maybe we can work together.

It's worth a try.

"I'm a retired policer. I'm here to find—somebody's daughter. She ran away and joined the Brotherhood."

"Not Shamat?"

"How did you know about her?"

"If Luctan had Tuke punish for disObedience every Brother who'd talked when he didn't think I was listening, he'd have no one left to do any work."

"Clear. No, not Shamat. Nobody you would know, either, unless—how long have you been a prisoner?"

Kayab was silent so long that Alanni began to fear she'd said too much. "Long enough. If you want to hear my story, let's go to bed. If we stay here longer than we'd need to shower together, Tuke may suspect something when he hears the tape."

Maybe al-Barahut didn't send Kayab a vision. But Somebody sent him brains, the Light be praised!

Alanni turned off the shower and bowed her head. "As you bid me, Eldest Brother."

After that her worst fear was that Kayab was going to burst out laughing before they were safe from electronic eavesdroppers.

They went straight to bed but neither slept nor soared.

Stead of either, they burrowed under the sheets and exchanged stories in whispers. Kayab's story was a long one, and he didn't leave out much, but Alanni's exhaustion was as thoroughly fallen-away as her clothes. She couldn't have gone to sleep with a Two-set stopper pointed at her, although she knew she'd have to sleep sooner or later.

(Otherwise she'd look dosed with tetrazombase when Miembra saw her in the morning. Others might see her too, and anyway she couldn't work on hurt people if she could barely stand. She'd be as big a menace as another riot.)

Kayab put in a lot of detail, but the main points of his life were simple enough.

A boy, who thought he was ugly and spent all his time studying.

A young man, who *knew* he was ugly, never came close enough to a woman to let one tell him otherwise, and went on studying.

A brilliant University student who won every honor on Hellhole and a few offplanet ones as well.

The youngest professor at the University, teaching history to two generations of students who were the only family he'd ever had. They chose him over big-name 'puter-program "teachers," too.

At last the aging professor who moved to Bassar to start a school of his own there. He saw too much misery and too few people doing anything about it. He also saw what would happen in the next big earthquake. And at last, because he was a historian, he saw the remedy.

"But—why—*found a religion?*" Alanni said.

"Simple. If I'd tried to work through the Fog Coast government, nothing would have happened. If I'd tried to found a non-religious relief agency, I'd have been as dead as Shamat inside a year. The Heller government doesn't like to be made to look bad. They don't have much money, but there are lots of bugs in Bassar who work cheap."

It *was* simple, when Alanni thought it over. Also quite sensible. No planet's government went very far in questioning even the oddest religions. People were more willing to rebel, fight, and die for their religions than for a lot of more sensible things. If the rebellions didn't bring the government down by themselves, it was not unknown for TGO to pay a visit and oblige the families of the government's leaders to attend state funerals.

A little of this kind of lesson went a long way, even with the muckwits who composed the average "government."

"Of course, once I had the vision of Tarf al-Barahut, people started listening. I had to have help." If one could *hear* a bitter grimace, Alanni heard one now.

"Luctan had been one of my students at the University. He followed me to Bassar, to be administrator of my school. I can't hold a crowd or run an office. Luctan could—can do both well. Why shouldn't I accept him, when he proclaimed his conversion to the Way of the Dark Lord?"

Alanni didn't have to imagine hearing bitterness.

The rest of the story she could have guessed without being told. Luctan made himself so indispensable that soon he could do things without telling Kayab bin-Tarf. When Tuke appeared, he had the Invisible Wisdom with him. With that and his martial-arts skills, he more than met Luctan's price for hiding him in the Brotherhood.

"Tuke was—is—a good judge of people like himself. He

found enough of them, brought them into the Brotherhood, made it impossible for anyone who opposed Luctan to accomplish anything. Sometimes he made it impossible for them to live."

Kayab hadn't wanted that fate "–although I still don't know if I was a coward or a sensible man. All I knew was that dead men solve no problems. So when they locked me up and wanted me to play idiot—I played."

Alanni nodded and remained silent. Judging was not her way. She had never seen any point in passing judgments on mistakes already made (if this had been a mistake) unless it prevented more mistakes. She couldn't see Kayab making this one again.

His feeling of guilt made him misread her silence as accusation. "Yimra, for the Dark Lord's sake! Can you imagine how I've felt facing the handmaids, knowing what they've suffered—knowing about the ones who have died or killed themselves? That's why I've tried to be kind to all of you." He stared with stricken eyes before he lowered his head. When he resumed speaking the pain and anger had left his voice.

"I was also hoping to find an ally in one of you. I never did," he sighed. "A month of kindness can't put back . . . all that's been lost in a lifetime."

His voice was distorted by the helplessness and guilt he obviously felt. Alanni reached for where she thought his hand was, found his shoulder. She gripped it firmly to tell him that she was there, that she understood, that she did not judge.

He sighed again. "I felt the worst about you. I knew you weren't from Bassar. You've known better men than rapists and unBrotherly cake-slicers before you came here. Not to mention Miembra . . ."

She heard something riding his voice and wondered; did he think there was something wrong with her, that she was able to soar with another woman? Some men did, but Kayab didn't seem the sort whose machismo ruled his judgment. Still . . .

"Oh. Miembra didn't give me much choice, I admit. But she's been as kind as if I'd been free to tell her to go to Iceworld and make it with a glacier." Memories made her giggle. "Good, too. Where she finds the energy after all the work she puts in, I wish I knew. She should leave her hormones to science."

"I wondered. One of the girls who killed herself—she did it to escape Miembra."

"The poor vacuum-brain!" *Of course—not all bigots are male!*

"How's *your* energy?"

Alanni didn't bother asking for what. She was too busy trying to keep from grinning so widely she couldn't talk. He was taking the initiative! *Finally*. And finally she said:

"Here."

"No, there." And the mattress quivered as he bent over her lower body. He seemed to hesitate, then she felt his lips and the brush of his beard on skin already anticipating their touch.

She hardly cared that he had touched down several sems from the nearest erozone. She was willing to wait and let him find his way. *So long as one of us doesn't go to sleep first!*

Ummmm . . . don't think it'll be me. . . . His lips had traveled to the right place and she wanted to shout. She did sigh, and he took that message and her tremor the way she intended. Beard brushed skin softly; tongue joined lips in tracing over her fluttery lower belly, her navel. Their owner emitted a grunt and slid a hand over his neck.

Not much practice, but the man has a lot of natural talent! And that was her last thought that deserved the name.

His hands held her flanks lightly while his lips traveled on down her belly until she twitched, gurgle-sighed, and opened her legs. Lips met lips, kissed . . .

And he sneezed.

She stiffened. Her breasts felt ready to melt, yet with nipples hard enough to stab through equhyde. And he had *sneezed*?!

"Sorry," he murmured. "Your . . . hair went up my nose."

"My–?"

She had actually forgotten! Like most Galactics, she was hairless below the eyebrows. On the planet she had chosen for her cover story, about one woman in four had a re-genengineered growth around her vulva, usually trimmed into some artistic or allegedly esthetic shape. To prop up her story, Alanni had done the same. Now she understood at least one advantage of a bare vulva more clearly than ever!

She began laughing and couldn't stop, didn't want to stop, and did not stop until her lover gave up on her lower lips and moved up to the noisier ones. He didn't neglect her lower lips while he kissed her into silence-but-for-sighing; his hand moved there, gentle and effective. Then she was pushing at his hand and tugging at him. His slicer took over the responsibility.

When it glided into its proper place—practically a lake, by now—she would have bitten off anything in her mouth if she'd been able to move it that much. She wasn't; he held her mouth captive and kept it the captive of his throughout their ancient slicing movements. When she wanted to scream and he wanted to groan, both of them nearly strangled. Their mouths were united and full. And that didn't spoil a thing.

Nothing did. She felt marvelously full, loved, and even used . . . well-used. Then her eyes were flaring, rolling up, and there was no way she could give a damn if they rolled out and went into orbit of the room. His mouth stopped her shriek when she flashed, big, and he kept right on moving, working his hips four ways at once, and then her mouth was catching his roaring groan of completion.

After a while she whimpered when he abandoned both sets of lips, then grunted.

"El . . . desst Brother . . . might this . . . Sisssterr ask a further favor?"

"I suppose I *could* nibble on your cake again . . ."

"Not that—please . . . could you get your elbow out of my ribs?"

He chuckled, shifted position, and put a finger to her mouth. She realized that they had thrown off the top sheets in the exuberance of their mating, while practically wrecking the bottom one. *Dear* Bro. Tuke's tapes would be lying in wait, doubtless actuated by human voices.

A happily naked Alanni started to pull the sheets back over them. They had so much to plan, so much they could do together that they never could have accomplished separately, so much to . . .

A gentle snore floated out from under the sheets.

A second one followed it.

She sighed, rested a hand on the nearest lump she could be sure was part of Kayab, and rolled over onto her side.

Both of them had to have a lot of sleep, that was what, before they could plan anything requiring more thought than the opening of a skweezpak!

14

Alanni turned the shower full on before she knelt by the plas door in the rear wall of the bathroom. Looking back over one reelsilk-clad shoulder, she nodded to Kayab standing in the doorway.

"Your service has been good, Sister Yimra," he began ponderously. "Yet you have failed in one of the Three Principles. Can you guess which one?"

If Kayab hadn't been talking just to cover the noise she was making, she'd have said "Silence." (How could she have been silent, considering all the plans they'd made, all she had taught him, and all the times they'd soared in the past twenty days?)

Instead she inserted the kitchen knife in the crack on top of the door, probing for her carefully-rigged fasteners.

She said, "This Sister is ashamed that she has failed, but does not know in what respect. She begs the Eldest Brother, the Chosen of Tarf al-Barahut, to enlighten her, that she may return to the seeking of the Way."

She swallowed an "Aha!" as the knife popped the first fastener.

"Sister Yimra, you have failed in Obedience, the greatest of the Three."

Is it? I hadn't heard that. Of course, I've never been curious about the theological fine points of most religions and this one less than most!

"This Sister does not understand how she has failed." *(Very thoroughly—sometimes I've treated the poor man like an awkward recruit. I'm not going to be here much longer, though. Maybe not after tonight. Kayab has to learn everything I can teach him before I leave, to stay alive until I come back.)*

She'd told herself more times than she could remember that she would come back to Bassar and help dismantle Luctan's leadership of the Brotherhood of Servants. She'd even told herself that she would be ready to trust Councillor Nortay's agent in Golden, rather than run the Invisible Wisdom back to him herself. Jay and Bouncy could take a *few* chances, and she really couldn't just build up Kayab's hopes and then leave him alone.

Are you sure he'll cooperate if you come back after stealing the Invisible Wisdom? Or will he feel so betrayed he'd rather die than trust you again? And if you're not sure about that, are you sure you aren't just telling yourself a pretty tale so you won't feel guilty about hurting Kayab?

Alanni decided she wasn't sure about anything. She also decided that from the way Kayab was looking at her, she'd missed a cue.

"This Sister fears she did not understand the words of the Eldest Brother concerning her disObedience."

The other fastener went *spunnng* and the door popped into her hands so suddenly that she nearly let it fall with a clatter.

Come on! You haven't been so nervous since the first time you went out with a boy you knew wanted to soar!

She was inclined to doubt that proposition (although she'd accepted the boy's), but didn't doubt that the prospect of actually seeing the Invisible Wisdom at last was making her a little thick-fingered. She lowered the panel to the floor and finished her ritualistic conversation with Kayab.

It ended in her elaborate promise to do her Duty, Obey Kayab bin-Tarf, and hereafter to be Silent when he spoke.

It was nearly too elaborate. She saw Kayab fighting not to break silence or Silence by breaking out into fatally revealing laughter. She stood up, went to him, rubbed against and kissed him until there was no danger of his having any breath for laughing.

This could be our goodbye kiss.

He squeezed her shoulder, and Alanni bent down to slip through the hole. Before she'd stood up in the low passageway behind the wall, the panel clicked back into place. Her world was instantly painted black.

Working by touch, she found the movable slab in the floor, hooked her fingers into the cracks at either end, and lifted. It came up with a *skrunk*. She took inventory of her cache of equipment, first by touch, then with the help of a tiny handlite. She also used it to be sure the door in the wall would look perfectly normal to anything but a very careful inspection.

Everything was as it was supposed to be.

No reason to expect it wouldn't be, of course. Security in the Brotherhood really depended on Tuke and about eight or ten Overseers. That number had no hope of watching everything that needed watching even above ground, let alone in the maze of old tunnels and rooms under the First Temple. (Alanni's briefing had mentioned this warren without indicating what it had been. A bombproof military headquarters made more sense than anything else, if not very much.)

As for the rest of the Brotherhood . . . the Children would be trouble only if she did something right in front of their noses. The Brothers were too busy guessing which stash they'd use next to be security-conscious. Unless Tuke told them. Even then, many of them would resent his telling them *anything*.

I have the perfect cure for them, Alanni thought. *When I'm finished with Tuke his manners will be perfect. He'll never say a harsh word again—or any other kind.*

She pulled off her skirt and top, pulled on pants and too-large shirt, looped on a belt, hooked on a pouch. She filled the pouch, tied up her hair, and donned gloves. She wouldn't use the skin-blackening cream tonight—it would just make her look *odd,* exactly the wrong way to look if anyone saw her. After she left the Temple, the black cream might have its uses. (And how had anybody ever done covert night work in the old days on Homeworld, if the legends were true about there being so many people as pale as Aglayans?)

Alanni added dried fruit and nut bars, spare socks, and the headcloth to the contents of the pouch. She didn't *plan* to have to redshift tonight, but she hadn't planned for most of the things that had happened to her on Hellhole. (She still wasn't quite sure whether her performance would have won a passing mark at the Academy. A lot of slaving and a lot of slicing. *Harrrd* work!)

The cache still was a long way from empty when she slid the stone back in place. It landed harder than she'd expected.

The *thunnnngggg* sent echoes rolling up and down the tunnel until they were lost in the darkness, and she absolutely froze.

She felt an absurd impulse to turn off her light, so that if the echoes awoke anything it wouldn't see her. She'd heard rumors (or at least rumors of rumors) that beyond the rooms and tunnels used by the Brotherhood a whole complex had been dug under the hills of the peninsula, in a warren stretching for kloms and kloms.

It was also too old (or so the rumors of rumors said) to have been built by any Galactic race.

Skepticism about rumors of rumors aside, Alanni knew that such tales existed about nearly every settled planet in the Galaxy. Some of them had to be true—otherwise, where had the Invisible Wisdom come from? Someday when she had leisure, energy, and a modest arsenal (everything short of long-illegal nukes) she wouldn't mind exploring the whole peninsula above and below ground.

Assuming these caves survive the next *big quake!*

Meanwhile, the human-built underground part of the Temple was the Light's own gift to one Alanni Keor. Without it, she'd never have had a halfway safe way of exploring the Temple, finding the Invisible Wisdom and planning her escape routes, or even hiding anything she couldn't swallow in an emergency (such as a search of Kayab's rooms by Tuke.) She'd have used the tunnels even if they swarmed with green monsters four meters tall, with six tails and four sex organs.

The arsenal that held the heavy weapons—stoppers, slavewands, slug-throwing pistols, plasmers—was the one place she hadn't been able to enter at least once. Otherwise she had collected her gear fairly easily over the last ten days—or nights.

(The only place where Alanni snatched by day was Miembra's office, and not much, and that with exquisite care. Miembra and Alanni were both able to contain their enthusiasm for ending up in Tuke's hands.)

Alanni wasn't as well-equipped as she could have been if her bag hadn't been plasmerized on Skyraft, but she should do well enough. *With a little luck.*

Ugru tried to show nothing, but thought he was being dishonored at Miembra's mention of "Initiation" and then "bath attendant." That faded when she gave him that smile and went to start a shower. He realized that she wanted him to attend *her* in her bath, and she did not mean as attendant. True, he was a little surprised; he had thought that a day that began before dawn and ended after sunset (as far as anyone could judge under this hellish planet's damnable clouds!) left no one the strength for slicing, licit or il-.

He had been wrong, he realized, on both counts. *Let it be as it must be. My blood is that of a clan never marked by dishonor toward woman.* Accordingly, he started to undress—and staggered when the whole room quivered. Plas containers rattled on shelves, a pile of medrecord printouts slithered off a side-table, and a couple of empty spray injectors followed. As he bent to pick up the papers, he noted dust motes that hadn't been there before, dancing in the pale yellow glow of the overhead light.

Ugru's own Terasaki was one of the most geologically stable of all human-inhabited worlds. Ugru, however, had traveled far and been briefed thoroughly. Hardly easy in his mind at the 'quake he knew he'd just felt, he wondered whether he should tell Miembra.

She probably is not aware of it, over the noise and vibration of running water. My saying anything could be worthy of suspicion. I shall keep silent, and let her take the initiative in this matter as in others.

Deliberately he began to ignite himself by anticipating pleasures soon to come. To see a man excitedly ready was flattering to a woman.

(The strains along the main fault line of the Fog Coast had been building for more than seven centuries. The slight shock Ugru felt—hardly more than a geological hiccup—had done very little to relieve the pressure within the planet.

(In fact, at a point along the fault line three hundred kloms out to sea and with two kloms of water adding its weight to the rock, Hellhole's hiccup had made matters worse. Two sections of tectonic plate that might have released pressure shifted, creating a whole new set of stresses that demanded relief.

(In the normal course of nature, that release could not be long in coming.)

15

Alanni reached the bottom of the spiral staircase and darted to the right, into the shadows under it. She hadn't heard anyone coming down the stairs behind her or along the tunnel ahead. She also doubted whether anyone could have heard her this way; barefoot; or seen her in these dark clothes.

Unless someone was deliberately trailing her.

If someone was, she wanted to give him time to wonder where she was and possibly make a move that would show him up. It was one kind of job to scout in the face of the normal nighttime population of the underground Temple. It was another to do it with Tuke or somebody trained by him after her. (And it would be a he; no chance that it could be female, in the so-male milieu of the Brotherhood.)

The second case would mean snatching the Invisible Wisdom tonight, then taking her chances with redshifting and surviving. There was a technical term for making a second try in the face of an alert Tuke.

Suicide.

(Not to mention the danger to Kayab. He was now almost as much a hostage for what might loosely be called her good behavior as Jay and Bouncy. *Almost,* because she was going to liberate the Invisible Wisdom and see that it traveled home to Eagle. The most she would do for Kayab was avoid anything else that would put him in danger. Or at least put him in danger without giving her the Invisible Wisdom.)

Alanni had just decided that nobody was coming when four somebodies came tramping down the stairs.

They were a Younger Brother and three Child-Sisters. The

Children were carrying plas crates whose labels proclaimed them freeze-dried fishcakes. Survival rations, if the Temple had to stand a real siege? No point in speculating ahead of the evidence.

Except that the evidence of really bad trouble to come is rapidly catching up. Best pack the Invisible Wisdom and redshift before Bassar turns into a real jungle.

The work party turned down the tunnel in the opposite direction from Alanni. She waited until they were out of sight, then began her slow stalk down the passage toward the storeroom that *probably* held the Invisible Wisdom.

(The Brotherhood had chosen the storeroom for its valuables before Kayab was imprisoned. Among the skills he'd always possessed that Alanni was now teaching him how to use was an excellent visual memory. Every piece of directions he'd given her so far had been accurate.)

The door was the usual roughly-finished wooden planks. Of course it was locked. No guard on duty, though. Just as well. If she had to Poof anybody tonight, it could be a disaster. Even the most stash-minded Brother might become security-minded after that. Not that suspicion would necessarily land on her.

The Brothers would most likely suspect some of the refugees or wounded. Still, if the whole Temple ended up patrolled night and day by Brothers at least trying to stay alert because they were afraid of being Poofed—well, Alanni Keor's life would be simpler (to say nothing of longer) without it.

A few meters from the door she stopped and catalogued what she saw.

Floor dusty—a few marks where something might have been dragged, but even they were old. Ventilation grille over the door—plas. A knife or tough wire should be able to cut it. No sign of any electronic security systemry was good news, though not completely surprising.

The Fog Coast had no local electronics industry and imports were expensive. The Brotherhood obviously didn't like spending stells that might make the Elder Brothers richer.

Not to mention Brother Tuke's pride in his ninjitsu *or whatever he calls it. He'd feel that he'd lost his slicer if he needed more than snooper-ears to give warning and bare hands to finish the job.*

And wouldn't you just love to make his feeling real!

Alanni crossed the last few meters, squatted, jumped, caught the ventilation grille with both hands, and peered into the storeroom. It was unlit, and she had to hang by one hand while she risked a quick look with the handlite.

One was enough. The Invisible Wisdom lay on the lower left-hand shelf of a double rack at the back of the room. Without her freak peripheral vision she might have missed it completely; she could never have gained an accurate sight line on it.

A tattered dusty rag tucked into the prass frame covered part of the artifact. The rag appeared to be a discarded pair of Children's shorts. For a moment Alanni actually managed a sympathetic thought for Councillor Nortay.

At least he'll give it a more dignified place in his collection than these bugs have!

Otherwise the treasure she'd come so far and endured so much to find was just as her briefing had said. In the poor light the prass frame with its carrying handle seemed to enclose a thirty-sem-square cube of empty air. The only thing hinting at a solid object was the way the rag hung.

The Invisible Wisdom weighed a good deal more than empty air, of course. Fourteen kilos ready to go, she knew. She'd hiked with twice that load, but not in a hurry. Definitely nothing to carry in her arms.

A rope harness—strong rope. And if I make a hook and tie it onto the rope, the carrying handle is sticking up just far enough. I can at least try hooking the Invisible Wisdom from here. If there's an alarm on the grille or under the Invisible Wisdom, I'll still be outside the room when it goes. Less time lost in redshifting!

Alanni no longer spent much time cursing herself for losing her gear. She could never have brought it "inside" with her, not without giving Luctan and Tuke the equivalent of a complete file on her. Still, she couldn't help a yearning thought for the hundred meters of monofilament rope and the twenty meters of wire, neither much thicker than heavy thread but both able to–

Alanni froze, gripping the plas grille so hard the rods gouged her fingers.

Something had made a noise, off there to the left. She relaxed her grip and let out her breath, but didn't drop to the floor. Sudden movement always drew the eye.

Best stay still, and hope whoever it is thinks its eyes are playing tricks . . .

Then it didn't matter anymore, as five people came charging out of the darkness of the passage.

Alanni was on the ground and in combat stance before the first of them reached her. Since he'd apparently never heard of combat stance, he was easy. A kick to one knee, a chop to his neck, and he was falling aside, and another man was closing in with a can in his hand–

The can *wsssssshhhh*ed and Alanni smelled Soothe. Smelled it and tried to blast all the air out of her lungs in a shout (jumping aside at the same time), collided with someone, had to breathe, and took in a lungful of the riot-control gas.

She still tried to cough it out of her while she also had to kick sideways at the man she'd run into. She heard him scream, but the satisfaction lasted about two heartbeats before she knew that the gas was affecting her. The heads of the others around her were distorted, and their eyes were enormous, round, dark, like insects'–

Goggles.

Infrared goggles. And one IR light far down the tunnel, lighting it up for anyone with the goggles while leaving it dark for anyone with normal-light vision.

All Tuke had to do was make this stretch of passage Forbidden Territory, then hook a vid pickup to the IR light and have it cybermonitored while he went off and sliced a Sister!

And I came bonking into it like a child!

At least she could take the turnout of five hostiles as a compliment to her. On the other hand, it tended to indicate that Tuke knew more about her than she had hoped.

The man with the Soothe was coming at her again . . .

And an Instrument of Obedience cracked across his wrist. The can ponged off the wall and the man gasped, holding his wrist.

"*Never dishonor me again by weakening an opponent. Never!*"

The voice was colder than Bleak's South Pole.

It was also Tuke's.

Alanni felt her legs turning into mush but kicked at Tuke anyway. If she could just force him to kill her–

Contemptuously, Tuke swung away from her kick, taking what was meant to shatter his spine on his hip, riding it around in a complete circle, then swinging the Instrument of Obedience again. With gruesome precision it smashed into her elbow. Alanni screamed.

She saw Tuke smile. Then she saw him raise his other hand and chop sideways. The hand bit into the side of her neck like a spade into a clay dike. Alanni stopped seeing anything.

16

Kayab came awake in a bed that shouldn't have been empty but definitely was. As quick a search as he could make while still half-asleep told him worse: his entire room was empty. At least it was empty of Yimra Tewao. He somehow doubted that no matter how sleepy he was he could have overlooked an object that large, alive or dead.

Yimra Tewao was quite a nice *solid* specimen of the human female. Kayab's thoughts ran warmly back over all the times he'd held that solidity in his arms and she'd held him in hers, while also holding his solidity 'way up inside her.

Then the warmth vanished, as he thought of why Yimra might not have returned from this night's little excursion.

It was just barely possible that she had found the girl she'd been sent to rescue and carried out her assignment. She and the girl might be on their way to the spaceport already, and offplanet by morning. That was a nice explanation—and the only one that required no action on his part.

It was also the least likely one.

Far more likely was that she'd been caught and punished—lightly if she was suspected of nothing worse than disObedience, more heavily if Tuke took a hand in it.

No, not *if*. *When* Tuke appeared. The man was no fool. A villain, but not a fool. Kayab could not believe that Tuke wouldn't have noticed something odd about Yimra, if only her fighting skills.

If he hadn't noticed it, Luctan would have. Luctan was another villain who was not a fool.

Yimra was in serious trouble. In fact, she was probably

right now suffering torments that no well-run Netherworld would inflict on its Damned.

Tuke was an expert at that sort of thing.

For a moment the most pressing matter for Kayab bin-Tarf was to reach the bathroom and empty his stomach. When he'd finished doing that and wiping the sweat off his face, he found that he'd somehow also decided what to do. He blinked, almost surprised at himself.

He was going to go out into the Temple and challenge Luctan for Sister Yimra's life, even if it meant risking his own.

Again, no *if.* Luctan could not afford such a challenge to his leadership. Not if it was made publicly. If it wasn't made publicly it would do Yimra no good, which was the whole reason for such an effort in the first place!

Kayab remembered Yimra's advice about starving the imagination by keeping busy. He went to the closet where hung his full regalia as Eldest Brother. For the first time in years, he began hauling it out. Checking each piece to see if it was intact really did keep his mind off what might be happening to Yimra now—not to mention what might be happening to him before the night was over.

The regalia was not only complete (Luctan must have been afraid of gossip if he'd stolen any of it) but wearable. The Dark Lord knew he'd paid enough so that it *should* have lasted, not to mention keeping himself trim too!

The saffron robe was thick silk, with hand embroidery in silver thread and a sheen that made it seem to glow in the proper light. The sandals were real leather, with fangface-hide straps and silver buckles. The staff of office was a little dusty, but all the coral and gold inlays were intact. So was the synthetic ruby at the head and the spiral of fish ivory around its middle.

Even the medallion of office, showing a dark hand raising a gold sunburst, was intact, although its leather strap was cracking and would not last much beyond tonight.

I may not either, Kayab thought, and swallowed hard.

Most important of all, the Eldest Brother's headdress was sound, although a little tarnished. No surprise about the tarnish—the headdress was only a gold washing over brass. Kayab couldn't afford a sunburst seventy sems wide in real gold, and he'd had to have a sunburst. The whole symbolism of the headdress was the Dark Lord's at last giving *light* by sending a vision to the Eldest Brother, his Chosen. Nothing else would do half as well as a sunburst.

The headdress nearly fragged Kayab's whole scheme by being a couple of sems too wide to go through the door in the bathroom wall. A little judicious bending of the frame solved that problem, however. Kayab nearly stopped breathing when one of the sun rays threatened to snap off, but fortunately it stopped short of that. Like the strap on the medallion, it would last the night.

The headdress now sat a bit loosely on his head, with a pronounced tendency to droop to the left. It seemed unlikely that anyone would notice, or care. Kayab hadn't worn the thing in public for more than three Heller years.

And I never would have thought of that, without Sister Yimra teaching me. Maybe a real spook, that lady?

Maybe. But I'm still going to save her if I can.

He had no night vision worthy of the name, but his staff of office made a halfway-reasonable cane. He tapped and stumbled his way along the passage, until he came out in a storeroom that was obviously long unused. Not surprisingly, he had to take off his sandals, hitch up the hem of his robe, and wade through ten sems of foul-smelling water to the stairs on the other side of the room.

The stairs ended in a well-lit, probably well-used hallway.

Kayab waited until he was sure nobody would see him leaving the storeroom, then straightened the headdress, raised the staff high, and strode out into the corridor. (More Wisdom of Sister Yimra: "If nobody sees you sneaking *into* a place, they're more likely to assume you have the right to be there.")

As he walked, Kayab chanted over and over again the mantra of the Brotherhood:

"The Dark Lord gives the Light of the Way."

"The Dark Lord gives the Light of the Way."

"The Dark Lord gives the Light–"

He broke off when four Younger Brothers and two Child-Sisters came out of a side passage. "Blessings on you, my Brothers and Sisters."

"Eld-d-duhhhh–" was all one Brother could say. The rest could only stare.

"The Dark Lord has given me a new vision," Kayab said, as loudly as he could. (The more people who heard him, the better.) "I must see Brother Luctan and Brother Chayim at once."

That should smoke out Luctan and bring one of the most respected and trusted of the Elder Brothers to his side. Unfortunately, it gained him only more silent staring. Kayab raised his voice to a shout.

"Is the Dark Lord now served only by the mute and the witless? Speak, if you value your place among his servants!"

He gestured with the staff, so wildly that he nearly brained two of the Younger Brothers. (He doubted that would have been any great loss.)

One of them remembered he had a voice and stopped waving his arms. "We—I—can summon Brother Chayim. Brother Luctan . . ."

"Brother Luctan will be summoned as well. Do you wish to risk his wrath as well as mine, by leaving him ignorant of this new vision?"

"Brother Luctan is in—he is seeing to the punishment of—of great disObedience."

"I will be the judge of whether the disObedience is great enough to be his first duty now." Kayab hoped it wouldn't be noticed that he swallowed and licked his lips before going on. "Who has been disObedient?"

"A Sister—a new Sister–" began one of the Brothers, then one of the Children suddenly screamed:

"It is your handmaid, Sister Yimra! I saw them carrying her to Brother Tuke's chamber. I saw them!"

Two of the Brothers glared at the cute-faced, too-thin Child-Sister. Kayab had a horrible moment of wondering what he would do if they attacked her—or him.

The moment passed. Kayab thanked Whoever was responsible, that his authority still smelled vaguely real when he waved it under people's noses this way. He nodded graciously to the outspoken Child.

"You have shown Duty and Obedience in breaking Silence, Your punishment shall be light, if any. Truly, the disObedience of my handmaid is a great matter. It is also something I must see to myself."

One of the Brothers licked his lips in a way that made Kayab want to smash his face in with the staff. *The little swine must think I want to have my share of the fun of torturing Yimra to death!*

Kayab took the medallion from around his neck and handed it to the Child. "Take this and my message to Brother Chayim. Lead him to where Sister Yimra may be found. Show Brother Chayim or anyone else who doubts you that medallion, and say that you speak in my name."

"As you command, Eldest Brother."

The girl couldn't have redshifted much faster if she'd been converted to tachyons. Kayab hoped she would reach her goal. She was a little more likely to be stopped than one of the Brothers, but much more trustworthy out of Kayab's sight.

"Now, Brothers," he said to the bright-eyed group. "Lead me to Elder Brother Luctan."

They formed up in the manner of an honor guard, two on either side and slightly ahead of him. He let the remaining Child-Sister fall in behind him—he could safely turn his back on her. She also wouldn't notice his sigh of relief on hearing that Sister Yimra wasn't dead or redshifted. He'd gambled his life for hers without knowing whether the prize was still his to win.

Now, just possibly, they might both beat the house.

As he marched off down the corridor with an impressive swishing of robes, Kayab still couldn't help wishing that he'd thought to put on trousers under his robe. A little extra padding might muffle the sound of his knees knocking together.

Alanni choked back a scream as the jointed frame creaked and squealed and finally turned so that she was facing up again. She couldn't quite keep back a groan. Alanni *hurt.*

What next? Back to slicing in front?

Front and rear, every one of the ten men in the room had driven into her as often as he could. The only thing they hadn't asked for was her mouth—or any form of lubricant.

Probably afraid I'd bite. I would have, too, before they put the gag in!

The gag was a complicated affair of spiked metal, designed to hold her mouth open. That way she couldn't bite off her tongue, by accident or by design. *Very Considerate.* It also gouged gums and lips horribly. Alanni tasted enough blood in her mouth to let her hope that maybe she would choke–

Luctan's too alert, except when he's slicing.

(That was a good part of the time, of course. No doubt about it—Brother Luctan was stimulated by a woman's pain to a prodigious level of performance. Alanni didn't find it terribly consoling that she was remaining a fine judge of men's quirks, right to the end.)

The gag wouldn't let her speak an intelligible word. It would let her scream her head off, if she wanted to. She did want to, because that would make the pain more endurable. She also refused to do so, because there were more important things to do.

Such as fragging Tuke's game, for one.

Tuke didn't care what he learned from her. He wanted to hear her scream until she ruptured her larynx and *died* screaming or maybe choking. Until he heard her scream, he would do whatever he could to make her, and the Maelstrom take learning anything from her!

Alanni knew that meant she was going to go out slow and nasty.

It also meant she could probably hide Kayab's secret and hers. It might even mean she could bring Tuke down with her.

If she died without giving the scrute, Luctan would have a perfect excuse for Poofing Tuke. "Excess of zeal" or some other phrase would do perfectly well.

Light, he could even have the fobber punished publicly!

Then Tuke could be replaced by Child-Brother Ugru—*if he's willing, and I suspect that Luctan's calculated his price already.*

Certainly the handsome (presumed) Terasak looked and moved in the way of someone capable of taking Tuke's place. Just as certainly, Luctan was studying him as if he wanted him either in bed or in a plot. Luctan being woman-minded when it came to bed, Alanni suspected plotting.

An Instrument of Obedience came down across her left nipple, then her right, then both thighs. All were swollen. Each time the horror landed on bruises, she tried not to flinch. It didn't help that her eyes were taped open, so she had to look at everyone slicing her in front while each could stare at her, never smiling while he lunged and ground in her. Serious business, this!

Apparently her pain did something to help at least Luctan and the Overseers. Not Brother Ugru, though—she'd noticed him closing his eyes while he was in her, whenever he thought Luctan or Tuke wouldn't notice.

He won't last long if Luctan gives him Tuke's place. He has principles. Luctan won't stand for such scut as principles!

Two Overseers adjusted the frame while the Instrument of Obedience in Luctan hands continued to come down on Alanni's exposed parts. She felt already strained muscles straining tighter, ready to tear. Around her rear entry, it was already worse. She felt as if a red-hot rod had been rammed up her.

And here came another.

I'll look as bad as Shamat by the time Miembra starts on me.

Stop hoping, Hope's something they can use against you, make you think you'll live if you're nice to them. You're not coming out of this one, Alanni. Miembra's never going to see you until they dump your body at her door. Don't hope and let them play with you.

A heavy fist sank into the pit of her stomach. The breath *wssshed* out of her and had there been anything in her stomach it would have followed. She fought for breath, started to black out, hoped this would be the end–

The frame was suddenly loosened, letting her breathe painfully. Luctan or Tuke must have noticed that she was about to go out, and signaled to the Overseers.

When she could breathe easily again, she could also see clearly. On the little table at the end of her punishment frame, Tuke was laying out equipment for the next stage. A slavewand—oh, of course. A spray injector—*containing what*? And . . .

No. Oh no.

Needles. Slim shining needles and a small mallet. A small mallet to drive shining needles in under her finger- and toenails—to start with. He wouldn't need the mallet to pincushion her breasts . . . would he?

She thanked the Light and her rapists that every other part of her insides was as empty as her stomach. Otherwise Tuke could have seen and smelled her fear, if not heard it.

Now he raised the injector, smiled straight into her unwillingly staring eyes, and pressed the injector against her belly just above the uppermost strands of wet, matted hair. He had plucked out only about a third of them. One at a time—slowly.

"This is a delightful double-action compound, made by Miembra-daktari with her own hands, miscreant! It will make her feel *so* good, when she understands what it did to you. What's that? Were you saying something? Oh, I don't imagine that she will miss you for *long,* wicked '*Sister.*' But while it lasts how the wicked sister will hurt! Oh, she will *hurt.*"

The injector hissed, Alanni twitched, and Tuke continued.

"The injection will make you more sensitive, you see—to pain. At the same time, it will also stimulate your vital systems, so the pain won't overload them to make you faint. At least not for longer than it would take otherwise. You will probably faint in time, but long after you want to."

"*gah.*"

Tuke seemed to be describing the injection accurately. Already she could feel the bruises on her thighs more acutely than before, and her battered rectum was coming alive. It seemed that blunt-toothed animals were gnawing at her, and her nipples weighed a half-kilo each. The rod behind her was surely turning white-hot and magically sprouting spikes and being dragged back and forth inside her until she was sure she could feel blood not just oozing but pouring–

Then Tuke drove in the first needle. One blow, all the way, and not under a nail either, and suddenly the world was very simple. It contained only two things. One, close to her, all around her and in her and through her, was the pain.

The other, a little farther off, was the sound of her own screams.

17

Ugru was not sure whether he wanted Sister Yimra to faint or not.

It would be a mercy for her, most surely. Her throat was raw, her face was a death-mask, and her body was slimy with sweat. Blood oozed from under all of her toenails where Tuke had driven in the needles. Now he was starting on the fingers.

Being forced to endure much more pain without being allowed the relief of fainting was likely to snap what hold on sanity the bound woman had left. Too, if this swine Tuke drove in needles everywhere he planned, she would be crippled for days . . . perhaps weeks, no matter how enduring her training might have made her.

That would cost her the ability to defend herself. It would cost Ugru a potential ally.

Potential, because he very much doubted that they served the same master. She might not be willing to make even a temporary truce. Much depended on what oaths she had sworn and on what plans she had made to carry out her assigned task.

On the other hand, as long as Sister Yimra was a shrieking, obscenely writhing, bloody, sweaty *thing* on the torture rack, none of the other people in the chamber received any attention. With even Luctan visibly excited by this torture, no one was paying any attention to Child-Brother Ugru. Nor would anyone, so long as he did nothing foolish such as allowing his face to show his revulsion.

Certain mantras recited mentally had so far permitted him

to remain seemingly impassive. Meanwhile he observed the people around him in a properly detached manner.

Tuke, Luctan, and three of the Overseers were in a state best compared to sexual ecstasy. Already Ugru had seen Luctan actually starting to fondle one of the Child-Sisters before he remembered that he had to hold on to a little of his dignity for a little longer.

Two of the other Overseers seemed to be taking the torture as a routine part of their job. Younger Brother Jirish seemed slightly ill-at-ease but more than slightly afraid to show it.

The two Child-Sisters who were attending the whole gruesome business looked scared out of such wits as their Initiations had left them. Ugru had an idea that their main concern was trying desperately not to soil themselves in terror. They knew how little it would take to persuade Tuke that they should succeed Sister Yimra as the object of his devoted attentions. (The swine actually used those words!)

As long as Sister Yimra's torture drew everyone's attention, Ugru knew he could shift position almost at will. A few more steps to the right, and he would be in the best position. He could deal with several people barehanded in a matter of seconds.

He could also snatch the slug-thrower from the belt of one of the Overseers.

(Ugru would have preferred a stopper, since the slugs might ricochet and hit unintended targets. On the other hand, he was not too unfamiliar with the characteristics of percussion pistols. Too, he would need some sort of weapon capable of striking at a distance. For all his pride in mastery of the fighting arts, he recognized their limitations—short-range effectiveness being among these. A slug-thrower could strike far beyond the reach of his arm.)

On the whole, it seemed better to Ugru that Sister Yimra *not* faint, as much as she might suffer. The work he would be doing, to avenge his honor as well as carry out his duties, would help her as well. A few minutes' more pain might buy her freedom.

Ugru hoped that his determination to avenge his honor did not reduce his chances of doing his duty. That would be substituting one form of dishonor for another.

He could know the answer after he acted. And Ugru *was* going to act.

The Brotherhood had dishonored him, by forcing him to rape a helpless woman. That was an insult that demanded blood.

No man to whom Ugru would have sworn an oath would deny that.

He took another step. Three more certainly, two more probably, and he would be in position.

Tuke wiggled one of the needles already inserted, producing a scream that died away to a whimper for sheer lack of breath. In the sudden near-silence, everyone in the room suddenly found its head jerked toward the door.

Someone was *knocking*!

Ugru took the last two steps while everyone else turned glaring eyes on the door. *Now if the man with the pistol will just stand still. . . .*

Luctan's face was working as if he was on the frame himself. It was impossible for someone to be interrupting him. It was also happening. Even worse, an interruption at such a time had to mean a real emergency. Ugru wondered . . . had someone above ground received warning of another earthquake or perhaps a *tsunami*?

If the rocks of Hellhole did bury us all, it would at least avenge my honor and give Sister Yimra a clean–

At a signal from Luctan, Brother Jirish and another pistol-armed Overseer went to open the door. As it slid wide, someone in the corridor shouted:

"Do honor to Kayab bin-Tarf, Chosen of the Dark Lord, Eldest Brother of his Servants!"

Luctan seemed to age years in the space between two breaths. A quick hand signal drew the Overseer back into the torture room. Another sent him to a corner . . . a corner with a clear shot at anyone coming through the door.

Ugru nearly went into action in that moment, but realized just in time that he could not let the shame of defying the Eldest Brother fall on him as well as on Luctan. It was just possible that Luctan might not be prepared to risk the consequences of simply shooting Kayab on the spot. More likely, he would delay a moment or two, to hear what Kayab might have to say. (Luctan was a man with a keen eye to the value of intelligence. This was known, and Ugru's briefing had emphasized it.)

That way, if Luctan acted, Ugru would have the appearance of *defending* Kayab bin-Tarf. "Under certain circumstances, the appearance of virtue has almost the power of the true article," was a saying of one of Ugru's less reputable instructors. (One he respected, nonetheless.)

Kayab bin-Tarf strode in, to Ugru's eyes clearly a man frightened half out of his wits but trying to hide it. He wished he could hope the fear would not be equally obvious to Luctan, then chided himself.

I must not hope for what may be.

I must do, according to what is.

One thing was—the visual impact of Kayab's ceremonial regalia. From sandals to vast golden sunburst (sitting a little awry on his head, Ugru noticed) it had been designed to draw the eye, and right now it was doing just that.

Four Brothers escorted Kayab into the room. A Child-Sister brought up the rear. Ugru saw Luctan's chosen assassin shifting from side to side, trying to keep his clear shot at Kayab.

Encouraging. They cannot suspect that there is anyone in the room capable of noticing what their man is doing.

"What is being done here?" Kayab snapped. (He managed to keep a quaver out of his voice.) "Sister Yimra is my handmaid. To punish her without a word to me—is this the way of the Brotherhood?"

"Revered Elder Brother," Luctan began. "Her crime was a disObedience so great that I am sure you will agree that we have been most merciful and generous, when you hear what she has done."

"Perhaps. But I will not hear your—tales—while Sister Yimra lies on that—device. Give me an Instrument of Obedience and release her to my guarding. *Then* tell me what she may have done."

Ugru thought Luctan was going to balk, but Kayab showed more sense than he'd expected, about holding the psychological momentum. "Brother Jirish. Release Sister Yimra and give her such Healing as you can." He turned to one of the

Brothers escorting him. "Go and see if Elder Brother Chayim has been summoned. Also summon Miembra-daktari for–"

Turning to speak to the Brother, Kayab took his eyes off Luctan. In that moment Ugru saw Luctan give a hand signal to his Overseer guard. The creep shifted to his left—toward where he would have an easy shot at Kayab. His hand eased down toward his holster.

Two steps before he reached position, Ugru chopped the Overseer beside him across the throat and snatched his pistol.

He snapped off the safety with one hand while he raised the weapon to position with the other. His extremely noisy shot took the Overseer through the head. (Hitting him in the body might still have given him time to get off a lethal shot of his own.) Blood erupted to paint a surrealist design on the man's yellow robes.

In the underground room of stone, Ugru's shot sounded like the Voice of Doom. Kayab nearly dropped his ornate staff of office. Jirish froze in the act of releasing Sister Yimra's left arm, while Luctan froze in the act of drawing his stopper.

This last was a serious mistake. Before Luctan could use the stopper on anyone, Ugru fired twice. *Boom* and *boommmm* again, and Elder Brother Luctan no longer had a face worthy of the name. And not much more of a head.

Ugru pulled the trigger again to dispose of Brother Tuke—and the pistol clicked in unsympathetic emptiness. Meanwhile Tuke was snatching up his master's fallen stopper and bringing it to bear.

He hadn't quite succeeded when Sister Yimra's free left arm snaked down and caught him by the collar of his robe. With more strength than Ugru would have thought left in her whole body let alone one in her arm, she jerked him backward. He fell nearly on top of her, one ear within range of her teeth.

Those teeth met in Tuke's flesh. He yowled in surprise at this sudden attack from a contemptible quarter. He shouted again when Ugru chopped him across the wrist to break his grip on the stopper. He also screamed very gratifyingly when Ugru kicked him in the groin.

(Ugru pulled that last kick, much against his inclinations. Tuke was the principle author of his dishonor, and he would gladly have kicked all the man's internal organs into jelly. Unfortunately Tuke was also the principle living source of intelligence about the Brotherhood. Ugru was not a man to underestimate the value of intelligence.)

Tuke slid to the floor in a faint. He splashed thickly in the pool of blood spreading around his late master. Brother Jirish had turned an interesting mottled color, rather like a long-submerged rock. But was still standing beside Sister Yimra. When Ugru came up with Tuke's stopper pointed in his direction, Jirish jumped several sems and returned to his work.

Training in Obedience has its uses.

Jirish was releasing Sister Yimra's bloody right foot when she gave up at last; the poor woman fainted. Even so, Ugru noticed the faint smile on her face.

Then he crossed the blood-splashed room to where Kayab was still standing as if turned to stone by magic. Ugru held out the pistol to him, butt-first.

"Revered Eldest Brother, if I have been disObedient in anything I have done, it is in your hands to punish me." (Not unless Kayab was carrying a weapon of his own. Thanks to Tuke's caution about letting his Overseers have ammunition, the pistol held only an empty magazine.)

Kayab took the pistol as if he wasn't quite sure it wouldn't bite. He held it for a moment before turning it end for end and handing it back to Ugru.

"Brother Ugru, your Initiation is complete. You have shown superb Obedience. Indeed, you have been the hand of the Dark Lord in bringing punishment to those who have shown disObedience to his chosen."

Ugru had the distinct feeling that if Kayab stopped speaking for more than two seconds his teeth would start chattering. When he spoke, though, the words came out full, round, magnificent—as if the former teacher really believed everything he was saying!

Kayab's speech held everyone's attention long enough for Brother Jirish to commence bandaging Sister Yimra and for Ugru to relieve all the surviving Overseers of their weapons. By the time he had done, he had accumulated quite a tidy little arsenal.

He'd also been taken with a strong desire to sit down, gulp some saki, and meditate for a few minutes. No matter how well-trained one was, such scenes as this did lead to a certain wear and tear on the adrenaline supply. He settled for pulling the charges on all the stoppers and emptying all the pistols—except for one of each that he kept for himself.

By the time he'd finished this job, Brother Chayim had arrived and Ugru knew the worst was over. He still had to explain to Chayim what had happened to account for all the splashed blood and the bodies littering the floor. While he did, he could not help stealing an occasional half-envious glance at Yimra.

She was being allowed to *sleep* through the whole messy business of tidying up!

18

Alanni's first sensation when she awoke was surprise that she wasn't dead.

She remembered seeing Kayab come in and Ugru demolish her tormenters . . . yet there had been a dreamlike quality about the battle. She couldn't be sure at first that she hadn't gone completely fobby from the pain, seeing what she wanted to see rather than what was actually happening.

Then she saw Ugru sitting in lotus position at the foot of her bed. Alanni realized that the odds were very much in favor of her being alive.

Alive . . . and sore all over. The bed was soft—Miembra's own, she realized, complete with the scarlet sheets and faintly perfumed pillows—but not soft enough to cushion all the bruises. Also, there were her fingers and toes. The fingers of her right hand were the only ones intact. The fingers of her left were spray-sealed, and all her toes were wrapped in bandages until they felt as thick as sausages. They also throbbed abominably.

Seeing that she was awake, Ugru rose with a grace she couldn't help noticing. He came over to stand beside her. "Sister Yimra, you wake?"

She grunted what she hoped would be taken for "Firm" and tried to sit up. Ugru put a well-shaped hand on one shoulder and effortlessly exerted a minim of pressure. Alanni stayed down, supine. Her frustration at being so weak made her want to curse—or cry. She also noticed a large tube feeding into her right arm.

"What . . . how long have I been out?"

"It is evening of the day after you were taken," Ugru said smoothly. "Before I say more, I will summon Elder Sister Miembra."

"Where is Kayab?"

"He is well and doing the work of the Brotherhood. He also may come, after Elder Sister Miembra has done her work with you."

Alanni resisted the temptation to swear or look around for something to throw. Since she was tubed up she might have internal injuries. That would be a real downer . . . and fact, with nothing she could do about it. She lay back, and discovered that once she'd relaxed it was easy to fall asleep again.

She awoke to find Miembra bustling about the room, reading vital signs, making tests, and generally being aggressively daktarish. Alanni suffered in silence, except for grunting when Miembra pulled out the tube.

"Well, Sister Yimra," the Healer said. "I'd always known you were tough, but not how tough. I wouldn't try eating spicy food or running races for a few days. Otherwise you're much fitter than I expected. Though I admit I've helped you along. Any infections try to get a hold in you, they'll run off screaming like Tuke's surviving jackos."

"Is *any* of those slimy creeps still alive?"

"Ugru could only be in so many places at once, Yimra."

Something about Miembra's tone made Alanni frown as she asked, "What about Tuke himself?"

"I'll call Kayab now."

"*What about Tuke*?" Alanni tried to shout and only squeaked. She went on more quietly, "Are you hiding something?"

"When I came in, Yimra, you were muttering something about 'call Kayab and have a council of war.' I'm doing precisely that. So what's your complaint now, my dear?"

Alanni sighed again. Obviously the woman was hiding something. Knowing Miembra, it was probably not a life-or-death matter. Also knowing Miembra, it was obvious that she was determined to take full advantage of her being the daktari and Alanni's being the patient.

And of course she was right. Ugru could indeed not be in

two places at once, and how many other trustworthy people might be among the Brotherhood was an open question. Had it not been for that, Alanni would have preferred that Ugru be elsewhere. Nobody who was so nearly certain to be working for some opposition should hear most of what she would say to Kayab.

Unfortunately, Ugru was the best and most trustworthy fighter the new leadership of the Brotherhood had. With Alanni/Yimra, Miembra, and Kayab all gathered in one room (and maybe Brother Chayim as well), Ugru might be the only factor preventing some desperate Luctan-lover from trying to Poof the lot of them.

Alanni compressed her lips. While hairbreadth escapes from death undoubtedly helped to prevent boredom, she was more than willing to struggle along without two of them in one Heller day.

She had put on a robe by the time Kayab arrived.

(She had also tried to sit in one of the chairs, but discovered that was not a good idea right now. For the next few days, she would have to lie on her side in order to be comfortable. The fact that Luctan was dead was emotionally satisfying—and did nothing to heal bruises and other damage, in intimate portions of her anatomy.)

Kayab, sans headdress while still magnificently robed, delivered his report with the dryness of an academic lecture. Much of it confirmed what Alanni had already suspected, and she was able to notice how Kayab kept licking his lips and swallowing as he reported murder, mayhem, and massacre.

Way over his head, she thought, *but determined to go down fighting.*

And now maybe he won't have to go down at all.

Luctan was dead, and so were four of Tuke's Overseers. Ugru had killed another one, Miembra had Poofed a third, and the fourth–

"He tried to take refuge among the Children," Ugru said. "It seemed that he thought they would be in too much fear of him to resist. He was wrong. They tore him to pieces, although he killed five of them before he died. Miembra has laid them out for burial—and thrown the Overseer into the garbage pit."

"The three Overseers who surrendered are tied up and sitting beside the pit, contemplating their late comrade's remains," Kayab added. "Miembra thought this might impress upon them that we mean business."

Too bad they aren't all there.

Alanni would have said that aloud if she hadn't had the sense of bad news coming. Kayab would also have the misguided kindness to try holding it back until Miembra chewed it out of him like a mining laser. Alanni decided to keep her mouth shut.

"The last two Overseers and a number of Brothers have fled, probably into Bassar. We have *not* sent their names to the BMP.–"

For which the Light be praised, Alanni added.

"–but we will announce a pardon for them if they return. Brothers Chayim and Jirish have been given charge of the administration of the Temples. Brother Chayim is using mostly the Child-Sisters for important work. He feels they are the most trustworthy."

Apart from those who may be here on the same kind of business as Ugru and I—pos they will be. Certainly they have more to lose than anyone else if the stash-hunters are turned loose again! A gold star for Brother Chayim.

Maybe another for Brother Jirish . . . if he keeps improving.

"I am going to recruit a few medical people from down in the city," Miembra said, taking up the reporting. "We can make them Lay-Brothers or Lay-Sisters or something like that. Once they're on the job, we'll be so indispensable to the city that it will takc bigger bugs than even the Fog Coast government to shut us down."

That had the sound of another excellent idea, which was just what Alanni would have expected from Miembra. She still had the impression of bad news being held back. The impression was even stronger now.

Time to take a firm grip and pull it out.

"Where's Tuke? Did he redshift or . . .?" *And I hope it's Or. . . ?*

"Tuke is in Brother Chayim's quarters," Miembra said, looking as if she was almost on the point of smiling. "He's under sedation, which means I gave him enough to stun a full-grown fangface."

Relief washed Alanni. *Pity you didn't give him enough to Poof him.*

Kayab looked at Miembra, then sighed. "Yimra, we have a problem with Tuke. We didn't kill him in the . . . torture room, because we needed to learn who his friends were. Not just the Overseers, but others, who could be relied on to make trouble for us if they were left free."

So far, not too bad. What's next?

"Tuke agreed to tell us, in return for a pardon. He'd even swear a public oath of repentance for his past sins and promise Obedience in the future, in return for the pardon. Otherwise we could do our worst, and the names of his friends would die with him."

"Let them die, then," Alanni said shortly. "Tuke is more dangerous than any ten of them put together."

"Since we don't know who they are, we can't be sure of that," Miembra said. (What she did not say was clear: *Yimra, don't make it any worse for us than you have to, even if you're right in wanting Tuke Fried, one sem at a time.)*

"Also, Tuke has another friend. Perhaps more than one," Kayab said slowly. "He—they—are in Bassar. If Tuke doesn't report he's safe every other day, the friend goes to the BMP. *With* a complete file on everything that's happened in the Brotherhood, updated every week or so."

Alanni didn't waste time wondering whether Tuke was lying. *It would be just like the wormspawn. In fact, in his place I might have done the same.*

Still–

"Suppose Tuke's friend did dump the scrute on the policers? What could they do, with Luctan and Tuke both dead?"

Miembra sighed. "Haul most of us in as accessories to our late friends' crimes if they wanted to. They'd probably want to. Either to squeeze bribes out of us for letting us go, or because the government wanted our hides. Remember, Kayab's a fine scam, disguising a welfare organization as a religion. The government won't like that kind of trick, *or* the people who played it on them."

On the basis of what Alanni knew of governments (which was extensive and unfavorable) she had to agree with Miembra.

"It looks as if Tuke has us by the short hairs." *Except–Pos. But if you raise this point, what about your cover story?*

The old one's dead. I'll just have to make do with the new one I told Kayab. Ugru may not like it, but I don't owe him that much just for saving my life!

With a nod, Alanni spoke:

"Has anyone thought to check the memory of the Temple's computer? It might have the *friend*'s name. If we had that, Brother Ugru might pay him a visit."

Kayab's face wrinkled up in frustration like a dried fruit. "We thought of that. But what if Ugru was caught? We'd be worse off than before, because Ugru wouldn't be free. Also, he did try to access Luctan's own personal computer. It was blocked. Next he tried to interface it with the main computer."

Alanni winced and Kayab shook his head. "No, it wasn't that bad. Brother Ugru saw in time that the interface would be a bomb for the whole memory of the main computer. We would have no 'puter at all then. That could also cripple us."

Which means Brother Ugru has just revealed how much he knows about computers.

"It is also nearly certain that there is another bomb in the main computer, placed there by Tuke himself," Ugru said. "He would doubtless have wished to protect certain data even from Luctan. Nor will it be possible to force him to tell us how to access that data without triggering the bomb."

Gazing at him, Alanni kept her face open, brows level. *How do you know? Probably because you can recognize a hypnotic block when you see one?*

"It seems better to let Tuke swear that oath," Kayab concluded. "All we need is *time*. Time to put our own house in order so we'll be completely indispensable. The government won't touch us if the alternative is complete chaos in Bassar. *That* fobby, they aren't."

I hope you're right.

"Firm," Alanni said. "But—I want to try my hand with the main computer. As Eldest Brother Kayab can tell you, I know my way around a board. It's the best thing I can do for now, since I'll be on light duty for a few days."

Miembra nodded. So did Brother Ugru. "The Dark Lord bless you, Sister Yimra," he said. "May this Brother offer to assist you, when other duties do not demand his attention?"

"Pos." *Why not? That way, he won't be able to get at the computer when I'm not around, and I may learn more about him. Besides, he's rather pleasant to look at. More than pleasant—damned fine!*

(Alanni had no plans to soar with anyone except Kayab, and not even with him for a few days. Still, admiring Ugru would be one of those little pleasures of being alive she hadn't really expected ever to enjoy again just a day-ess ago!)

"Then that's settled. The other thing: keep Tuke locked up. We can't let him escape, and the Child-Sisters probably want to treat him the same way they did the Overseer."

"I'm not that fobby either, Yimra," Kayab told her with dignity.

Alanni recognized wounded vanity in his voice and a suppressed giggle in Miembra. She knew she'd gone a little too far. Well, apologies could wait. She gave him only a kind look.

"I mean that. Keep him locked up, or by all the gods of the Galaxy the first thing I'll do when I can move is crawl down to Tuke's cell and Poof him. I'll bite his other ear off if I can't do anything else."

"Pos, Eldest Sister," Miembra said nodding, and now she couldn't suppress the giggle.

Alanni lay back on the pillows with an involuntary sigh. It was settled, as much as it could be now—and not one slicing word had been said about the Invisible Wisdom!

(Three hundred kloms out to sea and two kloms below the ocean floor, a fracture was beginning in a slab of ancient granite. It was not a large fracture, but it was in a crucial place.)

(When the granite split apart, the last barrier to a massive shift of tectonic plates would be removed. Seven centuries of accumulated stresses could find their long-sought release in a single moment.)

19

Alanni contemplated the sky over Bassar in its frowning menace. Oh, that seldom-pretty sky didn't make her more uneasy than any of the other things she could have contemplated. It didn't make her any less so, either.

Today the clouds looked a way she had never before seen. Even native Hellers said this weirdness was rare. They seemed to form broad bands of deep slate gray shot through with narrow bands of a lighter gray. Those eerie stripes in the sky seemed slightly arched, too.

It's like being inside the carcass of a giant animal, looking up at the ribs.

She wished she had not had that distinctly unpleasant thought.

Tired of contemplating Hellhole's sky in any form rare or common, Alanni looked downhill toward the Oath-swearing ceremony. Tuke knelt naked in the center of a ring of Brotherhood people, full Brothers and Sisters alternating with Children. He was covered from head to foot in ashes and garbage, while Elder Brother Chayim and a Child-Sister unknown to Alanni beat him about the shoulders with Instruments of Obedience.

Alanni noted that they were beating him only symbolically; they hadn't drawn much blood. Too bad. From Brother Chayim that was no surprise, but the Child must be showing extraordinary self-restraint. (Or perhaps Miembra and Chayim had been able to find a Child-Sister who didn't owe Tuke a blood-debt, hard though that was to believe.)

Alanni didn't need to hear the Oath. She'd spent several

sleepless nights helping to draw it up. She knew it so well that she could have recited it backwards.

It was an elaborate confession of unspecified but gruesome sins, an even more elaborate expression of repentance for them, and an incredibly elaborate avowal of willingness to suffer whatever penalties the Eldest Brother judged fit should Tuke break the Oath. He would sign the printout, too.

The computer was definitely fitted with a bomb. No doubt about it, in either Alanni's mind or Ugru's. They had no chance of learning the name of Tuke's friend in time to keep him from giving his lethal bag of secrets about the Brotherhood to the policers. None, zero, zilch, and several other expressions meaning that the new management of the Brotherhood was well and thoroughly screwed, not to mention crotch-deep in the slimepit.

Likely to stay that way, too. Miembra's sources in Bassar had put her on the trail of a portable computer *almost* large enough to handle the Brotherhood's business. If it could be purchased and a couple of trustworthy people found to run it, *and* if the old computer's vital data could be transferred to the new one, Alanni and Ugru were prepared to have another go at defusing the bomb. If it did blow, there wouldn't be much left in the old computer it could damage.

A lot of "ifs," and all of them likely to take time. Yet that was a commodity the Brotherhood did not possess, if it wanted to go about its business under the new management. It did; apart from that's being good tactics, there was one simple fact that impressed itself on all of them.

People in Bassar would die if they played games much longer.

More people, probably, than would die from the worst Tuke might do.

"If he does run loose, we have trustworthy Children with stoppers and pistols all over the Temple," Miembra said. "They may Poof him before he can sneeze. If we let him bring the BMP down on us, many people we could have saved *will* die."

Once you've decided to be a hero, Alanni thought and very nearly said aloud, *you're stuck with the job.* Not that she disagreed with the daktari.

So Alanni did the next best thing. She drew up the Oath so that in terms of the Brotherhood's rules and regulations, Tuke would be disObedient if he so much as went to the sitter without permission! (She loved putting in that part—even a Child-Sister could now make Tuke stand dancing while he waited for a nod from her.)

"If he violates this one we can have him up for misfeasance, malfeasance, nonfeasance, and space piracy," Alanni said, once she had finished the Oath.

Several of the people around her stared at the legal terminology. After all the dry weeks, she'd drunk enough beer to forget for a moment that not everybody within hearing was cleared for her new cover story. She'd also drunk enough beer not to care very much so long as none of the close-at-hand ears was Tuke's.

While she was playing back pleasant memories of writing the Oath and seeing the Brotherhood returned to something approaching its normal course, Tuke had finished his swearing.

He rose, and the Child-Sister sluiced him off with a bucket of water—*cold* water. Brother Chayim clothed him in a new robe—white, for the purity he was supposed to have achieved through repenting. Everyone cheered—somewhat raggedly and not at all enthusiastically, Alanni noticed. Then Kayab led Tuke out of the square and Brother Chayim led the first of the repentant Overseers forward into his place.

Even from her distance, Alanni could see Tuke stiffen when Kayab touched him, as if he'd been hit with a Stopper set on Freeze.

Brother Tuke is about as repentant as Councillor Nortay, and a lot closer to hand.

Two Child-Sisters came forward to shower the Overseer with ashes and garbage from the buckets they carried. A fresh bucket of ashes and garbage, a fresh bucket of water, fresh Instruments of Obedience, and a fresh white robe awaited each Overseer, thanks to Brother Jirish's care for details. He might be a little too zealous (to prove his loyalty to the new management?) but by the Light and the Dark Lord, the boy was doing his job!

Brother Chayim had just picked up a fresh Instrument of Obedience when Alanni heard a distant, dull *thump*. At the same time she felt a shock in the ground, coming up through the soles of her feet. It was as if she was standing on top of a thick wooden plank and someone had struck the underside of the plank with a mallet.

A small mallet—this time.

The mallet strokes came again, twice. The fourth time it was a rather *large* mallet, and she wished she had something to hold on to. A fifth mallet-stroke sent small stones dislodged by the first four rolling down the hill.

By the end of the third mallet-stroke, the people below had stopped talking. By the end of the fifth, some of them had begun weeping and/or screaming in fright, or shouting about the Dark Lord's anger.

The shouters scared Alanni much more than an earthquake—than *this* 'quake, she corrected herself. If Tuke had the sense to proclaim that the 'quake was the Dark Lord's vengeance for the overthrow of his loyal servants Luctan and Tuke . . .

Trouble is, there are too damned many people in the Brotherhood who really believe! So we have to pretend to be running things according to the will of the Dark Lord to keep them happy, not just to keep the BMP out of our hair.

Alanni started down the hill as fast as she could without anyone's noticing her. After a few steps she stopped to pull off the loose slippers she wore, to avoid putting pressure on her now-unbandaged but still-sore toes. The ground here was soft and she could move faster barefoot.

She moved on, keeping her eyes aimed at Tuke and her hand close to the butt of the stopper hanging from the sash of her yellow Elder Sister's robe. Before she was close enough to the crowd for anyone to notice, she flipped the setting to Three.

If Tuke so much as winks funny, I'll Poof him and argue the consequences later. We can deal with the policers better than with a hysterical mob led by Brotherless Tuke!

By the time she was close enough to Poof Tuke without hitting anyone else, the uproar was dying away. The fifth groundshock had been the last. After that, Brother Chayim went right on with the Overseer's Oath of Repentance as if nothing more than a shower of rain had happened. Alanni saw

Kayab watching with a glaze of sweat on his brown face and his eyes squeezed half-shut.

He still walked and spoke steadily when he went forward to greet the presumably penitent Overseer.

When the last Overseer had pulled on his new white robe, Kayab stepped forward again in all his finery. He lifted both arms aloft with a flapping of sleeves.

"Behold, the anger of the Dark Lord is appeased. He has seen the repentance of those who did unlawful deeds in His name and heard their solemn oaths. He has turned His anger aside from us, Praise the Dark Lord who rejoices in those returned to seeking the Way!"

"Praise him!" Chayim shouted.

"Praise him and bless his name!" Tuke shouted. "Let his mercy endure forever!"

"Praise him!" Alanni shouted, setting off the people close to her. In moments everybody was screaming, "Praise the Dark Lord!" in voices shrill with near-hysteria and complete relief at the passing of the earthquake . . .

Or at what they think is the passing of the 'quake, Alanni thought without missing a syllable of her chant of praise. *We're not out of this one yet. Meanwhile, though . . . thank the Dark Lord or Somebody for Kayab and Chayim's keeping their heads and their courage!*

Having them at her back almost made up for having Tuke there as well, even if neither of the older Brothers would be worth a bucket of muck if matters became physical.

Which they will. Let's just hope that the day comes while Ugru and I are still working more or less together. Let's also hope that Tuke isn't going to wait until either I or Ugru makes our move for the Invisible Wisdom.

It was not much of a hope. Whatever vices Tuke had, stupidity wasn't one of them.

At last the chanting wound down and Kayab gave orders for everyone to return to work, rejoicing in the new blessing of the Dark Lord. When everyone was on its way, he signaled to Alanni to join him. In a few minutes, the whole new management of the Brotherhood was gathered around Kayab, except for Miembra.

(She'd sent word that she was too busy dealing with minor

injuries and cases of hysterics from the 'quake and would trust them not to do anything stupid.)

"The daktari is most especially blessed by the Dark Lord," Jirish said.

His tone made Alanni frown, then shrug. It was hard to be sure whether he was a Believer or not, when he talked that way. Nor did it really matter, so long as he worked.

"I did not like that one," Brother Chayim said. "What do you say, Eldest Brother?"

"I don't think the Dark Lord . . . intended for us to like it," Kayab said. He licked his lips. "Nor do I think He is through with us." He swallowed, then took a deep breath and straightened into a position that would have done credit to a senior cadet at the T-SP Academy.

"Jirish, you are now an Elder Brother."

"Chosen, I am–"

"Oh yes, you *are* worthy. There was no great evil in your heart, and the Dark Brother has purged what there was. Now go to Bassar Municipal Hospital with a message for Hermosh-daktari. Tell him that we can feed only the sick and the hurt here in the Temples. All others must bring their own food."

"Hermosh-daktari, firm. My Obedience is to your will, Eldest Brother."

Jirish disappeared at a run. Kayab sighed. "Hermosh will spread the word better than anyone else. I wish we could take anybody who comes, but we simply can't feed half of Bassar."

"The riots did not make them flee, Eldest Brother," Ugru reminded him. "Need we fear their coming now?"

"If somebody knows what those shocks might mean and spreads the word—firm. And the Dark Lord forgive me, I don't know if I hope that somebody will speak out or not."

His eyes met Alanni's and the message passed between them: *Do we want them all to die mercifully and swiftly or save a few and see the others go the hard way?*

"Firm," Ugru and Alanni said almost together.

"Brother Chayim. Go to the Temple and put the Children to work taking all the tents down from the roofs and moving them away from the walls. Pitch all the unused tents as well. There may be enough tents to shelter everyone."

"We are not past the season of the summer storms, Eldest

Brother," Chayim said, respectfully but firmly. He seemed to have gained weight in the past few days, and fresh color in both his skin and the celldye around his eyes. It was as if no longer having to witness atrocities in silence had taken years off his age. "The sick and the hurt will not rejoice if the wind carries away their tents."

"They'll rejoice a good deal less if they fall down with the roof or the roof falls on them," Kayab said shortly. "Also, take Brother Ugru with you. Put him at the head of a team of trusted Children to remove all the valuables from the strongrooms. Set up a special guarded tent for them."

That's setting the swooper among the chickens, Alanni thought. No way to raise the point explicitly, either, but–

"The underground tunnels have survived through several 'quakes," she said. "Is what you have ordered necessary, Eldest Brother?"

"They may not survive the next one," Kayab told her. "Or some may fall and block access to others. Also, we cannot easily guard all the tunnels, while we can guard a single tent with ease."

"My Obedience is to your will, Eldest Brother," she said, in a voice just short of sourness.

Ugru was already out of hearing, loping up the hill at his usual effortless pace, powerful calves lashing under hitched-up robes. Chayim was following with more dignity but no sign of whether he'd heard the exchange and the tone of Alanni's reply.

After a moment, Alanni shrugged. The Invisible Wisdom was still important as the easiest means to her goal: saving Jay and Bouncy, her farm, and her home on Eagle. It wasn't the only possible means of saving her two friends.

Jay could find a place among the Brotherhood, and Nortay would find it hard to reach him there. The Outie didn't believe in any religion and also didn't disbelieve in any one more than the others. He could be relied on to make the right sort of noises, and he also had a dozen skills the Brotherhood could use.

As for Bouncy, Tilno would certainly be good for enough stells to buy it a ticket to some world with a fair-sized Jarp community. One Jarp looked much like another to most

Galactics, and Nortay would have a long search if he wanted to make one at all.

That, of course, would leave Alanni farmless, homeless, and a fugitive. Hardly the optimum solution, by any means! Yet she preferred even that non-optimum solution to leaving Kayab now, in the lurch. He was keeping his teeth from chattering and his knees from going like a slave dancer's bells only by sheer strength of will, but he was *doing* it. He would meet the crisis for which he had founded the Brotherhood—a crisis now coming at them with the relentlessness of a falling asteroid—on his feet.

What else could Alanni Keor do, except stand beside him?

(Alternate question: What was more troublesome than a sense of honor and loyalty?)

Not a slicing thing, she answered both questions, cheerlessly.

20

Kayab was giving Alanni a full-length massage when the 'quake hit. She'd been wondering where he found the energy and thinking they might soar tonight . . . when the bed began to shake.

First time I've ever shaken the bed just thinking *about slicing–!*

Then she saw that everything else in the tent was shaking as well. She'd just realized that this godforsaken, gods-damned planet's 'quake was on again, when the tent pole snapped and dropped what seemed a hectare of canvas on them.

Kayab grunted, then swore so loudly that Alanni was sure he couldn't have been seriously hurt. Not bothering to grope around for her clothes, she started to crawl out from under the folds of cloth. It was surprising how long it took. He could have sworn their little tent had *grown* while falling, until it could have housed a company of policers.

And all the while, Hellhole kept dancing to its inner spasms.

By the time Alanni poked her head out into the night air, people were crawling out of fallen tents or running out of still-standing ones all around the First Temple. Many were wearing no more than she. She had just started to stand for a look around when the ground seemed to heave itself half a meter into the air and another half a meter sideways.

Almost every tent still standing went down. People sprawled drunkenly on the ground, waving arms and legs like babies while they screamed about the wrath of the Dark Lord . . . or just shrieked wordlessly. Alanni didn't try to stand. She hugged the ground as tightly as she'd ever hugged Tilno or

Kayab while she listened to the screams. The errant thought came: she hoped no one would propose murdering Kayab now that the Dark Lord's wrath was upon them again . . .

Fortunately everybody was too busy screaming or praying to think about the fine points of yesterday's sermon. The ground kept jerking like blankets covering a patient in convulsions, rumbling with an awful guttural *roar* all the while. Other rumblings and boomings hammered Alanni's ears, along with incredible crashing sounds—the buildings of the First Temple collapsing.

Though she was facing away from the Temple, she knew what was happening to it as clearly as if she'd watched for every minute.

Stone ground and squealed against stone, wood crackled, plasteel beams screamed as they were stressed beyond their limits. Dust poured out in a choking cloud, as thick as fog and a damned sight harder to breathe. Alanni tried to burrow into the ground, filling her nose with the scent of wet grass and nearly filling her mouth with mud.

Only after what seemed enough time for a complete cycle of the Universe, the planet stopped quaking.

Alanni waited until she was sure her legs would hold her up before she stood. The first thing she saw was Kayab, lying just outside the tent and curled into the fetal position. She shivered, and not just because she was nude and the breeze was up. She was more afraid of Kayab's turning fobby or even catatonic than of anything else that might follow the 'quake, and whether that made sense or not—

He sat up and dug mud out of his left ear with his little finger. "Is it over?"

"I think—whups!" She went down on all fours as an after-shock made the ground quiver anew. It was a comparatively sedate quivering this time, rather like a bowl of thick pudding.

Kayab stood up and held on to her with one hand while he picked up his clothes with the other. She burrowed under the tent to retrieve hers—it was too chilly to spend the night in her bare skin.

By the time she came out again, Kayab had gone off about the business of calming people and counting casualties. He seemed to be succeeding at the first job, or maybe people were merely running out of breath. At any rate, the screams were dying. Alanni wondered how many people were doing the same. She saw no one obviously hurt within easy reach.

She looked downhill toward Bassar—and felt her stomach imitate the seismic lurches just past. Nothing worse—she was Captain Alanni Keor again, at least in the matter of coping with gruesome sights.

The clouds were patchy and both moons were up, so that she easily saw how the outline of Bassar had blurred and flowed.

Jagged points had sprouted to replace smooth lines. Here and there only a gap like a missing tooth marked the site where a whole streetful of buildings had squeezed itself into a heap. Lights still glowed in places; in other places fires were already spreading. (From stoves, electrical wiring, workshops and . . . Light only knew what other tools Kali had to work with here!) Smoke boiled up to thicken the cloud of dust already hanging over the city.

At the foot of the hill the land itself had dropped away. The last fifty meters of the stone steps, the pier, the guardhouse—all were gone.

In their place sprawled a canal now swollen to the size of a major river, a hundred meters wide at least. Looking along it as far as she could see, Alanni realized that it was deeper than a person could wade, and stretched from the bay to the south all the way north to the dikes.

The peninsula where the Temples stood had just become an island.

"Oh, *damn*!"

It was the best she could do.

She didn't know how long she stood there, watching the water slosh back and forth in its new channel, carrying its load of wreckage and bodies. She did know that it was long enough for the tide to start going out.

Except that it wasn't the tide, as Kayab told her when he'd finished his rounds and returned to find her standing as if hypnotized.

"The seismograph's still on line. I've plotted the epicenter. It was well out to sea, on the fault line I'd expected."

"So?"

It sounded to her as if Kayab was making pedantic small talk to calm either his nerves or hers. *Of course, maybe mine do need calming, or I wouldn't be standing here. . . .*

"So we have the great-to-infinity grandfather of all *tsunamis* to look forward to. And so do those poor bugs down there." He pointed to ruined Bassar.

Alanni nodded. "They won't reach high ground on our side. What about the causeway?"

"If it's still there, and it doesn't get completely blocked with wreckage or a panic-stricken mob so they're all waiting when the wave comes . . ." Kayab shuddered. "They'll have to take it, though, if they want to travel any farther in this world."

"Do you think there's a next one?"

"If I thought I knew the answer to that question, I would have founded a *real* religion, Yimra. I don't. I suspect it's either such an important question that the Higher Authorities are keeping the answer a secret, or such a silly question they don't care what strange notions we little mortals have about it."

"We may find the answer ourselves when that *tsunami* comes," Alanni said in a dead voice. Being able to say it aloud made her feel a little better. Not much.

"Neg," Kayab said. "We're a hundred meters above high tide. The only *tsunami* that ever went above sixty was the one on Resh, and that was almost certainly a meteorite strike. They didn't have the skywatch set up then. It apparently came in at a very low angle more or less out of the sun, just to make things more fun."

Alanni could think of a number of words he might have used to describe being overwhelmed by a wave sixty meters high. "Fun" was not one. She decided it was time to stop waiting for Bassar to die and do some useful work.

"Is there any security problem in the camp I should know about?"

He shook his head. "Neg—I think. Of course, I'm not sure I'd recognize a security problem if it came up and bit me in the slicer, but–"

She kissed him. "You can learn that too. I'll teach you.

Meanwhile, I suspect that if Miembra doesn't need help now she will soon enough."

Alanni was helping Miembra splint the broken arm of a refugee who'd swum the channel when she heard Kayab's voice outside.

"Everybody out of the tents! Everybody out of the tents! The Dark Lord's wrath against Bassar is not yet spent! Everybody out of the tents lest the innocent taste His wrath."

(That was the line Kayab was taking, to keep the believers of the Brotherhood from panic. The Dark Lord had forgiven those of the Brotherhood now that the disObedient had repented. Bassar's sins, however, were too numerous to be forgiven. It was a city without ten virtuous people, so it was doomed.

(So far the tale seemed to be working. Total casualties in the Brotherhood were only eight dead and about forty hurt, and most of those not badly. It wasn't necessary to be crawly-fobby about religion to suspect that the Brotherhood was in Somebody's good tapes.

(Alanni wasn't wild about the explanation by superstition, but this time it did seem best. She'd leave to somebody else the job of saving Hellhole from religion.)

She finished the splint, gave the man a trank—*something else we're going to run out of by tomorrow, at the rate we're going*—and went outside.

She joined Kayab, and while they routed people out of the tents he explained. "The impact of the wave may trigger off more aftershocks in local faults. Also, there's going to be an airblast."

At last the tents were empty. Even the people who didn't know what they were waiting for stood on the hillside, a dark mass spotted with the yellow of the Brotherhood, looking out to sea over the ruins of Bassar.

Kayab had just put his arm around Alanni's shoulders when suddenly the horizon bulged. They heard a distant sigh, which turned into a rumble. Too swiftly, it became a roar.

Then suddenly a mountain came marching out of the sea on Bassar.

The mountain reared fifty meters high and spread kloms wide, moon-gilded water amove and crowned with foam. It marched over the breakwaters as if they didn't exist. Perhaps they didn't; who could tell what the quake had done, and nobody would ever know now . . .

Alanni tasted blood from her bitten lips.

Then the mountain struck the ruins of Bassar and disintegrated as the land tore the roots out from under it. Billions of tons of water collapsed on the city with a roar like the Universe itself being torn open—and a blast of air that knocked Alanni off her feet.

She lay, trying to shut out the screams from the dying city, then telling herself that she'd been imagining them. Surely nobody could scream loudly enough to be heard over the roar of the wave!

It would have helped if she could have screamed herself, or wept. All she could do was try not to choke on the sharp-edged iron lump in her throat and pound her fists into the spray-slick ground.

At last Kayab pulled her to her feet. Where Bassar had been, a murky channel raged now, a good three kloms wide from dry land to dry land. Waves curled and boiled, leaped and spouted, flinging up crests of foam and also of dark things that might have been bodies or wreckage or the Light only knew what.

There really wasn't anything to say. They said nothing as they went uphill arm in arm, to return to whatever work the Dark Lord had left for the Brotherhood of his Servants.

21

A second *tsunami* struck before dawn. This one was no mountain of moving water. It was hardly even a decent hill.

Then the *natural* tide began going out. By mid-morning a good part of the three kloms of water between the ex-peninsula now-island and the mainland had drained back into the ocean. What it left behind was a soggy hellhole.

There was still no way anyone was going to cross to the mainland without a boat and good luck against its having its bottom ripped out by wreckage. Somebody with fish blood *might swim—or might have its alleged brains knocked out against a stone,* Alanni thought

There might be a demand for that sort of hero before much longer, but Alanni knew it wasn't going to be filled by her. Her swimming expertise consisted of an ability to keep afloat. For a while. If she had to.

For all the people in the Temples' care, it was either find a boat or perch on the rocks of the peninsula like seabirds until help came or the food ran out.

Kayab started the day hoping to find boats and people to handle them in the fishing villages along the coast of the peninsula. There were half a dozen of them, none holding more than a few hundred people, but those people lived by and for the sea.

"If they can just haul us a boatload at a time on to the mainland, we're safe. With Bassar . . . *gone,* and the harvest about to come in—the mainland won't be short of food. All those mouths that won't need filling now . . ."

"It might make more sense to use the boats to bring the

food out to us here,'' Alanni suggested. ''Here we have shelter and fresh water.''

While the First Temple lay in ruins, many of the tunnels and rooms carved out of the solid rock below it had survived—dusty and rubble-strewn, but still fit to keep the rain off. In the flooded storeroom Kayab had found the night of his prison break, an underground spring had broken through, to pour out tons of cold fresh water every day. Farther back in the hills, the Second Temple was nearly intact.

Alanni had even heard more rumors of rumors, that the way to the ancient caves built by ancient races under the peninsula now lay open. She discouraged such talk as much as she could. People were all to ready to start believing in ancient non-Galactics rising from the ground either to destroy or help them.

Any help the Brotherhood found, it was going to have to find for itself.

Therefore—Alanni's suggestion that they bargain with the mainland farmers.

''What do we have to offer them?'' Kayab said, with an elaborate two-handed gesture. ''Also, there's the government to think about. The minute they discover there's a food surplus, they'll decide to sell it off to fatten somebody's credaccount. If we're already on the mainland eating the food as fast as it's harvested, they won't find it so easy to rob the starving to fatten the overfed. Not impossible, since nothing's impossible to those bugs if they really want it. Not easy, though, and too . . . they're *lazy*.''

He had the right of it, Alanni admitted, as long as there were enough boats.

Very quickly, she learned that there were not.

The first refugees from the fishing villages staggered out of the hills early in the afternoon. The villagers were used to storms and high tides, and they'd taken the earthquake's warning. Most of them had been perched safely on dry hillsides when the *tsunami* swept away their villages.

Swept away their villages, *and* their boats.

''Oh, a few may have been carried inland and dropped without being smashed to pieces,'' one woman said in a lifeless voice. ''My husband is staying behind in the hope of just that. I don't think he'll have much luck, though. Any boat he finds, he'll need to repair, and all the tools for that are at the bottom of the sea."

Not quite all; the Brotherhood possessed a tentful. These would still be a drop in the bucket compared to what would be needed to repair enough boats to carry ten thousand people to the mainland before they starved.

The refugees from the villages kept coming all day and well into the night. The last to arrive were the ones carrying the injured, on improvised stretchers or sometimes on people's backs.

At least *all* the work of dealing with the casualties didn't fall on Miembra-daktari. Some of the villagers had basic medical training; they had to, living a dangerous life fifty kloms from the nearest hospital.

Also, Hermosh-daktari had sent a few of his people from Bassar Municipal Hospital to the First Temple the afternoon before the big 'quake. Whether he had planned to follow personally, they didn't know. Certainly he had not.

When Alanni went to bed that night, she could console herself with the knowledge that the refugees would have good medical care—until they commenced dying of starvation.

By breakfast the next day, Kayab, Alanni, and Miembra had decided that for the moment the most important thing to do was to hide the fact that they weren't quite sure what to do next. Kayab didn't like the idea; he said it was behaving in the manner of a government.

Alanni with her leadership experience and Miembra with her ruthless common sense convinced him otherwise.

"It's not as if we were planning to fog our people for our own profit," Alanni said. "We're not. We just don't have all the scrute now. When we do, we can act. Meanwhile, we have to prevent panic. That could frag everything."

By noon, she was in charge of a party sent to work its way along the shore of the peninsula opposite the mainland. Their job was to find landing spots for boats, salvage anything useful—and burn or bury as many bodies as they could.

She recruited mostly men from the fishing villages. They knew the sea—most of them could swim—and they had strong backs and (just as important now) strong stomachs. They didn't disappoint her, either. By mid-afternoon she was Captain Alanni Keor again, so happy at being in command of people who knew their business that she sometimes managed to forget why she was here for all of five minutes at a time.

A look toward the mainland, and the tidal flats and pools that had once been Bassar, was a guaranteed cure for her forgetfulness.

They were working along a wreckage-littered shingle beach three kloms south of the Temple when Alanni heard someone shouting, faint and far off. Her first instinct was to look inland, expecting to find another party of villagers. Then she realized that the voice was coming from out to sea.

She looked—and blinked, not sure that the long day in the sun wasn't scrambling her brains. The clouds were patchy and thin, with both suns pouring out heat most of the time. Even worse, the reflected glare off the water blistered skins, sucked moisture from lips, and left eyes aching and half-blind.

A naked man was sitting impossibly in the water a hundred meters from shore, waving frantically at her.

She blinked again, and he didn't go away. He also went on shouting. Most important, some of the other people in the party were apparently seeing him.

A not-unreasonable conclusion was that the naked sitter was *not* a hallucination.

Alanni pointed at the two best swimmers on hand. "Go get him."

"Firm."

They stripped off their clothes, plunged into the water, and churned off toward the impossible like fangfaces scenting prey. When they reached the man, Alanni saw that the impossible had a simple explanation: the near-naked man was sitting on a floating beam and paddling with his hands.

With his two rescuers kicking from behind to push it along, the log made fine progress. In a few minutes it was in water shallow enough for the man to slip off and, with the help of his rescuers, wade ashore. He wore dripping, sagging undershorts, torn so badly that they hid very little.

When he tottered up on to the shingle, Alanni once again

wondered if she was fraggy from the sun, the heat, and too many gruesome sights.

It was the young BMP policer from the terminal riot. The one who'd herded rioters along without hurting them, then played that little charade with her to keep her out of trouble.

He didn't look so young now. The slight plumpness was gone. So was any kind of uniform, dirty or clean. He had a Galactic-record black eye and a liberal distribution of minor cuts and bruises, as well as a bandaged left arm and a magnificent sunburn.

Alanni poured half a canteen of water and some salt tablets into him. By the time they'd started to work, he was able to explain his survival.

"I was on the north end of the causeway when the wave hit." He looked at his audience and nodded. "It was as bad as you think." He closed his eyes for a moment to shut out the memory.

"The wave hit," he repeated dully, and shuddered. "I grew up in Pearl Haven, which means I know something about waves. I saw it was going to lose some strength by the time it reached me. I can also swim. So I dived off the causeway and was in the water when the wave came.

"The wave itself wasn't so bad. What nearly fragged me—what did frag a lot of other people—was finding a place to *land*. I was lucky. I came down on soft ground, just inland from the policer barracks. I held on to a bush until it pulled out by the roots. By the time it did, the water was shallow enough for me to stand up. I ran up the hill and made it over the crest before the water rose again. I . . . don't know if anybody else made it or not."

The next morning he'd crept down to the BMP barracks, ruined by the 'quake and now standing in three meters of water. Knowing where to go, he had dived and found a couple of ration paks. They kept him from going hungry.

"Someone stole my clothes while I was diving, though. I decided that if this sort of thing was starting, I'd come over to the Temple and see whether anyone was left here. If there was, I could help."

Finding a floating beam to sit on and a piece of plas

sheeting for a paddle, he launched himself. He'd lost the paddle during the night but kept on, using his hands.

"I almost wish I hadn't found you people," he said shakily. "I would have liked to make the whole trip myself." Then he looked at Alanni's canteen. "On the other hand . . ."

She handed him the water again. "On the other hand, maybe you're just as glad we met you."

"Pos," he said, and swigged the canteen empty.

The news that the main policer barracks might hold salvageable material—and was in water shallow enough for easy diving—started everyone talking. Alanni didn't try to halt the talk, since most of the fishermen seemed to be thinking along the same lines as she was.

Weapons and charges for them in the barracks, unhurt by the water. A whole arsenal, ready for whoever reaches it first!

That has to be us. We can't trust anybody else. Other survivors could turn pirate. Mainlanders could try to hold the shore against us. The government–

Enough. I'm convinced. But what do we do for boats?

Try the villages. Send tools. If there's nothing there to be salvaged, maybe we can build rafts out of the wreckage.

This water looks shallow enough in most places that we can use poles to move them.

She decided to turn her party back toward the Temple. Apart from finding a survivor who really deserved to be one *(and where are your manners, that you haven't even asked his name?)* they now had some idea of what to do next.

Salvaging the police arsenal wasn't just busywork, either, to keep people's minds off the shrinking food supply. It would really do some good.

Best of all, it would let her go on being Captain Alanni. The more she could be that, the less she'd have to think of her Mission . . . the Invisible Wisdom.

22

Water, dry land and the company of reasonably unfobby human beings did wonders for the BMP man, whose name was Ram Ghaukari. That name had the feel of Ghanj about it. So did Ram's pale brown skin and wide gray eyes—which were very pleasant, Alanni thought, to look into.

Dam' fine eyes. Enough to make me forget that he's probably a good five years-ess younger than I am!

That's assuming that he's not on his second time around, and that's what I have to assume.

The brown skin was not quite in such good shape, even apart from the visible damage. It hung hound-loose on a set of very good bones, inevitable result of the Galactic-record crash diet of the sort Ram had been subjected to. The muscles under the skin were still toned and tuned, though, and they let him match the pace of his companions with ease.

If he is duty-fit . . . The Light knows we need more security, and he was a "protector" who really did protect stead of prey!

Ram and Alanni came naturally together at the head of the column as it turned inland, back toward the Temple. They fell to talking—or rather they slid into it, since the conversation began after Ram slipped and fell down the muddy bank of a creek. Alanni helped him out and up.

"Give a man new clothes and look what he does to 'em," he said, while she helped him scrape mud off his loose trousers, using a stick.

"Happens," she said. "You're descended from Ghanji migrants, firm?"

"Not bad guessing," he said, with a how-do-*you*-know-this look that demanded an answer.

Alanni had decided to tell him: "I'm in the same line of work you are—or were, Ram. I was in the Temple on a matter that even now only Kayab knows about."

"I thought you might be. Here—we'll let the rest of the mud go. It'll come off easily enough when it dries—if it dries. We heard of the way you handled that situation up onstation. My late . . . colleagues didn't learn anything more from me, since they didn't ask."

Bugs, Alanni started to say, and stopped herself. The colleagues *were* late. And for all that Ram was probably worth any six of them put together, he had served with them for a fair number of years. This was a time for not saying anything at all, good or bad, about the dead. Unless he did.

He didn't, and was not reluctant to talk about himself. Quite the reverse. With an audience, he seemed to need to talk to reassure himself that he was still alive . . . unlike nearly everyone else in the (late) city of Bassar. By the time they reached the First Temple, Alanni had learned quite a bit about Ramgup Ghaukari.

He was descended from one of Ghanj's well-known noble families. The founder of the Hellhole branch of the family, however, had been the bad fruit of his generation. Had an undue propensity for gambling and collecting other men's wives as trophies, back on Ghanj.

"After too much of that, he had to go offplanet. He was sent with enough money to honor his name here, but he gambled that away. Maybe it wasn't altogether for the worse, since he then turned to business—and made an honest living as a fish merchant."

The family had made honest livings of one sort or another in Pearl Haven for six generations. Only now in the seventh had they made a sufficiently *good* living to revive the Ghanjese tradition of service. Until recently they had been too busy surviving.

"I began working—serving—aboard one of my father's fishing boats. Then I was watchman in our warehouse. I studied, and at last I was sent to Bassar, to the Protector's School." Ram twisted his lip. "*Protectors*!"

Alanni liked the sound of that sneer. *All that goes a long way toward explaining why he turned out so differently,* she mused. *Heir to the Ghanji tradition of service and feeling the need to redeem his family's honor—of course he'd break his equipment trying to Do The Job! We couldn't have asked for a better man. So long as he doesn't worry himself to death over how much work there is to be done and how few of us to do it!*

Her happy mood was wiped out when they reached the Temple. The first news she was given was that Tuke had escaped.

Once she was through damning the persons responsible and their ancestors, not to mention their alleged sexual habits, she learned that the situation was not nearly as bad as it might have been. At least Brother Jirish had had all weapons counted and placed under guard. It appeared that Tuke had only the clothes on his back and his (admittedly formidable) hands.

Kayab had gone a step further. He had placed Ugru in charge of a reorganized guard-force, now divided into bands of four or six rather than the pairs and trios previously used.

"That won't save them if Tuke attacks," Alanni pointed out to their little summary council. "He can kill a half-dozen untrained people with his bare hands."

"If they all stood still to be killed," Ugru said, "true. They will not, however, stand still. Their orders are to scatter if attacked. Surely at least one will reach you or me, or the guards at the treasure tent—who have weapons."

Alanni could not entirely trust Ugru and she also could not deny his logic. Tuke was presumably (literally) holed up in the multi-tunneled warren. He might make occasional raids to spread terror and he might kill. He could not accomplish major damage, and sooner or later his luck would run out and he'd be so hungry that he was no longer fit to fight.

"We can manage," she muttered, and immediately realized: *We could manage far better if we could salvage weapons from the BMP barracks*! With a few rafts and plenty of people willing to sweat—and Ram's guidance—they could swing that. She said so, and "We can make the First Temple impregnable to anything short of a full-scale attack by the Hellhole Planetary Protectors—or a spaceship!"

"Would be only justice," Jirish said, "if Tuke was Poofed by some Child-Sister he has abused without her even having to work up a sweat!"

That brought grim semi-smiles, and they worked out details of the expedition, right down to who would guard each raft. Alanni noted that Ugru was always polite and deferential—and clearly had a better grasp of the matter than anyone else present. *Except me. Pity I couldn't have Ram sit in. I'd like his opinion on a number of things . . . including Ugru!*

It wasn't until late that night when she and Kayab were undressing that he mentioned It: the Invisible Wisdom. Alanni was only just able not to react. She hoped her face showed nothing when he asked her what she thought they should do with the artifact. Could it be used as bait? Was Tuke likely to be after it?

"Does it rain on Hellhole? It would be the monster's ticket offworld and three times around the Galaxy, if he could get his claws on it."

If he wasn't too cracked to think of it. The trouble was that they had no proof that he was, or was not. They thought about that while they stripped and exercised. Alanni pushed hers. Tuke was on the loose, full of hate. The next day or even hour might bring her into a battle to the death with him . . . a man definitely better than she. She would carry a stopper set on Three, and even that might not be enough; she couldn't walk around with it in her hand! In that case her body might have to do the job—or become Tuke's prey.

That thought sent prickles up her bare spine and she lengthened her exercising.

Not until they had both worked up a good sweat did Kayab speak again:

"If the University will take It, I'd like to give it to them. It may or may not be anything important, but it merits study! It wasn't about to be scientifically studied here even before the 'quake. Now . . . two generations will pass before the Fog Coast even has the facilities."

"I hadn't realized that Planetary U. was much better than the Fog Coast, in research on alien artifacts."

"Where do you think you are, a barbarian planet? Besides . . . if they can't study it here, they can certainly *sell* the Invisible Wisdom to someone who can, for a nice new balance in the University credaccount. Just as certainly some of that profit would belong to the Fog Coast, for rehabilitation. You see?" he said with a grunting chuckle. "I can do simple arithmetic, you know."

Alanni laughed. Flat on her back, she bumped her butt up and down and extended a hand in his direction. "Like two-body problems, for example?"

Kayab's facial celldye did a lot for his pretended scowl. "Shameless hussy, get thee behind me!"

"Now *that* would be a new position, if we could accomplish anything!"

He made an exasperated sound. "I am *serious*! Would you act as courier for me, Yimmeh?—take the Invisible Wisdom to the University if they want it? Our courier would have to be a fighter, just in case. That means you," he said, popping up to squat over her and set the tip of his right index finger on the dark crest of her breast.

A tremor ran all through her, and he knew only part of the cause.

He would trust me *with the Invisible Wisdom? Ah Light, Light—and entrust the milk to the cat for safekeeping! All I'd have to do is buy a ticket for Shaitansford stead of Golden, look up Nortay's agent, and finish my job right here on Hellhole! Piece-of-cake easy!*

Right . . . easy to betray Kayab?—frag his trust in you, maybe his will to go on? What happens to the people he's leading, particularly since you'd never be coming back? Ram's good and so is Ugru. But Ugru might also shift goodole Mudhole if the I.W.'s no longer around.

Of course, she could always make sure that Kayab didn't learn of her treachery. Living a lie was better than not living at all, or killing innocents through murdering this man's shaky self-confidence.

Hmm. Nortay's agent should be willing to help her with that sort of cover-up. In fact, probably delighted even to mark her up . . . *uh-huh. And take that information to Nortay along with the I.W.! Then the wormspawn would be able to hold it over my head as long as the Brotherhood is important to me.*

Which would be . . . as long as the Fog Coast needs the Brotherhood! Face it, *Alanni dear dummy . . . you* care. *This time you really give damns.*

And what about Jay and Bouncy? Everything she believed in—everything she *was* demanded that she find a way to do her duty to them and this man she realized she really cared for. Find a way, find a way . . .

Kayab smiled. ''We can talk about it in the morning.''

''If there's time before we have to get to work,'' she reminded him throatily.

''There will be time, if we don't stay up talking all night.''

''Uh . . . my dear . . . I wasn't thinking of *talking*.''

There was always strength for that, and both of them proved it. Later he was nuzzling-nibbling-nursing when she thought, *Please . . . please let me wake up with an answer . . .*

23

Kayab was still asleep next morning when she awoke. Giving him a fond smile, she dressed and trotted down to the treasure tent.

One look inside made her stiffen and take a second while all the juice seemed to flow right out of her. That second look told her the worst.

The Invisible Wisdom was gone.

With the bottom missing from her stomach and her legs trying to go rubbery, she pulled her face into an uncommunicative mask before she emerged from the tent. Whatever had happened to the Invisible Wisdom, she could accomplish nothing by starting a panic.

She sent a guard off to fetch Ugru—*and please, let's hope he's there to be fetched and not gone with* It—and took the woman's place. The guard hadn't come back when Alanni saw Brother Jirish come hurrying toward the tent, followed by the new watch of four guards.

"Brother Ugru is not to be found," Jirish said. Between excitement and his rushing gait he was half breathless.

The bottom dropped out of Alanni's stomach again. "Have you told anyone else?"

"I have not."

"Well done. Let's don't. The Invisible Wisdom is also gone."

Jirish frowned. "Do you think Brother Ugru–?"

Yes, I think Brother Ugru, she thought, but said, "Brother Ugru must have gone on the trail of the thief the moment he found It missing."

Jirish put his head on one side. "Without telling anyone?"

Brother Jirish, please don't be so damned smart! "He probably didn't want to give the thief a head start."

"If there is more than one, though . . ."

"Brother Ugru probably took a stopper. Anyway, he's as good as four men even without a stopper or anything else."

"That is so," Jirish said, while his eyes studied hers.

Alanni wished she could be *sure* she hadn't heard skepticism in his voice. Still, as long as he was Obedient to any order to keep his guesses to himself, no harm would be done. She wasn't about to say "What else could it be?"

She said, "Send–no, please go yourself to the tool tent. See if any tools for boatbuilding are missing. I doubt that the thief was planning on swimming to the mainland with fourteen kilos of Invisible Wisdom on its back. Likely enough, it–all right, let's say 'he'–was going out to one of the villages, repair a boat if he couldn't find one to float, and reach the mainland that way."

That is, assuming the thief is either Ugru or someone as intelligent as he is. If by some chance he is a plant with a Mission, we've probably seen the last of the I.W. Which won't break your heart, O gray ex-policer of conflicting loyalties and tender scruples!—will it?

Do tachyons move fast?

Jirish hurried off, taking one of the Child-Sisters with him. Alanni noted that he was willing to turn his back on her, even though she was carrying a stopper. Both were also doing the eyes-always-moving routine . . . clumsily, but well enough to cut their chances of being taken by surprise.

Give Jirish another ten years and a few women to beat him about the head and shoulders when he needs it, and he won't be a bad specimen of the human male.

She settled down to pace her guard-route around the tent and consider what to do next.

One thing didn't need considering. She would do everything short of getting herself killed—and not much short of that—to save Ugru's reputation. If he had stolen the Invisible Wisdom, he would have to be tracked and caught. He might have to be . . . placidated. Poofed. *Probably* would; the odds were that he had sworn oaths he could not break, to snatch the double-damned thing.

Otherwise it would be known that she had simply let him get away with It. *Known widely enough so that sooner or later darling Councillor Nortay would hear of it,* she thought, very grim of face and tight of lip.

And Councillor Nortay would be pleased. So. Tracking Ugru and then doing whatever was necessary to recover the Invisible Wisdom—that was inevitable. She would do what she had to do. At the same time, she wouldn't let it be known that Ugru had been the thief. *(If he is, Alanni, if he is!)* He might have to die, but he would die with his reputation intact: the man who had slain Luctan and saved the Brotherhood.

Not to mention saved her, directly, and indirectly all the people the Brotherhood would save here. *Although that might not be many, if we can't get either the people to the mainland's food or the mainland's food to the people . . .*

Pacing (and so deep in thought that she was not doing so pretty good a job of guarding, if it came down to that), she tried to plan how she would airlift the people around the Temple . . . if she had or found or could steal anything that could fly. Surely they had no aircraft and no prospect of any. Thus her thinking was merely a mental exercise to keep her occupied until Jirish returned.

It did, and he did. "Certain tools essential for boatbuilding have indeed been taken," he reported, looking a little sick. "I could not swear to their use myself you understand, but the men of the village said that is what is missing."

Alanni looked at him with an open, resigned expression, and sighed.

And so the hunt begins, she thought, without cheer.

She thanked Jirish for his prompt Obedience to the call of Duty, and returned her attention to her guard-track by way of dismissal. Jirish departed. Back on her sentry-go, Alanni considered who to take with her on the hunt for . . . the thief. The unknown thief.

She did not consider long. She knew quickly that there was one answer: she must go alone.

The only people she could trust to be discreet were Kayab,

Chayim, and probably Ram Ghaukari. The first two were not fit for a cross-country trek, and Ram was needed here. They'd have to have him to direct the salvaging of the BMP arsenal. Not to mention fighting off Tuke if the wormspawn decided to put his nose in at such an eminently inconvenient moment!

So. Go alone then, or risk making Ugru's name stink. That was her choice. He was a choice containing too much opportunity for getting herself killed, because Ugru wouldn't be slow with hand *or* stopper and Tuke was probably out there somewhere, too.

It was still what she had to do.

The first hard part was saying goodbye to Kayab.

It was even harder because she had to explain the whole situation to him.

She did. He understood, and did not even try to keep her from going.

"Maybe there is a Dark Lord or some other Upstairs Neighbor who watches over people who have to do illogical things because honor demands it," he said very quietly, and tried to smile while it was plain that his eyes could not. "Whoever it may be watched over me, the night I went off to save you—against all logic. I'll see what I can do about a real prayer, *Yimra*; that It do the same thing for you."

Alanni kissed him, starting with a light peck to the cheek. When his arms came around her like telepresence waldoes, she shifted to his mouth. She sighed and pressed to him. *Oh damn, Kayab—I don't want to go either!*

"Yimra, do what you must," he said softly, "but come back!"

How could she say it: *If I'm really lucky I won't ever come back—and if I'm not lucky I won't either, because I'll be dead*. She could not.

She pulled out of the embrace. Already she had given . . . *him*, the thief—too much head start. She had to redshift, and at speed, although here was Kayab and she might never slice or flash with anyone again. She told herself she was making things easier by turning and rushing out. What she was doing was fleeing.

• • •

Ugru probably hadn't been able to ask the fishing villagers about gaining a boat, for fear of exposing the game he was about to play. Whatever that was. Too, he would be slowed by fourteen kilos of Invisible Wisdom and twenty kilos of tools and equipment.* Tough as he was, that was a respectable load to lug many kloms over terrain both rough and unfamiliar. Particularly with someone on his heels who was just as tough but carrying no more than a stopper and minimal survival gear. *Of* course *he'd think of that!*

Alanni was able to ask the questions that Ugru couldn't and hadn't.

She learned the names of four villages that might have intact or reparable boats. She decided to head for the farthest and work her way back toward the Temple. That would also let her travel inland on her outward trek, with trees and rugged ground offering plenty of cover for her. Along the coast, wide stretches of open ground alternated with patches of upcroppings and boulders that could easily hide a whole squad of ambushers who would be able to spot her out in the open terrain as obvious as a fly on a plate.

Ugru certainly had a stopper. Tuke might have acquired one by theft, or stolen some sort of hunting weapon from some village or villager no longer around to mention his loss. He might even have made himself a sling or bow. Alanni wasn't going to make herself any more vulnerable than she had to.

After a bit of thinking she added a slug-thrower to her equipment. It had the edge over a stopper in range. It was harder to aim but certain to inflict damage if it hit at all. It was also a lot harder to control the *degree* of damage from a slug chewing its way into someone's anatomy at shocking speed. A slug aimed at a leg could smash it—or puncture something vital. She was not wild about the old percussion weapons, then; Alanni felt a professional's distaste for not being able to control the effects of her weaponry.

She took the pistol anyhow. She felt an equally professional and more acute distaste for being killed.

With the slug-filled weapon thumping tediously against her

*34 kilograms; 75 *pounds*, Old Style.

hip, she tramped uphill and turned to look down at the Temple for a moment. Next she directed her gaze across to the mainland. Then she stepped back, unpacked and drew on the loose and nicely long pants she had (stolen), turned, and vanished into the hills of the peninsula.

She found Ugru at the second village.

A gray-blue twilight was already spreading over the calm sea and beginning to creep over the land when she saw him. He was sitting on the roof of a ruined cottage, his legs dangling over a three-meter drop. Below was the bank of a little stream that still gurgled down to the sea.

Tied to a flagbush on the stream's bank was a leaky, patched boat. Alanni could see the Invisible Wisdom in its bottom, in a few sems of brown water.

Above the moribund cottage, the hillside was strewn with boulders that remained because they were too deeply imbedded to have been shifted by the quake. Among them the soft and moss-grown ground muffled the barefooted steps of Alanni Keor. She had a clear stopper-shot at Ugru before he was aware of his stalker.

"Don't move, Ugru."

He turned slowly, one hand creeping toward the stopper resting on the edge of the roof—and drawing back empty as he saw Alanni's leveled weapon. Even more slowly, he stood. His was a beautiful animal grace made all the more impressive because he wore only a lioncloth. The rest of his clothes lay in the boat. Alanni had noted that they were black with sweat and grime.

He had worked hard all day, and he was standing below her on insecure footing. She *should* have the edge—not much, but enough.

"Damn, Ugru. What am I supposed to do with you?"

The words were only just out of her mouth when she realized that she shouldn't have said "I." Letting him know that she was alone might tip his judgment in favor of trying to jump her—in which case he'd get himself Poofed.

He stood quietly, however, a magnificently built man with what might have been a smile on his face, while Alanni told him to thump the stopper with his foot. He did, without looking down. When he heard it land, he spoke:

"I do not know, Sister Yimra. Or would you rather I called you by your true name?"

Again Alanni braced herself. That request could be a gesture of honor toward someone he knew he was about to kill. (Never mind that he had mighty little chance of succeeding—*how far and how fast can he jump?*—that sort of confidence was a weapon all by itself.) If he kept bringing her to the alert and letting her drop back, he might confuse her enough to gain the seconds he needed to shift for better footing for launching a flying attack . . .

Now she wished she'd told him not to get up. Now she wished her stopper was set on Two. That could keep him nicely out of mischief without killing him, while she–

He squatted, she lowered the stopper, and he came erect and flying all in an instant flurrying of uncoiling springy limbs that defied the physical limits of his footing and the uphill-downhill angle and Alanni squeezed the stopper and his hand smashed it out of her grasp. Since he also crashed into her and kept moving, she missed. And right now she had no time to consider whether she had really wanted to shoot this man . . .

Before his other hand could destroy her and without even thinking of wasting the effort to draw the other pistol she'd never have time to use, she went into her own flurry of movement: jabbing at his eyes, kicking at his loinclothed groin, trying to break either arm (who cared which) and all the while shrieking like ten evil spirits. All at once. She couldn't afford to be deliberate and scientific about fighting this time. That would mean she would be dead, and she couldn't afford that either.

She knew she had only one small chance to survive against this man who had already accomplished the impossible in pouncing to disarm her. That was to inflict enough damage to *slow him down.* Left at full speed, he could kill her with the ease of a *sensei* throwing a brash child.

The blurred motion continued, without thought for it; all the while she knew that if he hadn't been determined to take her stopper out of the game first, she wouldn't have even this chance. She'd already be dying of shattered ribs thrust into heart and lungs at about the same instant she learned that she was in danger. And the flurry of blurred movements continued . . .

At the end of ten seconds' fighting—maybe eleven—Alanni was somehow on the roof and kneeling at its edge, looking down. Her green shirt was mostly ripped off and one eye was half-shut and her lip leaked blood where a broken tooth had gouged it and her arm ached beyond aching and she wished the world would stop swaying in front of her good eye.

Three meters below, Ugru lay on the ground in disarray. One eye was bloody pulp. One arm dangled-lay uselessly. And he seemed to be having trouble with his right leg.

And yet Alanni again had the notion that he was smiling at her.

She said, "Do you yield honorably?" and he shook his head.

Damn. She lurched to her feet. She'd have to go down and retrieve her stopper or his and stun him with her Outworlder Two setting even if he had taken injuries that would make it dangerous to put him out. She had done plenty of damage, all right . . . and the amount he'd inflicted was so frightening, so close to *enough,* that she had to force herself to think with reasonable clarity.

"Look out, Alanni!"

He could yell, all right! She jumped and drew the lethal pistol then—and stopped. The shout and use of her real name must be Ugru's trick to distract her while he reached for his stopper–

Under her bare feet the roof creaked, groaned, and shifted. She flung herself backward, clawing desperately for solid ground as the precariously-balanced roof slid away from under her.

She found solid ground, with a *whoof.* She even held onto the pistol. Meanwhile the roof fell, noisily.

She heard metal twang, wood splinter, stones rumble and crash, and then an ugly thumping sound and a peculiar grunt. She rose again, grunting herself, spat out a mouthful of (gravel?). and looked down thc slope beside the ruined hut.

Ugru lay even uglier, now, with the edge of the roof pinning him to the ground. Even from up here Alanni could see that it had chopped halfway through his body, like a gigantic but dull knife. Already blood was trickling from his mouth.

She was never certain how she reached his side. Surely it wasn't by mere walking! She knelt beside him, and all thoughts of her aches were gone.

"Couldn't let you," he murmured, gasping, "d–after–dishonored you . . . couldn't . . ."

A silence stretched so long that she thought he was gone. Then:

"Tell the Commodore."

Blood accompanied every word from his lips. More flowed now. The pulse in the wrist she held faded, faded, and then she couldn't find it. She lowered the dead hand to the ground and stayed where she was, kneeling by his side with her head bowed on her chest.

The . . . Commodore . . .?

The Invisible Wisdom is yours and you have a clear road out of here. Just climb into that boat and start rowing for the mainland.

The boat? I can't handle a boat! Are you trying to kill me?

Isn't that what you want?

Alanni shut off the internal conversation with the not-so-still voice of her self because she realized that the concept of rowing out to sea and not coming back didn't appall her as it should. Her death and the disappearance of the double-damned I.W. had the smell of something that would solve a lot of problems for a lot of people, starting with Alanni Keor.

I am so double-flainin' tired of being gray, *and when it means killing the man who saved my life–!*

She also knew that being tired enough to feel sorry for herself was not a good excuse for dying, when that death would also create a lot of problems. Kayab, the Brotherhood, the refugees, Jaykennador and Bouncy . . . they all needed a live Alanni Keor and would go on needing her for quite a while.

Possibly for longer than I can last, she thought with a sigh.

Nevertheless she couldn't just piss her life into the ocean. That would be going out as coward, and Alanni knew her conscience would say so in her final moments.

Since you can't die happy, why die at all?

If we put it that way, I suppose I might as well live, Voice.

Wearily she retrieved both stoppers—crawling, bared left breast dangling and dancing. Wearily she jacked herself to her feet and walked—wearily—over to the stream. Again she sagged to her knees, this time to wash her face in running water that even considered being almost cool.

As a matter of fact, she realized as sweat evaporated, the air had gone cold. She commenced looking for a place to build a fire, for warmth and for light to show up anyone who might try sneaking up on her in the night. One brief attempt told her that she could not move the roof and thus could do nothing with Ugru . . . Ugru's body. Meanwhile she was *not* going to try hauling the Invisible Wisdom back over rough and barely-known country in a darkness that might hide Tuke.

She had just dumped the first armload of dry driftwood and pieces of hut in her chosen place when a shout came from inland and spun her as if it had been a physical force.

"Yimra!" it called, and she dived behind a boulder so fast that she nearly broke her nose before she realized she had heard Ram Ghaukari's voice.

"Here!" she yelled, and for some reason tucked one stopper into the back of her loose pants.

He materialized out of the deepening shadows with a drawn stopper in one fist and a club in the other. Behind him Alanni could only just distinguish other moving shapes. She licked at her split lip, which thc water had stung.

"You're not alone, Ram?"

He shook his head. "Brought five of the village people with me. Had no idea what or who we might have to face." He looked at Ugru's body. "Uh. Or bring home with us! Did he–"

"Don't touch him, please," she said, moving a hand when he started toward Ugru. *How long till you grow cold enough not to give me the lie, Ugru poor Ugru who once saved my life?* "He must have caught up with whoever stole the Invisible Wisdom and lost the fight or been trapped. Maybe the thief heard me coming then and redshifted—at any rate there's the artifact, there in that boat."

She indicated it without turning. The pale illumination of twilight was behind her, and she could just make out the skepticism on Ram's face. She assumed that he could not see her closed eye or swollen lip; at least she'd washed away the blood. Abruptly she remembered to look down.

"Sorry, Ram, I forgot. Tore my blouse and strained myself too, trying to move that roof off him. Couldn't."

"Uh," he said, looking studiedly at the dead man while she strove to get her bare breast covered with the tattered remnants of her shirt. "Could anyone defeat Ugru, d'you think, except Tuke?"

"I doubt it."

He squinted about. "Then Tuke can't be far off. We found no traces of him—which proves nothing." He half-turned his head then and yelled "TAG!" with such suddenness and volume that she was startled. "Signal," he told her.

Human shadows rose from behind boulders and came hurrying downhill.

"Three men on guard all the time," Ram told them, "and the biggest fire we can build. In the morning we lift this roof off Brother Ugru and take him back to the Temple for burning."

"Firm," came from all around Alanni, and one of the voices called off two names to join him as guard.

About then Alanni realized that she would faint if she stood any longer. She sat, back to a chunk of rock and head between her knees, until the dizziness faded. She muttered something about straining herself with "that flaining roof." Her conscience was perfectly clear about leaving matters to the (former) Bassar policer. If there were better hands within twenty kloms to leave matters in, she couldn't imagine whose they were.

She thought it would be lovely to lean on his chest and weep so that his arms would come automatically around her. Really *cry,* for the first time since landing on this arsehole of a Hellhole. Ugru deserved that tribute, even if he had been working against her for someone called "the Commodore."

She also knew that she was not about to weep, not now, or lean on Ram Ghaukari either.

The Commodore . . .

The name sounded vaguely familiar, somehow. Where had she seen it? T-SP files? And who had it referred to? The Commodore. . . . She fell asleep trying to remember.

Ram had to stretch her out and roll her up in one of her own blankets. He even studiously avoided anything except the most professional and necessary touches of her, but Alanni neither cared nor knew.

24

"One, two, three—*Heave*!" Alanni shouted.

The men on the plas-rope heaved with a chorus of grunts.

"One, two, three—*Heave*!"

Again they obeyed amid throaty sounds of effort.

On the fourth try, a two-meter length of crate broke the scummy green surface of the water. Alanni's shout stopped a general rush to the side that would have let the big plastoc box sink again, probably on top of Ram Ghaukari. Slowly they manhandled it onto the raft. Water oozed from cracks in the crate's corners and around the lid.

Alanni didn't worry about the cracks. The label indicated power cells for stoppers and other portable hand-equipment—all waterproof for years, no matter how poorly packed. This looked well packed, and it had been underwater only a few days. . . .

Ram's goggled face popped out of the water. He rested a beefy arm on the edge of the raft until he had caught enough breath to climb, with help, out of the water. It was Alanni who helped him. She found the play of muscles under his brown skin good to look at and better to feel, even briefly.

I must be recovering from Ugru's death.

About flainin' time, too! So men think they have trouble with celibacy, hmm? Huh!

It was about time, and surely Ugru would have been the first—well, second—to say so. He had been a professional, too.

"That's the last we're going to haul out without blasting," Ram said, mopping stenchy scum off his face and finger-combing it out of his hair. "We have one crate of grenades, and I suppose I can extract propellants from some slugs . . ."

"Oh no! We're going to need every weapon we can make function, and ten more besides!"

He looked at her, now wringing water out of his hair. "Can't argue with that, Yim."

He wouldn't have done so in public, even if he'd had a case. Ram Ghaukari was another professional, if at a different level. Unlike Ugru though, he was alive and doing five people's work to keep others the same.

It doesn't matter, Alanni thought. *If we can't get* food *to our people or people to our food, a lot of them are going to die and a hundred Rams won't make that much difference.*

She was looking for a towel to wipe the scum off her own bare arms when she saw a light flashing from the cabin of *Chrysalis*. A second look told her it was the signal light, and she stared, translating.

—MESSAGE FOR SISTER YIMRA. CONFIDENTIAL. URGENT. CODED.

That was it, and it was enough for Alanni. She forgot about the towel and ran to the edge of the huge raft. Hurriedly she climbed down into the skiff that was taking the salvaged crate out to *Chrysalis* just before it shoved off.

The thirty-meter coastal freighter Alanni had seen fitting out in Bassar on her first day there had ridden out the quake and the *tsunami*. On the evening of Ugru's death, her captain Mava Payno brought *Chrysalis* in and offered her ship and crew to the Brotherhood.

"There's not going to be much coastal trade for awhile, not with a third of the Fog Coast's people down there," she said, indicating the waters hiding Bassar. "I'll be taking *Chrysalis* across the ocean to Treasure Trove in time, I suppose. Meanwhile, there's work to be done here."

"Indeed there is," Alanni had said simply, and they had a ship.

Chrysalis's drawback was that she drew too much water to come in close to the barracks without running hard aground. She could still tow the rafts, convey the children and the sick to the mainland, and haul salvaged equipment. Captain Mava and her six crewmembers were earning more than they would ever be paid.

(That did not prevent Alanni from posting a couple of reliable people with stoppers on *Chrysalis,* just to make sure the craft went where Captain Mava said it would.)

Mava Payno's vessel also was equipped with the best radio within reach of the Brotherhood, and the only one that could receive signals from Treasure Trove—or a ship in orbit, even—and handle coded messages. A little doubt lingered determinedly in Alanni's mind: how and where had the big woman with the short, shaggy hair acquired the financial backing to equip her ship so thoroughly and so well?

Since she probably wouldn't like Cap'n Mava's answer to that question, Alanni refrained from asking it. And now she headed for the ship aboard a skiff with only two oarsmen (the powerpak for the motor had run out yesterday and too much other equipment needed the new.) Alanni had plenty of time to wonder futilely what the message for her might be, look at the sky (morosely sullen as usual), and wonder for the fiftieth time if the food would last.

Everyone was already on half-rations, except the salvage workers. She had put herself on that restricted diet in order to set an example, and now she stayed hungrier than ever she'd been in the Brotherhood. (She had also had to argue Brother Chayim out of going on a complete fast. She couldn't help wondering whether the man was fobby, didn't care, or thought such a sacrifice might accomplish something. (*Sure—his death, most likely*. Already the only way he could cast a shadow was to hold his breath.)

The boat ride out to *Chrysalis* could have lasted ten times as long without providing her time to answer any of her questions. The Fog Coast was in deep trouble and since Alanni had made its problems hers—damn her damned empathy anyhow!—she was in deep trouble, too.

It didn't improve any once she was on *Chrysalis*. The commsystem operator had the message printed out for her. It said nothing. It was indeed coded—except for the three numbers at the beginning: 698.

Kali's own time to have to break a flaining code, even if it turns out to have been a good idea! And . . . is 698 *a key, or is it in code, too? Might be that* 698 *means one-two-three or even . . .* wait *a min!*

Wasn't there a T-SP *code numbered Six-Nine-Eight back when you were Captain Alanni Keor?*

Excitedly Alanni punched in what she could remember of Code 698 into the CS computer. And waited. Whole seconds passed. Then the chatter of onscreen printing commenced:

FROM THE COMMODORE TO CAPTAIN ALANNI KEOR, GREETINGS–

–At which point she slapped the computer into silence.

Everything dropped whirring into place, starting with the identity of "the Commodore." She remembered it now, clearly: the title was one Captain Shieda had grandly conferred on himself some years back.

Shieda. Born on Terasaki. In an era when extra weight was purely a matter of choice for a million out of every million-and-one persons, Shieda was a fat man. He was also a thoroughly polished spacefarer and ship's master, a connoisseur of beer and women (preferably, she recalled, young enough to be called girls) and an adept at the archaic form of martial art known as *sumo;* a form of wrestling.

"Commodore" Shieda was also a well-known pirate.

Alanni left the computer shut off while she worked at the decoding by hand. It would take longer, but that was less important than secrecy . . . assuming that the message was what she was damned near sure it would be. Meanwhile she had a thoroughly unpleasant feeling that things were about to get worse before they ever got better—assuming they ever did.

"So," Alanni told Kayab that night, after she had explained who Shieda was, where he was, and what he wanted (the Invisible Wisdom, as she had assumed correctly). "It's a standoff, for now."

"How so?" Kayab asked, while she adjusted the headband that valiantly and vainly tried to keep sweat out of her eyes. She wore nothing else and Kayab even less. It was that kind of night, on charming lovely Hellhole.

"He knows we have the Invisible Wisdom, Kayab. And don't ask me *how* he knows that; I don't know." *Which is a flat lie,* she thought with some self-accusation, *because it had to be Ugru who told him, which means that Ugru was Shieda's man all along on the same mission here as I am, and please, Kayab, don't poke your nose down* that *trail!*

He said, "Uh. No chance of making him believe the Invisible Wisdom was washed away by the *tsunami* or buried in the 'quake?"

"None I'd care to bet much on."

Kayab sighed. "Firm. So explain the 'standoff' if you please."

Sarcasm, she wondered, *or just fatigue? Either way, he sounds ready for a fight. Another honeymoon ends in the face of strife!*

She said, "Shieda can keep us from sending the Invisible Wisdom offplanet. Maybe even off the Fog Coast. He–"

"Off the Fog Co—can he pick up boats or flyers? And how would he know which one was carrying the Invisible Wisdom?" He answered his own question: "Oh, I see. The same person who told him that we have it would be able to tell him when it left, is that it?"

"Right. As for stopping a boat or aircraft—Shieda's ship is *Kirin*. There isn't a thing in the Heller system that could stop him from taking it wherever he wants. Good ship, good crew, a better-than-good Defense Systemry—that's guns, Kay'b—and computry system."

"I know what DS is and I'll take your word for the rest of it, Yimra. But—doesn't TGO frown on pirates raiding *planets*?"

"More often than not—sure. On the other hand if we try sending a message Shieda's going to catch it first and—do something we won't be able to defend against. After that, well . . . TGO might or might not bother investigating something that happened on a very nearly wiped out area on *Hellhole*. The people of Delventine Colony never got a thing after a raid by Captain Hellfire, and I haven't heard of any big TGO search-and-grab operation that brought her in, either. See, Shieda knows all this better than we do, Kayab. He's already considered all of it, you can assume that. He would know that he's not running a big risk—at least not in proportion to what someone might pay him for the Invisible Wisdom."

Un-selfconsciously naked, Alanni brewed some tea while Kayab chewed on that and, she hoped, digested it. Between sips of an honestly good local brew, she finished her explanation.

"Shieda can stop us from doing anything with the Invislble Wisdom, Kay'b—and I wish you didn't object to my saying just 'I.W.!' We, on the other hand, can keep him from taking it."

"Look it or not, I am all ears."

She smiled at the totally bald man. "He can't just Poof the whole camp from orbit, or come down into atmosphere and try it either. That *would* have TGO on his fat arse, my dear."

Kayab raised furry eyebrows. "That might also result in the destruction of the Invisible Wisdom."

"True. He doesn't have the people to spare to send down and fight it out on the ground. Not after we've handed out the Bassar policers' arsenal!"

"But we haven't–" He broke off to stare at her for about six seconds before he moved, fast. First he picked up his robe and shook it out. Swarms of crawling, creeping, buzzing *things* had been driven from their beloved marshes by the *tsunami,* and had invaded the camp. So far no one had died or taken sick of them. Most people did itch a lot.

Whipping the robe over his head, he hurried outside. Alanni sipped tea and smiled. Thank the Light she'd been able to manipulate him into swift action! Soon everybody would be armed. She assumed that Shieda's only infiltrator had been Ugru. If on the other hand the obese "merchant" had another—then she or he would be armed, too. Wasn't there some old saying about having to break eggs in order to hatch chicks?

He returned wearing a grim little smile. "What next, O Advisor Yimra? *Other* than to tell Shieda that the Invisible Wisdom is his as a gift."

That might be best, she thought, but kept it to herself. She said, "Hide it. Somewhere only we two know about. Otherwise Shieda's plant may be able to give him enough information to tempt him into a raid he doesn't really want to make. Or—somebody may decide to snatch it for himself."

"Tuke?"

She flipped her fingers. "More likely an ally he left behind as sleeper."

Kayab opened his mouth to protest, paused, and turned it

into a shrug. "That would be like Tuke, yes. Ah! Suppose that we are right now arming that . . . 'sleeper'?"

"Better than if we didn't pass out the firepower and Shieda thinks we're an easy mark, my dear. Tuke is *bad,* but he doesn't have *Kirin* and enough expertise *and* 'Defense' Systemry to toast half the planet!"

"Unless Tuke allies himself with Shieda?"

Alanni shuddered. "Oh, Kay'b! One nightmare at a time, if you please! Now . . . where shall we put that oh-so-troublesome Invisible Wisdom?"

They hid it so far back in the caves that Alanni wasn't quite sure she'd be able to find the way back herself. She was relying heavily on Kayab's excellent visual memory, in the event they did have to do something with the I.W. in an unholy rush.

It did not help that even portions of the tunnels she had explored before seemed to have changed. Ceilings were lower and there were bends she didn't remember, not to mention the layer of rubble slurring underfoot—and the dust that rose in choking clouds. Her handlite could barely cut through it. She wished sincerely that she had a filter mask. Judging by his coughing, Kayab must be wishing the same.

"I wonder if the caves of the Old Race have opened up," he said, during one halt. His tone didn't indicate that he was joking, either.

"We won't find out this trip, I think," she said, ducking a nasty mini-stalactite. "Or do you think we should try to find out now? They might come out and want the Invisible Wisdom back."

Squinting off into the dust-shrouded gloom, Alanni decided that it had just become sinister and she wished she hadn't said that, especially as a joke.

Maybe that was why Kayab didn't answer.

They burried It under a pile of rubble large enough to hide it and still look natural. By the time they'd finished shifting stones and dusty dirt, both of them were coughing like lung-fever victims and Alanni's teeth were nearly locked together with dust. She'd run out of saliva long ago. Sweat didn't wash the dust off their faces, either. It just made muddy tracks.

The first thing the thoroughly messy pair wanted when they returned to the inhabited area of the tunnel-warren was a lot of water. Bent on that goal and swallowing drily, they were turning a corner toward the underground spring when they nearly collided with a Younger Brother. His eyes were wide and streaming tears. He was also stammering so badly that Alanni could make no sense out of what he was trying to say. She resisted the urge to slap the poor downer into coherence.

She didn't have to. Kayab lost his temper and thundered, "In the name of the Dark Lord, whimpering child, will you speak sense or must I summon Miembra-daktari to heal your wits?"

The Younger Brother might just as well have been slapped. He rocked back on his heels before stammering out coherence that no one wanted to hear:

"Mi–Miembra—T–Tuke has her! Torturing her. Wants the Inv–visible Wisdom or he–he'll kill her!"

Jaws firmed while eyes exchanged silent messages.

Kayab's was: *I should have had the filthy swine killed and be damned with his friend in Bassar!*

Alanni's was: *You had no way of knowing that it would be safe*. (And: *The BMP would be a lot worse than a dozen Tukes. We only have one of him*.)

She turned to the trembling youth. "How many people does Tuke have with him?"

He was able to state coherently that he did not know. Not more than four—probably. Not less than two, certainly.

Alanni nodded, thinking. The odds were within the bounds of reason, although not by much. She thanked the Light that she'd brought her stopper into the caves—and hoped that the dust hadn't done anything to it. She forced herself to sound much calmer than she felt at the concept of Miembra in Tuke's bloody hands—and what those hands might be doing to her even now.

"I'm going to do my imitation of a *ninja* and try to find a good firing position against Tuke," she said. "Why don't you go and negotiate with him. Don't let him get a clear shot at you or come close enough to snatch you too!"

"Firm," the Eldest Brother said, with never a trace of frown at her choice of words. "I think I should wash myself first, though." He saw the question in her eyes and added, "We want to give Tuke no clues as to the location of the Invisible Wisdom. If I go to him all dusty this way, he'll start thinking of caves."

Alanni *did* kiss Kayab for that wisdom, and under circumstances less grim she'd have laughed at the Younger Brother's elaborate efforts to look anywhere other than at them.

"You do that, Eldest Brother! I won't bother—with any luck, Brotherless Tuke's going to be dead before he has another good look at me!"

She slipped off before Kayab could ask her what might come about if she wasn't granted the luck she mentioned.

25

Tuke would have preferred better men at his back than these four. Two were villagers who had chosen to turn outlaw after the 'quake, and proved willing to follow him as leader. The other two had been his allies in the good old days of his power in the Brotherhood, before even the planet itself turned against him.

None of them was the fighter he would have liked. Still less could any of these bunglers be trusted once Tuke had the artifact in his hands. They would have to go. He anticipated little trouble with ridding himself of their presence, once he had the Invisible Wisdom. The only complication was that he had felt it necessary to give two of them stoppers rather than knives. The truth was that without the longer-range weapons they'd be completely useless rather than just almost.

Aside from the lamentable quality of his henchmen, Tuke could not say that he had much to complain of. He had a good chance of escaping Hellhole with his life. He was working on a reasonable chance of escaping with the Invisible Wisdom. And he had an excellent chance of killing Miembradaktari or at least leaving her horribly multilated, regardless of what else he did or did not accomplish. That did a lot for Tuke's mental attitude.

A glance told him that she was conscious again. Good.

The string-thin polymer cords that bound her wrists to the tent pole and her spread legs to the pegs driven into the ground would be cutting painfully again. (Good.) She was bleeding in only two or three places. The new pain might still be endurable.

That wouldn't last long. If the artifact weren't brought to him quickly, Miembra would start dying. Slowly. *Her screams should bring matters to a conclusion in my favor.*

Now if only I had as good a chance of finishing that bitch Yimra–!

At the thought sweat popped out on his forehead, and it didn't come from the heat of the evening. The prospect of having Yimra spreadeagled naked in Miembra's place was more than exciting.

Meanwhile, impatience ate at Tuke. He gave in to it and walked over to Miembra. Again he drew his knife.

At Miembra's fourth shriek, a robed shape detached itself from the ring of watchers around the tent. As it approached the scene of horror, it became identifiably human. Glancing around with eyes dilated by excitement, Tuke recognized Elder Brother Chayim. Tuke frowned. He had little love for the man who'd given Kayab so much aid. Yet he had no blood quarrel with Chayim, either. *Time for a conciliatory gesture, then.*

Tuke wiped the blade of his bloody knife in Miembra's hair and turned from her.

"Brother Chayim, this is no place for you. I have no quarrel wi–"

"I have a quarrel with you, Brother Tuke. You are foresworn and cursed by men and the Dark Lord alike. Yet you may redeem yourself in the eyes of both by letting me take the place of Miembra-daktari."

"Take the place–?" (Take her place? *What pleasure does he expect me to derive from torturing a* man?)

"Of course. It is my Duty now to endure such pain as you choose to give," Chayim said, stepping closer, "to keep you from destroying the important one—our Healer. She has much work to do here, work pleasing to the Dark Lord. My own work is not–"

Tuke tuned out the old flake. He noted how Chayim kept easing closer. Chayim had no weapons—at least none visible—and he was too old for hand-to-hand combat. Still, letting him get in so close was one more unpredictable variable in a poorly-programmed situation in which Tuke was already juggling too many . . .

"Stop, Brother Chayim. Return to your Children. They need you more than Miembra."

"The Dark Lord be witness, that is not so." Chayim shuffled closer.

"It *is*! Stop, Brother!"

"Will you swear to do no more harm to the daktari, if I return to the Children?" Chayim asked, gaining another shuffle-step.

And lose my bargaining point? He is *insane!* "Neg."

"Then I must do my Duty."

Tuke was drawing his stopper, hating to stab the old man, when one of his knifemen panicked in the face of Chayim's cyberlike advance and determined words. He charged Chayim, knife in hand and blade coming up from the hip.

Ran at the oldster, passing *between* Tuke and Miembra.

And stabbed Chayim. The shining blade slid upward smoothly between the fourth and fifth ribs.

Then the fool froze, as Tuke screamed a curse and simultaneously hit him with a Two-setting.

"Tuke!" A new voice, shouting, female.

The Two-beamed killer staggered free as Tuke turned blazing eyes and stopper toward the voice. Then a Three-set stopper sent Tuke (Elder Brother, Brotherhood of Servants, dishonorably discharged) to the Dark Lord as a rapidly expanding cloud of molecules.

Alanni hadn't been worried about hitting a Miembra who was tented out on the ground. Even shooting from an angle where only her freak peripheral vision let her shoot at all, she could aim high enough to miss the Healer. She had had to hold her fire only for fear of hitting that dam' fool Chayim. He might be determined to be a martyr, but Alanni did *not* want to help along his way.

She had held her fire until suddenly it didn't make any difference; Chayim was stabbed and collapsing and she had a clearer shot at the monster than she had expected. Something made her call out his name so that he turned to look at his death, for an instant. Exit Brotherless Tuke.

Alanni had no opportunity to feel relief. Adrenaline pumped and yet she did not want more men reduced to dust. A daunting fury with her filthy, sweat-streaked face and filthier clothing, she charged the four creeps before they were over their surprise.

She kicked one in the groin almost *en passant* and tossed another so that his head smashed into the tent-pole. The tent collapsed onto him and Alanni whirled to kick the still-writhing lump before rushing the other two. She wanted prisoners, but didn't particularly care about the shape they were in as long as they could answer questions.

The trouble was that the late Tuke's other two bravos didn't choose to stay and fight or face the hideous apparition. While many others scurried aimlessly, those two fled. Alanni had a stopper set to kill and could not use it as the two plunged among the former watchers of torture.

Ram Ghaukari was better positioned, and bolder. He went to one knee. His percussion pistol swung up in both hands. The two burst out the other side of the mindless mélée converging upon Alanni—who heard *pahpahpahpah*—four old-fashioned gunshots so close together they sounded almost as one.

One of the running men threw up his hands and fell. (Five or six people promptly pounced atop him to make sure he stayed down.) The other ran on, hobbling, and Ram fired that noisy slug-thrower again. The fugitive not only went down, he vanished. A faint *splutch* told Alanni he'd fallen into a ditch.

One I helped dig, I hope, she thought, while everyone cheered.

Except those close enough to Brother Chayim to see the hilt standing from his chest and the way he was leaking more scarlet into the red lakelet he lay in.

Alanni spent only enough time on Chayim to feel for the pulse that wasn't there. That was time enough for one of the Healers from Bassar Municipal Hospital to come up and take charge of Miembra and the other casualties, friendly and otherwise, and to start organizing stretcher-bearing squads.

Alanni rose slowly, feeling the excitement slide away.

On the other hand, Miembra needed better care than the first aid she or Ram could provide. The knifework on her left breast would leave horrible scars if it weren't treated properly, and maybe even if it was. Other sadistically inflicted wounds were nearly as bad. She would live, but Alanni wanted her happy as well. She and too many others owed Miembra too much to want the valiant physician to be a freak depressed by her scars.

On the other hand if I don't keep busy I'm going to have the worst case of the shakes since the first time I killed a human.

Which was strange and *wrong*, for of all those she had since slain in line of duty—and she needed both hands to tally her toll—none would be missed less than Tuke. Or had made her feel so good to . . . placidate.

You've been stretched to the limit too long, 'Lanni girl. What you need is about a month's vacation with a good man.

A good man was ready to hand; Ram Ghaukari strode up to her, holstering his reloaded pistol.

"Sorry to have put some of your people in danger. Anything seemed better than letting that monster's henchmen escape."

If you talk, maybe you won't shake. "I don't think anybody was in much danger, except those two brotherslicers. Light! —where did you learn to shoot like that?"

He flipped five. "Spending my own money for rounds, mostly, using hard hard-plas ones. If you're given a weapon, what is there to do but learn to use it?"

As she thought *What, indeed?* he went on: "Sister . . . Yimra. I want to talk to you," and there was no doubt about his hesitation over her alias.

The man under the tent was unconscious and no one else was within hearing of quiet words. They said them, while they hauled the bug out, checked his injuries, and tied him up.

Ram had been asking a few questions and putting answers together in the best two-plus-two fashion. Most of what she had fondly hoped were secrets no longer were. (An exception was the cause of Ugru's death. *Thank the Light for small favors . . . since it's too late to hope for any big ones!*)

"I can't help you as much as I'd like to, Yimra. Too much depends on your being able to go on working with Kayab. You have to be the judge of what will let you do that. I did find one bit of scrute that might help . . . after the incident over the collapse of PishcoeCorp–''

''–When you saved a couple of hundred people, fact?''

Ram was speechless for so long that she was considering whether to apologize or kiss him for such charming modesty. He grinned and humped his shoulders boyishly.

''Call it what you will, Yim. BMP went in and investigated PishcoeCorp's files. Not thoroughly—I suspect some fairly High-Placed plants were involved in ways they didn't want us peasants to know. But not just a glance, either. We found mention of a Shieda, who was going to deliver three heavy-duty transport flyers to Pishcoe. If it's the same Shieda, and the records were correct–''

''Heavy duty? How heavy, Ram?''

''Uh, forty tons of cargo in atmosphere, ten tons to or from orbit. I don't know about passengers. I don't even know if it's the same Shieda . . .''

This time Alanni's impulse was to sing and dance. ''I can't imagine there being two Shiedas, much less their coming to Hellhole so close together! Besides, Shieda has always been the type to take a profit from either side of the law impartially. He's as happy hauling slaves and booty as he is hauling machinery. Bargains just as hard, too!''

''You're thinking–?''

''I'm thinking that I want to race right out and contact that fat man in orbit and I'd better find Kayab instead. Ram—can you sit on these pigs tonight? You or someone you trust?''

''Of course.''

''Then I'll see you in the morning.''

She hurried away with no thought to bad manners he didn't deserve. She *had* to think out what she was going to say to Kayab before she saw him!

He was in the tent and raised his head when she entered. He blinked.

Dust and dirt coated her except where sweat had washed it off, streakily. The right sleeve of her formerly-white shirt and the left knee of her even browner-than-before pants was torn. Kayab saw grass and rusty stains on her bared kneecap. She was dragging off the shirt as she came in.

She also looked beautiful. Much too beautiful, the disillusioned bald man thought, for him. He said the first thing that came to his mind.

"Come to look at a murderer?"

"A mur–?" She stopped her disrobing, ruined shirt in one hand, to stare at him. "What—you mean Chayim?"

"Who else? If I'd had Tuke killed–"

"We've been over that, Kayab."

He very nearly voiced his thought: *Can't you even let me feel guilty about causing the death of an old friend, Queen Yimra the Rock?*

"We also went over the Invisible Wisdom," he said, "and much good it did poor old Chayim. If I had agreed to sell it to Shieda, it might have been out of here before Tuke could have used it and Miembra as bargaining points. Chayim wouldn't have had to try nobility and die to save her from my mistake."

Without a word she turned away to take off her pants. When she turned back, looking marvelous, she was, incredibly . . . smiling!

"I'm not sure it was a mistake, Kay'b."

"What? You think Chayim is better off dead?"

"Nothing of the kind, and will you stop wallowing in self-blame long enough to hear what I just learned?"

"I am *not*–" he began with heat, but broke off. "Firm. I'm listening."

He did, and hope rose until by the time she had finished he knew that he was smiling, too. He wanted to jump up, dance a turn or two around the tent, and rush out to thank a former Bassar policer.

"Now we can sell It for something that could save all our people," she finished. "Those flyers! If Shieda has them and lets us use them, we can have everybody on the mainland in three days! Even if he doesn't have 'em, they'll still be on planet somewhere, and he might be able to call them back. We can't lose anything, my dear! And we could save everything—and everybody." More quietly she said, "Of course, if you still wish to hold onto the Invi–"

"No!" What he wanted was to hold this younger, fantastically competent woman and not let her go for years. Instead, he said, "After it as good as killed Chayim? If I believed in curses, I'd say the Invisible Wisdom had one on it! Yimmeh, this—Shieda—can't have any laboratory or research facilities of his own. To collect any stells for the Invisible Wisdom, he'll have to sell it. Who knows? Some perfectly legitimate university might meet his price."

"Not–" she began, and stopped, still unable to tell him that she had been sent here to steal the artifact, and hadn't given up yet.

Kayab saw that tears were filling her eyes, then streaming down her face, making even more mud on her skin. She wept silently in her own guilt until he went to her and pulled her down onto the bed beside him. After that she sobbed aloud.

This must be the first time she's been able to cry since she landed on Hellhole, Kayab thought, misinterpreting, and his own eyes were misty.

They mourned Chayim together, and eventually slid into gentle lovemaking. Later he held her from behind while she slept and his thoughts kept him awake.

She is young enough to be my daughter. Even if she chose to remain with me, our years together would be few. They might end before I do . . . in which case I hope I'd be strong enough to let her go with dignity. She is "too much woman" for me, and stronger too—and how I love her and want her!

On one of those dreary Hellhole mornings when daylight merely grayed the sky from the black-indigo of night, Alanni and Ram Ghaukari shared good news.

His was that Tuke had used up his last charge with his try for the Invisible Wisdom. Dead or alive, he had no more allies. This Ram had learned by doing things to the prisoners that he was not happy about doing or having done.

"The difference between you and Tuke," she said, placing a hand on his shoulder. "Tuke *enjoyed* it! Now hear this! I'm just back off *Chrysalis,* or I'd have been providing you moral support in the interrogation, at least. We have our bargain. We give Shieda the Invisible Wisdom, and he sends down three flyers to lift our people to the mainland. We will also have hostages, you see. Six of his people—each flyer needs a crew of two."

"Six isn't so many . . ."

"It's more than Shieda will care to lose! Let a pirate captain acquire a reputation for being careless with the lives of his people, and he doesn't keep them long. Or he acquires a thorough alternation of his molecular arrangement."

"Like Tuke's?"

"Exactly like Tuke's. Anyhow, Shieda isn't a madman. Also I promised him a hostage."

Ram stared. *"What?"*

"Well," she said, glancing away, "actually he demanded. And we're short of bargaining power. Know where I can get my hands on a keemo?"

"You're the hostage!"

She nodded, but signed him to silence. "It's *done,* Ram, Now you see, he knows of me and knows what I look like. So–" She shrugged. "I'm supposed to be honored."

"The rotten pirate swine!" *The lucky bastard!*

"But what a lucky one, hmm? Now look. Shieda likes submissive women—*girls,* really—and he also appreciates practical jokes. That's why I want a Terasak robe. A keemo. No no—please, Ram. Don't ask, and yes, I am serious."

Ramgup Ghaukari sighed. "I hate it. And I'll try." He started away, then glanced back. "I suppose yellow won't do?"

Alanni merely raised her eyebrows and stared until he turned and went on his way. Then she returned to the tent to start plucking those brows.

26

Captain Shieda made a final survey of his cabin, adjusted the embroidered silk drapery over the bedside computer console, and nodded in dismissal to his steward.

"Thank you, Commodore." She smiled and pushed a straying lock of hair into place. Since the graying gene, along with the one that directed balding, had long ago been removed from her family as it had from most Galactics, she had performed the strange act of dyeing her hair the color it would have been anyhow: gray. "Of course, if I didn't know by now what you mean when you say you want a 'Pleasure Pit,' I wouldn't be fit for my duty."

"True, Xhosa. And since you're too old to be occupying the bed, stead of making it . . ." He smiled to take the sting out of the words.

"Commodore, the saying about old dogs also goes for old bitches. If you're placing bets on that, don't bet anything you can't afford to lose."

"I'll remember that. Dismiss'."

She threw him an open-palmed nearly-mocking salute and departed.

Shieda loosened the sash of his silken robe of blue silk. He sat, forcing huge legs into lotus position, in the center of the haiku that was embroidered in black on his cabin's red plush carpet. Seldom had he looked forward to a week with as much certifiably-pure pleasures.

Kirin was in orbit around Hellhole, close enough both to the planet and to its station Skyraft to make communication easy and surprise attack impossible. He'd already bargained his way to the Invisible Wisdom. He was in the process of bargaining his way to a good deal of more legitimate if less profitable business. (Refugees from Hellhole would pay tidy sums into his various credaccounts for space onboard *Kirin* There would be a lot of that, with the flyers left on Hellhole. He might even charter a freighter for extra space.)

He had also performed the ''humanitarian'' act of at once accepting Alanni's commed-up-from-planetside request re: their wounded and much-needed Healer. She lay cocooned in *Kirin's* shipdoc now, with the cybernetic daktari on its way to making her scarlessly perfect and healthier than she'd been in years.

All this was in accord with Shieda's motto: ''Never miss a chance to make a friend. Make enough, and you can afford more enemies—which you'll have whether you can afford them or not.''

He regretted never having met ''Captain Cautious'' Jonuta. Shieda felt that they'd get on rather well. They brought the same philosophy to their chosen occupations, both mostly outside the law: that it *was* a business, which should turn a profit just the same as selling vegetables or high-protein insects in the market or repairing cyberbartenders on luxury-class starliners.

He was also giving his crew shore leave (for the six now down onplanet crewing the flyers) or at least a change of scenery. That would help morale, which would have to be high to take *Kirin* on the Tachyon Trail crammed with people who had decided that anyplace was better than people-hating Hellhole!

Shieda rose with a subdued tenor grunt. He stood, contemplating what a week with the fascinating Alanni Keor would do for *his* morale. He also contemplated pouring himself a medium-cool Thebanian beer.

He was occupied in more than contemplating the Starflare Gold when the door chime sounded. He swallowed half the skweezpak's contents at a gulp, wiped his mouth, and called ''Enter.'' The word automatically unlatched the door.

He had decided to be standing when she entered, mainly because of his imposing bulk and height; Shieda was well over 193 sems tall, and weighed just under 147 kilos.* He stared down at the woman who minced in and was glad the beer was well on its way to his stomach. Else he'd have choked.

Her shimmering black hair had been teased and twisted up into a Terasaki coil that was tied in place with at least a meter of purple ribbon. That tall coiffure was further decorated by a comb of gilded wire teeth fastened to an iridescent green seashell of indisputably phallic appearance. Her robe was clearly intended to imitate a keemo. Red with yellow stripes, spots, and patches. Sashed in red, high under the breasts in obi style. A closer look showed the sash adorned with a highly obscene erotic verse painted rather roughly on the cloth.

Her face was vanitized into a dusty white mask on which the eyebrows were mere lines of gleaming jet. Two large black eyes were rimmed with green geometric shapes that Shieda was afraid to look at very long; they might be intended to hypnotize him.

Somehow she still managed to look about fifteen. With this woman, clearly anything was possible. Ugru had never reported that "Alanni Keor of Eagle is capable of anything," but Shieda's own report on her, along with Ugru's reports of her work with the Brotherhood, should have taught Shieda that.

He would not again make the mistake of underestimating her. Such an error seemed to have had fatal consequences for a goodly number of people. Already she had been trebly scanned and since she was here he could be sure that she was not armed. Nor were there any weapons in his cabin, which she would not leave save "playing slave"—meaning with her wrists tied not tightly but securely behind her.

She tiny-stepped across the carpeting, knelt sinuously before him, and bowed gracefully until her eyes were directed at the rug. And even farther, until her forehead actually touched the red plush. Supple as a genengineered dancer in freefall, he thought—*and the more dangerous for it!*

Lips glowing orangely lightly brushed his left big toe.

*193 centimeters and 147 kilograms: 6 *feet* 4 *inches* and 326 *pounds,* Old Style; the same weight as that of President William H. Taft.

Unable to keep his laughter inside any longer, he reached down to wind his fingers into her tall-standing hair. He started to pull her up—and somehow she didn't stay on course. Insead she slid up under his robe.

Shieda felt her breath on his genitals, and then an impossibly warm and agile tongue dancing there, over his flesh.

"Arroo!" The cry escaped him when her comb jabbed into his thigh, and he exaggerated it because he had decided to get rid of the comb anyhow, as a potential weapon. (Of course Xhosa's job for the week was to monitor his cabin at all times—probably fingering herself the while. And he'd play the tapes, once this week was ended.)

"Woman, if you castrate me with that damned comb I don't care what happens to my hostages. You're going back to Hellhole in pieces!"

Shieda thought that tiny-whiney voice said, "Forgive me, Master," although it was worse than muffled both by his robe and by the fact that she spoke without taking her tongue away from his growing slicer.

His reply to her apology was less coherent still, since by then she had taken him into her mouth and was working even harder—"work" in the technical sense of expending energy. Lots of energy. He was spending just as much energy to remain standing and in a condition that would keep her at "work" with that delicious, wonderful, maddening, hot hot mouth.

The inevitable came, as did Shieda.

She nuzzled a now-relaxing slicer and held it against her cheek. Again came the voice of a courtesan of his remote Homeworlder ancestors of *Nippon*: "Will my master forgive his clumsy servant now?"

"Pos," he said, and smilingly added, *"Hai, Alanni-san.* But you cannot justify this behavior—unless you are ill. You must be ill, and therefore will have to go to bed and recover from your sickness. I prescribe a week in bed."

Shieda squatted and lifted her without even taking a breath—she was about one-third the weight required to make him really work. He held her under one arm while he undid the obscenely poetic sash with the other hand.

Under the robe he was happy to find undecorated Alanni

Keor. That was plenty, although Shieda was vagaely disappointed . . . he had expected something on the order of a celldyed OPEN THIS END, right over her stash.

All he found in a profoundly thorough search was solid woman—almost too solid, with muscle. *A few decorative kilos wouldn't harm her a bit. Considering the way she's lived these past few months, no wonder she's wiry as an aerialiste! I'll feed her so well and see that she indulges herself in so much Starflare and saki that she both gains, rounds out—and is less danger as well—stuffed and boozed to the eyebrows!*

Having felt her so assiduously, Shieda was again ignited up to here. The robe dropped to the carpeted deck as he lifted her, swung around, and tossed her onto the bed. She *yiped* in pseudo fear and landed rolled into a ball, which bounced.

She kept up that bouncing while he threw off his robe, moved to the bed, caught her on the fifth bounce, and popped her onto an entirely ready and willing erection. Her eyes went huge. Powerful legs clamped around his thighs with such strength that he hardly needed to hold her up. He did anyhow, to have more of the feel of her, the ripple and play of muscles, the breathing that quickened in time with his own . . .

You can turn a girl into a woman, but you can't turn a real woman back into a girl! And Shieda knew that he was much looking forward to the next week, even more than before.

He was right, too. It was one hell of a week for both of them.

During that week she proved her sense of honor and trustworthiness while both of them proved their stamina and potency. During that week the move of the Brotherhood and rescued victims of 'quake-and-*tsunami* to the mainland proceeded perfectly and the farmers cooperated beautifully. During that week Alanni was provided numerous demonstrations of the colossal strength of this overfed ox . . . who was also a superlative lover! During that week he also brought up the tightened security on Skyraft, after they had found a body in a storeroom, awhile back. Did she have anything to do with that body? She decided to tell him, and she did, leaving out any reference to Trafalgar Cuw. No, the attacker had not been in Shieda's employ, and not, he assumed, TGO.

"Had he been TGO you wouldn't be here, Alanni. More likely he was one of Ramesh Jageshwar's—or TAI. Of course now they have no reason to be interested in you. They may be in me, because of the artifact . . . but they'll try to buy it first. You, uh, aren't still cherishing a thought of getting away with the Invisible Troublemaker, are you?"

Alanni sighed. Again she decided to tell Shieda the truth. "I still did when I came up here to begin this week of stuffing myself and being stuffed," she said, stroking his semi-relaxed stuffing instrument. "But now . . . no, Shieda. Want me to swear?"

"I really believe that isn't necessary," he said, reaching for a nipple that might be ready to perk again. "We aren't the first enemies who've wound up trusting each other—even liking each other, you know."

I know, Alanni thought. *Of course you won—you're the one gets the Invisible Thing. I get the safety of a bunch of people I should never have let myself start giving damns about—uh! And I get laid again, too! Who could know that all those youngsters Shieda takes up with here and there are*—lucky!

"Hello, Alanni," Kayab said. "Welcome back."

He stood in sodden robes in the rain, wearing a nice smile and the Invisible Wisdom in a sling across his back. It was soon in the hands of the "Commodore's" agent who had come down with Alanni in the planet-lander.

"Hello, Kayab." She squinted out at the gray sheet of rain. "Nice day."

"You're, uh, well, Alanni?"

She smiled. "Doesn't it show? I'm probably better fed than anyone on Hellhole! Shieda made sure I kept my bargain, and he kept his, too."

"More than kept it," Kayab said, nodding. "Miembra is in wonderful shape! Too, Shieda's leaving two of the flyers with us! That gives us the only air transport to the Fog Coast, and a lot of bargaining power."

Very aware that they had not even touched and that each had a foot off the ground, unsure of her plans, she said, "It's also something the pardon-the-expression 'govment' would love to get its tentacles on."

"Uh. Ram has been training the guards and they are training others. The govs will have to fight if they want those flyers. They'll have a hard time trying to round us up, too. We're scattered all over the Fog Coast! I was able to arrange that with farmers and several small towns, getting people close to food in exchange for assurances that the Brotherhood will provide plenty at next harvest, and share. No one place is swamped with our people."

"Congratulations, Kay'b! That took some real negotiating!"

He allowed himself a small smile. "I can argue well enough over a commlink, when I don't have to face an audience. It also kept me out of sight. It occurred to me that Shieda's people might try to grab and force me to give them the location of the Invisible Wisdom. Would have saved them a lot of work. Shieda may be honorable, as pirates go, but I didn't want to tempt him." He looked away. "It was hard enough, just knowing that you were . . . with him."

Alanni swallowed and covered: "This Sister believes that before long the Chosen Kayab will know all there is to know about plots and conspiracies, O Eldest Brother. And be more than competent to handle *anything*!"

"I'm . . . afraid there's one thing I can't–" he began, and was interrupted:

"We have the artifact and it is the *artifact,"* an electronics-damped voice said, from a nearby outspeaker on *Kirin*'s ingrav-boat. (Both Alanni and Kayab jerked in surprise, if not quite jumped.) *"Clear our takeoff area; we are returning to* Kirin, *well-satisfied."*

When Alanni looked at Kayab, he was staring at her and not looking happy. At last he said, "Well . . . I guess it's time to . . . you're going up on this lander, Alanni?"

"No," Alanni said, and took his arm and her go-bag, and they got themselves out of the way.

The lander's jets rumbled to life, sending mud fountaining and turning the rain into a shimmering golden curtain as they spewed flame. The craft lifted with a howling roar. Madly dancing patterns of light chased each other over the shiny hulls of the two flyers parked on the far side of the field.

Then that was gone, and so was *Kirin*'s lander and the Invisible Wisdom. Gone. Gone off Hellhole, and gone from Alanni's life.

Alanni and Kayab picked their way across ruts and puddles to firmer if not drier ground. She had no doubt that Shieda would keep his promise to get word to Jay and Bouncy. Probably he'd already initiated that. They'd be both shaken and disappointed, maybe angry. Alanni felt some guilt, yes. It was just that she could not be responsible for everyone she had ever come into contact with, and she didn't dare to go back home to Eagle so long as Nortay lived (there was a nice thought—an un-living Councillor Nortay!), and now she was at last sure where it was that she did want to be.

Of course, she mused, *it's possible that darling Nortay wasn't behind all this. I owe* somebody *one—but I'd hate to spend months or years hunting down the wrong wormspawn!*

"Alanni," Kayab said quietly, dolorously, big bald scholarly Kayab, who had at last become brave and assertive—because of her; for her, when she was in jeopardy. "Alanni . . . I have to ask. How long? How long before you leave? I mean . . . today, or do you plan to . . . stay awhile?"

"Oh, Kay'b!" She shook her head and her smile held no mirth or derision; it was a whimsical smile. "Oh, Kay'b! I do not plan to leave today or tomorrow or next month or the month after that, my dear. What I am thinking of right now is of tonight, in a dry bed, at home with you. And other nights, and days."

He nodded, looking straight ahead as they walked. The rain that pelted their heads and streamed down their faces was fortunate for both of them; each thought the other could not see its tears.

When of a sudden they broke, and dropped the go-bag to grab each other in a straining embrace, and each tasted the other's tears, it didn't matter. Alanni was home from the spaceways.